THE LOST RAINFOREST

MEZ'S MAGIC

ELIOT SCHREFER

KATHERINE TEGEN BOOKS
An Imprint of HarperCollins Publishers

Library of Congress Control Number: 2017934898
ISBN 978-0-06-249107-7

Typography by Carla Weise
17 18 19 20 21 PC/LSCH   10 9 8 7 6 5 4 3 2 1
❖
First Edition

For Charlie and Simon

Excerpt from
THE SONG OF THE FIVE
(Translated from the original
Ant by Rumi Mosquitoswallow)

Caldera has ever been thus:

Creatures of sun   Creatures of moon

Separated by the Veils of dawn and dusk.

[Only the ants walk both day and night

. . . and are despised for it.]

Fear is an eager rule maker, and these are Fear's rules:

To cross the Veil is to be

Unnatural

Aberration

Abomination.

To walk in the wrong half of time is to be worthy of death.

What, then, will happen . . .

to those animals . . .

born during the eclipse?

W*HAT'S WRONG WITH ME?*

Mez curls and uncurls her paws, worry springing her eyes back open each time she tries to scrunch them shut. All of the other panthers in the den are asleep, as any normal panther should be. It's daytime!

So why is she awake? Why is she on the wrong side of the Veil?

She starts counting ants, hoping that will make her sleepy. No creature can know any place better than Mez knows this den. It's a thick warren of brambles and vines, crawling with leaf-cutter ants and nestled deep within the intersection of two ancient trees. Snug and safe from any daywalkers that might do them harm.

Maybe Aunt Usha would be safe if she slept outside—Mez couldn't imagine any animal alive foolish enough to attack *her*. Usha's long, muscular body, covered in lustrous brown-black fur, is curled protectively around her nurslings. She snores softly, the vibrations spreading calmness over the sleeping cubs.

Mez eases away from Aunt Usha and pads to the far side of the den. There, she nudges aside brambles to create a triangle of blue within the roof, so she can see the sunlit sky. Mez shivers. Day is a time of legendary creatures, monsters no nightwalker has ever seen.

She stares into the light blue, a shade that simply doesn't exist at night. Even the butterflies keep their azure wings shut while the moon is in power. Mez gets lost in contemplating the color, and has no idea how much time has gone by when the blue triangle suddenly flashes green and tan. Mez recognizes the scales of an emerald tree boa—but boas are nightwalkers, like panthers, so no boa should be awake during the day. It's another animal up during the wrong time, like her! Mez darts to her paws, whiskers perking.

Chumba sighs and shifts in her sleep. Even though Mez knows her sister—like any proper panther—can't wake up during the daytime, she crouches, motionless, until Chumba settles back down. Sure enough, she rolls from Mez and burrows her whiskers and ears under her foreleg, soon snoring away. By the time Mez looks back up, the exposed triangle of dayworld is blue again. The mysterious snake is gone.

Mez's stalking posture relaxes and she lies back down, thrashing her tail and flicking her ears in irritation at the flood of adrenaline with nowhere to go. Heart still racing, she lowers her head to her front paws and goes back to counting ants. Why are there always so many of them? Her cousin Mist claims there were no ants at all in Caldera until the night Mez and Chumba's mother died, when the sisters came to live in Usha's den. Mez doesn't believe that, because how would the Ant Queen's constellation have gotten into the sky if there hadn't been any ants before? All the same, it *does* seem like there are more and more leaf-cutters wandering through the den each night. She traps one under her paw, to give herself something to do, then feels bad and lets the ant continue on its way to wherever it is that ants go.

She's not even aware that her tail is still flicking until it runs under Chumba's nose, making her sister sneeze in her sleep.

Wake up, Mez pleads.

Usually the ants zig and zag along the rainforest floor, but now they've started streaming along the ground in a straight line. She wonders what they're racing toward—or away from. As she watches the insects, Mez's thoughts unravel, moving from the strange behavior of the ants to imagining the night's hunt: chasing moths with Chumba and sniffing through musty thickets in search of plump rodents.

She snaps to attention when she sees the flash of green and tan again. The boa is back!

Mez is instantly on her paws, body rigid and teeth bared. She listens for the snake, but any sounds of its passage are muffled by the murmurs of the daytime rainforest, the constant patter of rain, the droning cicadas and shrieking birds.

Usha had carefully placed her family's den along a nearly impenetrable alley of vines and brambles. It's unlikely this boa would simply happen on it. Is he *hunting* them? All Mez wants to do is race out to investigate this intruder. But she can hear Aunt Usha's voice in her head: *The day is the wrong side of the Veil. Any animal who crosses the Veil has broken the natural laws. Any animal who breaks the natural laws must be exiled.*

One of Mez's cousins from Usha's latest litter had made constant whining noises. He didn't seem able to help it, or even aware he was making them. He had still been a mewling kitten when he spoiled too many hunts: Usha carried him from the den and then returned without him. They never heard from him again. Wrongness will be punished, there's no question about it.

Mez must not be caught daywalking.

No more sign of the green-and-tan intruder. Mez wishes Chumba were awake to talk to about it, but there will be no rousing her sister until dusk. Instead, Mez's mind conjures up all sorts of fearsome cub-hunting daywalkers. She hasn't gotten a good view of any yet, but imagines monsters with many heads and spiny backs and exposed skulls covered in fire.

Finally the blue above her dims and grays, the shadows of twigs and branches patterning the den floor. Dusk is finally here! Mez flicks her tail deliberately, making Chumba sneeze again. When the little cub returns to snoring, Mez goes right back to tickling her nose. By now, the Veil has dropped enough that Chumba comes awake.

"Come on, Mez, don't scare me like that!" Chumba lets out a big yawn, exposing her sharp teeth. "Why are you so perky right when you should be just waking up?"

"Happened to wake right after the Veil dropped this time, I guess," Mez says. "Look—it's the two of us, Chum! Like before."

The two sisters stare at each other, unspoken memories of their mother passing between them. Although only nurslings when she died, they remember her warmth, the scent of her. All the other cubs in the den were born to Aunt Usha.

The intruding boa haunts Mez, but she can't mention it to Chumba without revealing her secret, so she finds somewhere else to put her mind. She gets into pounce position, head down low and eyes bright. "Let's play a game!" she says.

"You can't be serious," Chumba says, yawning and stretching.

"Yes! How about tail chasers, or whisker taunt, or maybe two-paw-bluff, or—"

"Slow down, slow down," Chumba says, stretching out her forelegs and lowering her chin to the ground. "Still . . . waking . . . up. And you *know* I hate two-paw-bluff."

Mez bites her lip. The game of two-paw-bluff is a sore point. In addition to being the smallest of the cubs, Chumba is missing one of her front paws. The leg simply ends in a stump, covered neatly in a beautiful little patch of soft tan fur. Chumba barely lets it slow her down, but Mez knows the nub on her leg causes her pain in the mornings. Chumba shakes the pawless leg, gives it a few good licks, and then places it resolutely down on the den floor. She closes her eyes. Mez gives her a loving nuzzle.

When Chumba's eyes open again, they're full of playfire. She growls and pounces, knocking Mez flat. They tussle around the den, pawing and growling, rolling right over their cousins in the process. Usha's nursling triplets—Yerlo, Jerlo, and Derli—don't wake, but Mist does. Mez knows he's up when she hears a loud hiss and feels a claw tearing into her ear.

She whirls, hissing back.

"Watch out, will you?" Mist growls. "It's time you two runts learned how to behave. Do you want to wake up Mother?" Mist is the eldest cub by only a few nights, but makes sure everyone knows it.

"Aw, did we interrupt your precious sleep?" Mez asks, tail thrashing mischievously. Most panthers have soft browns patterning their black fur, even Usha, but Mist was born with fur of the purest white. He's the color of the inside of a freshly broken mushroom, from his whiskers to the tip of his tail. He spends long stretches of the night grooming the most luster out of it.

"Sleep is vital," Mist says haughtily. "If you don't want to keep relying on my mother to hunt your food for you, then I suggest you rest more to give you better reflexes. You two need whatever advantages you can get."

"You should try sleeping all day and all night, then," Mez mocks, wagging her paw at Mist. "You light up like a click beetle out there."

Mist gives a tortured sigh, baring his teeth at Mez. What he's failed to notice, though, is that Chumba's worked her way into perfect pouncing position around his backside. Mez's attention flicks to her sister—for a moment, but long enough for Mist to notice and whirl, his jaws gaping wide open as little Chumba hurtles through the air at him, giggling all the while. Mist dodges at the last moment . . . sending Chumba crashing into Usha instead.

Long and sturdy, her body stretching from one side of the den to the other, Aunt Usha barely moves when Chumba soars into her. While Chumba falls away, Usha gives a long yawn, exposing her sharp teeth as she cracks open her green eyes. They soon glitter in annoyance when she finds Chumba splayed out flat beside her. Cringing, Chumba slinks to the farthest corner of the den.

"What is going on here?" Usha asks.

"Mother, I'm as baffled as you are," Mist says, sitting up tall, an angelic expression on his face. "I was sleeping, trying to marshal my energy for the coming hunt, when out of nowhere Mez and Chumba came *flying* into me. They could have put us all in danger, they could have revealed the den to daywalkers, I can't believe they would—"

"No one likes a tattletale, Mist," Usha interrupts. She gets to her paws, stretching. "Come, cubs. The Veil has dropped, and night is here. It is time to start the hunt."

As Usha starts out of the den, Mist shoots a glare at Mez and Chumba before falling into formation, his head right behind Usha's tail.

Usha's latest litter is still asleep. Mez and Chumba rush around the den, nudging Yerlo, Jerlo, and Derli awake, ignoring the youngsters' sleepy protests. "Come on, Usha's on the move," Mez says. "I know you're tired, but you don't want to get left behind, do you?"

Yawning and stretching, the panthers make their way into the dusky early night. Mez and Chumba take up rear guard. Usha isn't one to slow for stragglers, so the cubs hustle to keep up. Even so, Mez takes a moment to soak in the surrounding rainforest. The trees are enormous columns framed in roots that emerge like wings before sinking into black and loamy soil, their trunks lancing far into the sky before any branches begin. Vines, trapped in years-long combat against the trees, twist in the night breezes. Roots grow from them too, forming nets in the air that extend all the way down to the dead leaves that cover the jungle floor, where mushroom buds wink in the moonlight, lighting the panthers' path enough for their darkvision to pick up every detail they need.

Usha is blackest, only a hint of brown competing on her fur. Yerlo, Jerlo, and Derli are nearly the same jet-black, though patches of gold shine within it. Eventually they will be sleek and strong like Usha, but right now her littlest ones are still puffballs, fur sticking out in all directions. The only way Mez can tell which way is front or back is by looking for the tail or their bright blue eyes.

Mist is as pure white as Usha is pure black. Despite Mist's malice toward her, it's hard for Mez to take her eyes off him. His fur is so radiant that he catches any bits of scant sunlight remaining in the dusk, giving him a constant luster. Mez watches him flow along the ground, like a creature made of some otherworldly magic.

In comparison to their cousins, Mez and Chumba are sloppy patchwork creatures. At least Chumba is jet-black on top, until it dissolves into flurries of brown and yellow spots around her legs and paws. Mist might make fun of Chumba for her coloring, but Mez loves it. Mez doesn't even have the jet-black top going for her. She's a complete mess of calico. She's learned to avoid her reflection, taking the long route around ponds and puddles whenever she can, shunning the sight of all those clashing patterns and colors. Maybe she deserves all the scoffing she gets from Mist. But her coloring reminds her of her mother.

She wouldn't give it up for anything.

Mist is right behind Usha, nearly noiseless as he high-steps through the broad snail-covered leaves strewn on the ground. Yerlo, Jerlo, and Derli are louder, their paws too big for their legs. As Chumba passes, her club leg spears twigs and leaves, making rustling sounds. She winces at each noise. Mez makes reassuring purrs each time Mist glares back.

Once, when Mist thought he and Chumba were alone, Mez caught him pinning her sister to the ground and hissing at her: *No panther can survive with only three paws. You should have been killed at birth, like the noisy cub.* Mez had attacked him for it, biting savagely at one of Mist's ears, but Chumba had pulled her off. Her message had been clear: *Let me fight my own battles.*

Mez growls whenever she catches Mist glaring at Chumba. She will do everything she can to keep her sister safe and happy, even if somenight it means going right up against Usha's prized son.

Aunt Usha's territory is in the densest part of the rainforest, the part with the most brambly thickets. Here they're far from the open waterways with their caimans and anacondas, away from the broad trails with their spine-trampling capybara. With no dangers to worry about here, Aunt Usha can lead her family through the inky night, concerned only with hunting, holding quiet and still with her cubs while they wait for prey to move and reveal itself.

As she slinks through the moonlight, ears and whiskers alert to Usha's every movement, Mez looks out for the green-and-tan patterns of the emerald tree boa. But greens and tans are everywhere.

The next time Aunt Usha pauses, listening for prey, Mist speaks up. "Do you sense something unusual, Mother?"

Usha says nothing, but Mez can scent pantherfear in the air. The others pick up on it too, going silent and watchful. When Usha turns around, her lips are set in a worried line. "Keep close to me this nighttime," she says. "No one stray."

With that, she turns and stalks off into the jungle, the cubs struggling to keep up. There will be no more discussion of it.

2

HUNTING PRACTICE.

The sky is cool, dark, and thick, clogged with low-hanging clouds and swirls of stars. Wheeling around the panther family are the creatures of the night: swooping bats, both the agile kind that eats mosquitoes and the ponderous, fat fruit kind; hooting owls; scrounging possums; lurking tarantulas. With the fearsome reptiles and birds of the day asleep on the other side of the Veil, night is the time for the proper creatures of the world to thrive. Mez is proud to be one of them.

Mist takes the position right behind Aunt Usha. Mez doesn't mind too much; she gets to spend time in the back with Chumba, and it's easy to keep track of

Mist. After Usha and Mist spot and kill a forest antelope before Chumba and Mez can even get there, though, Mez struggles to get rid of her irritation. She finds a way by stalking low through the underbrush until she's out of view of Chumba, then making a flying leap at her sister. They go rolling through the night grass, landing in a lagoon and getting soaked through, giggling all the while.

At the splashing noise, Mist comes stalking through the night, a spiny rat carcass in his mouth. "Shmudda in hoo," he says around it.

Mez gives Mist a long and somber look. "I'm sorry, I don't speak monkey," she finally says.

The sisters try to keep straight faces, but then Chumba falls into giggles that grow into guffaws as she rolls in the reeds at the swamp's edge. Mez breaks out into laughter too, and falls in beside Chumba, sending up a spray of mud that splatters Mist's glossy white chest. He gets an almost wistful look on his face at the sight of the two sisters rolling in the mud, and then his usual haughty expression returns.

"It. Should. Have. Been. Two," he says as carefully as he can, never dropping the carcass of the rat. Its long tail, partially detached, drapes along the ground. "I'd have caught both rats if you hadn't made so much noise.

I honestly don't know why Mother ever allowed you to stay alive."

"Shmonestly shmon't shmo shmy shmother schmever shmallowed shou shtay shmalive," Chumba says, wagging her paw at him.

"Come, young ones," Usha calls. "Time to return home."

Even though the sisters didn't catch a single animal during the night's hunt, irrepressible Chumba has a bounce in her step as she scrapes through the narrow opening of brambles to enter the den, giving her bum an extra wiggle at the end.

Mez is more distracted. After she's settled in beside Chumba in the corner of the den farthest from Aunt Usha, she doesn't even pretend to close her eyes. She's exhausted, but her heart is racing—once again, the Veil is about to lift but she's not sleepy. Mez starts counting ants, her mind wandering over the events of the night, finally to her memories of her mother, a remembrance of warmth and presence, though she can't recall her actual face anymore.

There are more ants than ever in the den, and Mez soon loses count. She stares up at the opening, where the triangle of light reveals the coming dawn. When she takes her eyes away to make sure Chumba is sleeping comfortably, she sees that Mist is still awake. From his prized position directly under Aunt Usha's chin, he watches Mez, eyes glittering. He seems to be trying to force himself to stay up, but no nightwalker can stay awake past dawn.

Except for Mez.

Though she's terrified of going out on the wrong side of the Veil, Mez knows she won't find out what's worrying her by staying in the den. This daytime she'll see if she can discover anything about the mysterious constrictor. It's time for a spy mission.

Once dayrise is over, once the sun is high in the sky and currents of heat have begun to curl the edges of the den, Mez gingerly lifts Chumba's leg off her chest, placing it across Jerlo instead, and gets to four paws. She stares up at the triangle of exposed sky. Long moments go by, and Mez never moves, falling deep into a hunter trance. Then—there!—she sees the flash of green and tan again. Nose low to the ground, Mez slinks toward the opening.

The walls are thick enough to keep the den dark, but there are points of light behind the brambles, like stars. Mez takes one last look at her sleeping family, and then pokes her way through the narrow ring of vines.

She pauses, blinking.

At first the world outside is pure and dazzling white. Adapted to darkness, her eyes are too flooded with light to tell her anything. For a long moment, all she can do is listen. The birdcalls are different in daytime, more songs than hoots. No frogs croak. There are more sounds of flying insects, more whining sounds of tiny wings. As she holds still, eyes streaming tears, the dayworld comes into better view.

It's so *bright*! She's relieved that at least it's still the jungle she knows out there, that the shapes are the same even if the colors are saturated and loud. Here are the same treetops draped in liana vines, the same broad-leafed ferns, deep green mosses even darker in contrast to the radiant blue above.

Mez's gaze darts through the flood of daylight, flitting between the movements of individual leaves, the columns of ants streaming across sun-drenched ferns, a pair of shrikes following each other from branch to branch, singing all the way. Under such an onslaught of information, she has to muster her courage to take even a step.

If she doesn't move soon, though, the emerald boa will be long gone.

She puts a paw forward. Then another.

Mez feels so small and exposed, so open to predators. "It's okay to be in danger, if it means getting answers," she whispers to herself. She scarcely believes her own words, and hopes speaking them aloud might give them more weight.

She creeps along the column of ants running beside the nest, going in the same direction the snake went. They're thick and fast on the ground, like a brook down a hill. Even though following the ants takes Mez through places she's already been many times, by day it's a whole new journey. She pauses frequently as she goes, keeping as best she can to the dark spaces beneath fronds and leaves, to the narrow crevices between fallen trees. She goes by memory through this flipped world, keeps her whiskers near the ants to better track their mysterious journey.

Where is the snake?

While she follows the ant column, an intense headache starts up between Mez's ears. She could handle the strangeness of daylight when it was a triangle of blue sky surrounded by reassuring darkness. But taking in all this brightness at once sets her heart to skipping, gives her a constant panic at the sunlit wrongness of this world. Her path takes her by a fallen tree, a mossy decaying trunk that took many other trees down with it and created a clearing in the woods. Passing through will mean leaving the shadows entirely.

She sinks her claws into bark and scales the fallen

giant, sprinting along its length. Imagining birds of prey in the dazzling sunlit sky above, Mez's head begins to spin and her paws start to feel uncoordinated, barely connected to the rest of her body. She continues to put one in front of the other, but has to close her eyes and go only by feel. The rotten bark of the dead tree, already giving rise to bright green weeds, is soft under the pads of her paws, and she concentrates on that familiar feeling as she continues forward. She narrows her eyes to slits and only fully opens them again once she's reached the far side of the fallen tree.

Mez locks eyes with a serpent.

The boa constrictor must have slipped forward while Mez was walking blind along the giant trunk, and lies coiled before her, right where she would dismount. Stunned by the unexpected sight, Mez goes motionless, as if there's any chance it hasn't noticed her.

The constrictor is huge: since it's coiled up, Mez can't quite see how long it is, but it's as wide as a full-grown fig tree. A cub like Mez could slide easily down that gullet, whole and struggling.

The serpent stares at her, waiting for Mez to move first. Though all of her muscles are tensed, she remains perfectly still. The reptile's eyes, surprisingly small compared to its body, glitter with calculating intelligence, but Mez has no idea what thoughts are passing through the emerald boa's brain. Maybe it assumes an adult panther like Usha is nearby. Maybe that's why it hasn't attacked yet.

Even if Usha were here, it would be hard to imagine her lasting long against a snake this size. And of course, Usha is nowhere near. Mez is far from her aunt's strength and fighting skill. If it comes to combat, she has no chance at all. But she's gotten what she asked for: she's found the other nightwalker awake during the day.

3

A S THE LONG stare between panther and constrictor continues, Mez edges backward, ears flat against her head. The snake doesn't budge, but its eyes remain fixed on her. Mez knows that boa constrictors kill by squeezing animals to death, and this one is enormous and strong; if it wanted to, it could streak forward now, encircle her body with its own, and crush the life from her.

But even as Mez continues to retreat, the strange snake holds still, jaws wide open, heat releasing in waves from its mouth and warbling the air. Maybe it's eaten recently. Maybe it doesn't like the taste of panther cubs.

Or maybe it, too, is feeling out of place here. Maybe

this constrictor is also overwhelmed by being in the dayworld. For, to Mez's astonishment, it closes one of its eyes and then opens it again. While a horrible smile creeps across its face, the constrictor does it again.

It *winks*.

Mez's mouth drops open in shock. She tries to form words, but fear is scrambling her thoughts, making her legs move on their own accord.

Before she knows what she's doing, Mez flees back toward the den, scarcely aware of the jungle floor passing underpaw. She breathes a sigh of relief when she sees familiar leaning boulders, even though day makes them a brilliant gray-green instead of their nighttime black. At the sight of home, Mez feels her heart rate begin to return to normal for the first time since she left the den.

Until a shriek splits the air.

She's heard eagles before while lying awake in the daytime den, her fur standing up on end at their shattering cries. But she's never seen one.

Mez expects to see the eagle high overhead. But the bird of prey is right at the opening to the den. To be so close to a daywalker! The eagle is regal and strong, beak long and hooked, muscled body covered with sleek blue-gray feathers. It hops in the air, too heavy to take flight.

Because it has something furry between its claws.

Chumba.

The Veil keeps Chumba trapped in dayworld slumber, unable to awaken despite the eagle's attack, eyes shut even as talons dig into her rib cage. Her chin shakes, mouth opening and closing, trying to find the source of the pain in her dreams.

Open attack is not the panther way: Usha has taught them always to ambush, never to confront. But the sight of Chumba in danger puts Mez beyond thought. The eagle leaps and surges its wings, using brute muscle to try to rise into the air. Chumba unbalances it, though, sending the bird pitching from side to side. The eagle tumbles back to the ground, rolling on one shoulder and momentarily releasing Chumba.

That's when Mez strikes.

She streaks forward, fast and agile, and sinks her front claws deep into the meaty back of the eagle's leg. The raptor cries out in surprise and beats its wings frantically, buffeting Mez on her sensitive nose. She recoils, instinct telling her to release the eagle for her own safety, but at the thought of helpless Chumba, Mez holds on, climbing the eagle's body until she can sink her teeth into the joint where wing meets torso.

Mez gets mostly oily feathers in her mouth, but when her canines find flesh, she bites down. The eagle cries out, beak raised to the sky as it shrieks. The noise is meant to terrify Mez, and it works; she imagines the bird clawing out her eyes and almost lets go of the raptor. But she manages to hold on, clamping down harder and harder.

It's almost like the eagle can't see her. Its beak gnashes over open air, making clattering sounds. As the movements become more and more frantic, Mez feels her grip slipping against the buffeting wings. She keeps her ears back and her jaws locked, but it's not enough. The eagle throws her, and she goes skidding across the soil.

Mez struggles to get to her paws, but she tumbles back to the ground—her back paw has looped itself in a vine. She tries to yank it free, but she knows it will be too late. She doesn't need to look to know the eagle is arrowing toward her, powerful wingbeats sending up sprays of dirt and insects. Mez scrunches her eyes, waiting to feel talons raking her flesh.

But the pain never comes.

Rustling and crashing, then silence. She opens her eyes to a harrowing sight: the eagle has wrapped itself in a vine, and is bound tight to the jungle floor.

Or, wait. It's not a vine.

The constrictor has wrapped itself around the eagle, weighting it to the ground. Emerald-green scales cross and slide across one another as the snake tightens its grip, pulling ever more ferociously around the bird. Blue-gray feathers stick out between the muscular coils.

Mez has been saved. By a boa constrictor!

Surrounded by down and flight feathers, she collapses into the mussed soil, gasping in air. Once she's caught her breath, she staggers to Chumba.

Her sister lies on her side, still in full daycoma, eyes darting beneath her lids as she sleep-flees. Mez's eyes have adjusted to her initial dayblindness, but with the exertion of combat the light has grown intense again, her headache thundering in her skull, powerful enough to make her want to shut her eyes and block out everything. But she keeps her eyes open and approaches her sister, vision drumming as she examines the gash on her nape. The eagle's sharp talons and beak broke the skin, but not too deeply—Chumba's wounds are already clotting.

The snake wraps itself again and again around the eagle, so that the two of them are rolling along the ground, the eagle disappearing entirely in the churning scales. Mez shrinks back in fear, bringing Chumba with her by dragging her tail gently between her teeth.

But the constrictor makes no move toward her. Nor does it seem to be interested in eating the eagle. It stills and stares at Mez, eyes glittering.

Then, shockingly, it speaks. The voice is low and throaty, with a slight purr to the end of each word. He sounds surprisingly like a panther. "You and your sister are safe now."

Wounded and panicky, scared that the eagle will soon emerge from the constrictor's grasp, Mez wriggles backward toward the den. Her hindquarters are already inside when the constrictor speaks again. "This eagle is no more danger, and this young panther's wounds are minor. We both know she won't wake during the day, unlike you and me. I've come a long way to meet you— please stay and talk to me. My name is Auriel."

Mez continues to drag Chumba back into the den. There's so much she'd like to ask this snake about, but the eagle attack has spooked her.

Auriel opens his mouth but then closes it, peering at the ground. While she tugs on Chumba, Mez follows his gaze. What does he see? Big puddles are forming from the constant rain, but she's barely even noticed. They're in the season when it's *always* raining. Then she spots where Auriel is looking: the broad column of ants has shifted so it passes swiftly along the ground beside him. Almost like it's traveling *to* Auriel. "What do you know about the Ant Queen?" Auriel asks Mez.

She ignores his strange question and tucks Chumba into the den instead. After pawing vines so they cover her, she then eases back to poke her head out of the opening. There's no way she's getting any closer to the constrictor.

Still wrapped around the eagle, he closes his eyes, head swaying. "Let me explain my question: I have the ability to listen to ants. They are the only animals that exist throughout Caldera, in all times and all places—including in your den. They do not speak, but communicate by chemical, one to the next. News travels quickly and with little distortion. Listening to them has told me something very interesting about you, Mez."

"You know my name," Mez says, tail thrashing.

Auriel nods.

"*Ants* told you to come here? And to find *me?*" Mez asks.

"Yes," Auriel says. "You've never really been alone. They have been watching."

"Those leaf-cutter ants I count each day," Mez says, "they've been seeing everything . . . and reporting it back to you?"

"Yes. The ants told me that a special panther has been born here. One who, like me, has magical power. A shadowwalker."

The drone of the cicadas begins to die off. The Veil of dusk will drop soon—and with it Mez's family will awaken. She must be inside by then, if she doesn't want to be caught.

"What's a shadowwalker?" Mez asks.

"Why, it's what you and I are," Auriel says, lowering his crepey snake head onto his coils. He's breathing heavily, and the ants swarm over him with renewed vigor. "About a year ago a strange event occurred. When the sun was at its highest point in the sky, the moon cut across its path, and their powers combined. The daywalkers remember this moment well, as their world went dark in the middle of the day. The nightwalkers experienced only a moment of wakefulness."

"I don't remember that," Mez says. Now that it's become clear that the giant snake doesn't mean to immediately suffocate and swallow her, Mez allows herself the luxury of taking a good look at him. Though he's covered in bands of emerald and tan, his scales have a milky cast to them, almost as if they're covered in fine cobwebs. Strangely, one of the scales on the side of his head is a glossy charcoal color. When he speaks, his mouth reveals flapping gums, pale pink. No sign of any fangs at all. Mez wonders what happened to them, not that it makes him any less dangerous. Auriel's body is dense with power. Who needs fangs when you're as large as that?

"You wouldn't remember it, and neither would I,"

Auriel says, winking. "Because we were busy being born. I would have known none of this if I hadn't been able to listen to the ants and learn from them. But because I have, through the shared memory of their immortal colonies I've been able to access knowledge beyond the reach of normal animals. The vital energy of the night comes from the moon, and the vital energy of the day comes from the sun. During the eclipse, those vital energies were doubled. It allows us to walk during both day and night, and it's resulted in magical powers. Exactly what that magic is depends on the animal."

"Well, you're wrong there," Mez says. "I don't have any magical powers."

"By listening to the ants I have already located over a dozen other young eclipse-born, and they are on their way to the Ziggurat of the Sun and Moon, deep in the center of Caldera. Most don't know their powers yet. Come with me there, too. One of the first other eclipse-born I met has shown powers of divination—we'll see if he can find your magic. If you do not have any after all, then we'll get you back here, safe and sound."

More and more of the daylight falls away. It will soon be nighttime. Mez looks fearfully up at the sky. She has to get inside before it's too late. But she also needs to know what's going on inside *her*. "I don't have much time!"

"Hide your sister away in your den and come with me," Auriel says. "Come join the rest of our kind. We shadowwalkers need to stick together."

Mez shakes her head, ears flat and trembling. There's no way she would leave Chumba for this stranger. Not for anything.

"I know it's daunting," Auriel says, unwinding from the limp corpse of the eagle and easing toward Mez. "But we need to combine our eclipse magic to stop the Ant Queen."

"The Ant Queen?" Mez asks, her wide eyes going to the dusky sky, where the stars of the mythical ant's constellation are already winking awake. The queen is in the center, her minions points of light scattered across the rest of the sky. "She's just a constellation panthers make up stories about to scare cubs. She's not real."

"I would have thought that too," Auriel says, "if my eclipse magic hadn't allowed me to spy on the ants. I have learned from them that their queen is the greatest evil Caldera has ever known, and she is about to emerge." As if he can sense the coming danger, a glossy charcoal scale on the side of Auriel's head begins to glow, standing out from the surrounding green. His head wags from side to side. Mez has to look away when she realizes that ants are now crawling over the milky membrane covering the snake's eyes as he continues speaking. "She has been imprisoned for thousands of years, through the magic of an eclipse that happened eons ago. After the most recent eclipse, the same combined magic that has made you and me shadowwalkers also started her release from her bonds."

As the sunset spreads its pinks and oranges along the jungle floor, rain begins to fall, drumming and pattering the ground. It dots Mez's whiskers and glitters on Auriel's scales.

"Only by returning the eclipse magic contained within us to the Ziggurat of the Sun and Moon can we hope to renew the prison containing the Ant Queen's evil," Auriel continues. "It's up to us, the shadowwalkers."

The last of the sun's rays are disappearing under the horizon. If Mez doesn't get her and Chumba back to Usha's side soon, they'll be found out. Exiled.

"I'm sorry, but I can't go with you," Mez says. With that, she darts into the den, dragging Chumba along behind her.

M EZ TUGS DESPERATELY on Chumba's hindquarters, trying to pull her deep into the den. But
the warren is so thick with brambles and vines that it's
impossible. Each time she gets one of her sister's limbs
free of an obstacle, another one gets stuck. The whole
while Mez keeps an eye on the den's opening, checking
to see whether Auriel is following.

Though the Veil has fallen, the air of the den still
bears the hot stifle of day. Usha is asleep on her side,
her cubs pressed into her belly for comfort. Mist is stir-
ring. His back is to Mez, but he's licking his front paws,
beginning the day's work of keeping himself pristine.

He'll move on to the back paws next—and when he does he'll spot Mez.

Before he can, Mez drops where she is, pretending to sleep.

She hears Mist continue his licking, then pause.

Mez doesn't move. She lies on the floor of the den, her mind spinning over the fight with the eagle, the fierce buffeting of its wings, the sharp and snapping beak, the feel of its muscle and sinew beneath her teeth, the sight of the daywalking emerald tree boa wrapped around it, her strange conversation with him.

Shadowwalker. Her!

As she lies there, running through her conversation with Auriel, one puzzle presents itself over and over: No daywalker has ever located the den before. And yet, the same day Mez walked out, an eagle found its way in to attack Chumba. What kind of a coincidence was that?

The most likely explanation comes to her, terrible in its simplicity: The eagle knew where the den was because Mez came strolling out of it in the middle of the day. Because she showed that monster precisely where her family was hidden away.

Mez nearly killed her sister. If she didn't already know there was something terribly wrong with her daywalking, she is sure of it now. "Oh, Chumba," Mez whispers, licking her sister's wounded nape. "I'm so sorry."

Even if Auriel never returns, as soon as Mez has a good opportunity she will tell Chumba everything. This is her fault, and she needs to own up to it.

Mez's skin grows cold and clammy, and her eyes dart beneath her lids. What if telling the truth gets her exiled? How will Chumba survive without her?

Mez watches through slitted eyes as Mist pushes the still-sleeping triplets out of the way so he's right in front of his mother's face. When Usha finally smacks her lips and yawns, he is the first thing she sees, sitting calmly on all fours. "We have a serious situation."

Aunt Usha looks at Mist steadily, then takes in the dozing cubs, Mez, and finally Chumba groggily shaking her head in the den's opening, still bleeding from the eagle's wound. "Round up the little ones."

Usha slinks out, leaving Mist presiding over the other cubs. Even on a normal night, Mez hates it when Aunt Usha leaves him in charge. But there's a reason for it—as Usha's eldest, Mist will somenight be leader of the panthers in the area.

Dread filling her, Mez rises to her paws, but before she can get her sister up and standing, Mist leans over Chumba and bites her on the nub where her paw would be. "How did you get all cut up?" he asks. "And what are you doing sprawled half out of the den? You're going to *get it* from Mother."

Chumba squeals and scurries away from him. "Hey! That hurt! And I have no idea what you're talking about."

"See for yourself. It looks like you lost a fight with a mouse or something."

Chumba whirls, but she can't spot the wound.

"You've got a cut," Mez whispers while she licks the spot. "It's not too bad."

"I don't understand," Chumba says. "How did it happen?"

Mist scowls at Mez while she continues to lick her sister's neck. "Once we get outside, you two will have to be the ones to tell my mother that Chumba got injured and doesn't even know *why*. You two are total wastes of fur."

One elegant paw after another, he heads out of the den.

Mez quivers in anger. Getting in a fight with Usha's son won't help matters any, though, so she forces herself to hold back.

"Are you in pain, Chum?" Mez asks her sister.

"It's not too bad," she says. "I'm confused more than anything else."

"At least there's *that* to make us feel better," Mez says, pointing her paw at Mist's departing tail. A big gooey yellow slug is suckered to his white fur.

"Should we tell him?" Chumba asks as Mez gives her wounded neck one last lick.

"Not a chance," Mez says. "Ready to go?"

"I'm always ready to go," Chumba says. "As long as I've got you."

Mez nods solemnly. "Okay. Let's get the triplets up."

The calico sisters poke around the den, prodding the other cubs awake with gentle taps of their noses. The little ones yawn, then once they have their minds about them look around fearfully for Mist. When they don't see him, they let out sighs of relief. Though Mez and Chumba get the worst of it, the triplets have often been nipped by their big brother.

"Time to go," Mez says softly. "Aunt Usha's waiting for us."

When they emerge, Mist is pacing in front of the den's exit. He turns on them, extending and retracting his claws. "You're late. Mother must have gotten frustrated with us and gone ahead."

"You might have helped us wake the little ones, you know," Mez says.

Mist looks back at her balefully.

"Never mind, forget I asked. After you, fearless

leader," Mez adds dryly.

Mist stalks away along the jungle floor, but goes only a few feet before he stops short. "Feathers!" he exclaims.

It's the dead eagle. It doesn't look as fearsome at night, but here are the powerful wings, the cub-killing beak. The bones are at twisted angles, pale birdflesh visible where the emerald boa's muscular coils yanked out the feathers. Even more mysterious: Auriel might have killed the eagle, but he left without eating it! What a strange snake.

Neither Yerlo, Jerlo, nor Derli seems to want to look at the bird's corpse, instead peering around nervously for Usha. Chumba seems just as confused, nose bobbing as she investigates the dead eagle. "What *happened* to it?" she asks, ears pressed back in confusion and wonder.

"One daywalker killed another," Mist says. "We've seen their corpses before. Small loss. Come, we need to catch up to Mother."

"It's no easy thing to take down a bird this big," Chumba says.

"I would agree," comes Usha's voice. Mez looks up to see her aunt emerging from the tree line, ears back and eyes wary. "Come, little ones. To my side."

Is that *fear* in Usha's voice? Mez and Chumba pad to Usha's flank, keeping the three tiny triplets protected at the center.

"It was just a daywalker killing another daywalker, right, Mother?" Mist asks, not sounding nearly so certain anymore.

"Mist, if you are to lead this family somenight, I expect more from you. Those are panther claw marks on the eagle's throat. The scent of pantherfear is all over its feathers."

Mist's ears go flat with shame.

"I *thought* I smelled pantherfear!" Chumba says.

"Shh," Mez whispers. She knows her sister is only trying to help Usha figure out what's going on, but she can see the fury rippling the fur along Mist's back.

"We are the only panthers anywhere near here," Usha says. "So it had to be one of us who killed this eagle."

"But Mother," Mist says slowly, "if one of us killed the eagle, then one of us was daywalking. And a panther who daywalks—"

"—is unnatural," Usha finishes.

"And an unnatural panther must be exiled," Mist says. He points his nose at Chumba. Usha follows his focus, and sees the wound on the cub's neck for the first time.

5

MEZ LOOKS AT her aunt, then at Mist and Chumba, waiting for one to speak up. "What's happening?" Chumba asks, confused. "Why are you all staring at me?"

The nursling triplets whimper. Despite her fear of what might be about to happen, Mez senses their confusion and forces her ears forward, so the nurslings won't be too frightened.

Aunt Usha paces around the eagle's body, examining it, but not touching the evidence. Mez can sense her calculating what to do next. Panthers who are unfit are killed or cast out. Crossing the Veil is deeply against the natural order. But Usha, like Mez, probably always assumed that such a wrong could never actually happen.

Mist follows behind his mother, mimicking her solemn air as he prods the eagle corpse with his nose. "There are other scents here, Mother," he says. "Something acidic, like ant—"

"Something helped a panther kill this eagle," Usha says, stopping up short. Mist isn't able to halt in time and bumps into her, the thick fur of Usha's tail bushing over his face. He hisses, sidesteps, and immediately starts grooming his fur back into place with a forepaw.

Mist shoots a dark look at Chumba as she struggles to contain a giggle. "That's right, Mother," Mist says once he's recovered himself. "Why don't we let Chumba explain who helped her?"

Chumba stops giggling. "*Me?* What are you talking about? I told you I have no idea about any of this!"

"Your wound is from an eagle's beak. How do you explain that?" Mist presses.

"I woke up with this after daycoma. It doesn't hurt too much, by the way, thanks for your concern." Chumba's words might sound daring, but Mez knows her sister too well, can see the fear bringing her haunches low, drooping the ends of her whiskers.

While she waits in dread to hear the word "exile,"

Mez clenches her mouth tight. Biting down so hard brings out the taste of blood in her mouth—her struggle to stay clamped down on the flailing eagle must have gashed her gums.

Usha's expression becomes unknowable as she scrutinizes Chumba. "You should know that I'm of two minds. That daywalking raptor could easily have taken one of the triplets. Defeating that bird was an act of bravery, even if daywalking is an act of shame."

Mez's heart races. Is Usha setting a trap? Confess and then the real punishment comes down? Mez wouldn't put that past her. She opens her mouth. Whatever happens, it will be a relief to tell what she knows, and bear the consequences.

But Mez clamps her mouth shut, because Mist speaks before she can. "Mother," he says. "I can hold the truth back no longer. It was me! I killed the eagle that was hunting our cubs."

Mez stares at him, mouth falling back open.

Usha's eyes narrow. This was clearly not the panther she was expecting to hear confess.

"I will one night be leader around here," Mist says, looking humbly down at the ground. "I need to learn how to protect all the panthers around me."

Usha looks at Mist with something like worry in her

eyes. "Mist. I know my eldest son is not a daywalker. So tell me, how did you accomplish this?"

"No, of course I can't daywalk. What happened was, um, what happened was this. I've been working to train myself to be the first to wake up when the Veil drops, the moment that sunset comes," Mist says. "I . . . noticed Chumba was missing, so I peeked outside the den, and found her daywalking! Even worse, she had led an eagle right back to the den's entrance, where it attacked her. I jumped in, and—and killed it, and . . . as soon as we got back to the den Chumba started pretending like nothing had happened. It all happened right when the Veil was lifting, before you'd even gotten up; it was over so fast, Mother!"

Chumba and Mez stare at their cousin, dumbfounded.

"I—I don't know what to say," Chumba stammers.

"It's not true!" Mez says.

"How do you know?" Usha asks, cocking her head at Mez. "Were you there too?"

Mez would be happy to let Mist take credit for killing the eagle if it meant taking the heat off Chumba. But not if it meant Usha would suspect Chumba of daywalking. Not if it meant Chumba would be banished.

Mez looks at Usha's expression to see if she's caught on to Mist's terrible lying, but her aunt's gaze is trained only on Chumba. "Even though you were missing your paw and were therefore unfit, I took you and Mez in as a last favor to my sister," she continues. "But the rules of the panthers are clear: If you are daywalking, you are unnatural. And if you are unnatural, you must be exiled."

6

AUNT USHA EXTENDS her claws and tugs at them with her teeth to sharpen them. Usha knows exactly the message she's sending by doing so now.

As if an invisible paw has pushed them down, the triplets nestle beside their mother, mewling as they nurse for comfort. Chumba is next to sit, plopping right where she is behind Usha and the triplets, wonder and fascination on her face as she waits to see what will happen next. It's like she hasn't pieced together that she's going to have to leave—she just knows that she wasn't daywalking, so she assumes the truth will release her. Heart quaking, Mez positions herself carefully so she's blocking her smaller sister from Usha's view.

Mist is the only one who does not sit, instead glowering at his mother's side, ready to spring into action once she passes judgment.

Usha speaks. "Chumba. This is your last chance to come clean and defend yourself. Tell me now: How did this eagle die?"

Despite her best effort to hold quiet and still, Mez lets out a groan of fear and brings her body low to the ground, nervous claws scraping through mushrooms and leaves. The scent of her own pantherfear rises around her.

Somewhere out of view, a tree splits with a sharp and wet cracking sound. As one, the startled panthers get to their paws, wheeling and staring, tails low and teeth bared. Even Usha loses her usual composure, fear revealing the whites around her eyes. "Show yourself!" she calls.

There is no answer.

Of course, none of the panthers suspects what Mez suspects—that Auriel is somewhere out there, watching.

One by one, the panthers sit back down. It's Chumba who speaks first. "Why would it be so terrible if one of us were daywalking?"

Aunt Usha gives her a scathing look, like Chumba has just admitted guilt. Usha hasn't noticed what Mez has—that Chumba's telltale right ear keeps flicking in

Mez's direction. Does Chumba know her secret?

"You have seen the constellation of the Ant Queen above," Usha says. "Legends tell that she was awake during night and day alike, and once ran amok over Caldera, enslaving the other animals and feeding those who resisted to her minions. Even now her ants can cross the Veil at will, a constant reminder of the danger their queen once presented."

"That . . . Ant Scene was powerful enough to *conquer all of Caldera*?" Chumba says in awe, looking up at the night sky.

"Ant *Queen*," Mez whispers, shivering and huddling tighter against her sister's side.

"But . . . you raised me, Aunt Usha," Chumba says. "You would really exile me for daywalking?"

"I would," Usha says flatly. "As if I needed any more proof that crossing the Veil is dangerous, your mother, my sister . . . gave birth to you during the eclipse, during the moment of wakefulness that resulted. But panthers are not meant to be awake during the day, much less give birth, and her labor went wrong. She went feral, her eyes rolled back, she lost control of her body. Most of her litter didn't survive. Only you two."

"And one of you was . . . ruined," Mist adds. "Mother, you should have known that Chumba would turn out to be the unnatural one. And with their patchy colors, too—it's time we winnowed out the unfit."

Mez shrinks in horror at the thought that their births had caused her mother's death. Usha's words continue to drive into her, warbling her darkvision and weakening her legs. Mez knew that her mother died soon after she was born. But she didn't know it had been because of the eclipse, because of the strange power from the sun and moon beaming down from the sky, and that there had been other newborns in her litter who hadn't survived. Usha had always refused to talk about it, claiming that what was past was past.

Surprisingly, Usha whirls on Mist. "Watch your tongue. Some panthers prefer a cat with some color to it. Male cubs can't even produce such a diverse range of colors. Only females are ever calico."

"Only female cubs are ever *ugly*, you mean," Mist grumbles.

"You're just insecure about your white fur," Mez says hotly. "If Usha wasn't your *mother*, we might be talking about how that white fur of yours could make *you* the unfit one."

All the panthers, even the triplets, stare at Mez. Ears flattened and heat flooding her cheeks, she studies the grass.

"Chumba, I'm still waiting for an explanation," Usha says. "The eagle was killed during the sunset border time. Mist rescued you from it. But what were you doing out there in the first place?"

Mist doesn't flinch. Apparently he's sticking to his story.

For a moment, Mez keeps her eyes down on the greenery and the black loamy soil. A bright yellow caterpillar climbs a leaf. "It wasn't Chumba who was daywalking," she finally says.

Before Aunt Usha can respond, Mist cries out, "Of course it was Chumba! It has to be Chumba!"

"Mist!" Aunt Usha scolds. But she doesn't move to protect Chumba. She will let this power play work out on its own—that is the panther way.

Mez's mind races. If she lets Chumba go into exile, they'll be separated. If she tells the truth about her day-walking, they'll be separated. There is no way out—she's going to lose her sister either way.

Mez runs to Chumba and has her teeth around her sister's nape, as if to carry her to safety like a little kitten. The triplets watch her strange behavior like it's a game of catch-the-frog, their rapt eyes going back and forth and back and forth.

Aunt Usha's tail was already flicking, but now it thrashes and jabs, sending wet leaves flurrying about the clearing. Then suddenly she is on all fours, teeth bared. "Enough! Here's what will happen: Chumba, you will not return to the den."

"No!" Mez cries.

Mez feels Chumba's warmth next to her, and then nothing. Her little sister has gotten up to stand on all fours. Though Chumba looks calmly into Usha's eyes, as though she has nothing to fear, all the hairs on her calico body have pricked up. "As you wish, Aunt Usha. I will go," she says resolutely.

"No!" Mez cries again.

Usha silences her with a simple look. "You cannot always speak for your sister," Usha says. "Let Chumba make this decision herself."

"She doesn't need to go!" Mez says. "Please don't do this—she needs me!"

Mez pulls back in shock as Chumba whirls on her. "Stop it!" she cries. "Stop trying to protect me—let me help you!"

There's a secret message in Chumba's eyes. The others wouldn't see it, but Mez knows her sister so well. *I know it's you. But you have the best chance of surviving anyway. Let me be the one to be exiled.* "But no cub can survive on her own," Mez whimpers.

"I wouldn't call spending all her time hiding behind your tail 'surviving,'" Mist says.

Aunt Usha casts a frustrated glance at the night sky. "I'm tired of being lied to, and we need to hunt this night, or the triplets will go hungry," she says. "This conversation is over. Chumba, you stay here, and we will go. By the time we return, you must be gone."

"Come on," Chumba whispers to Mez. "Don't fight this anymore. You've got the best chance of the two of us. My nights have always been numbered, anyway."

Tears stand in Mez's eyes. She bares her teeth at Mist, at Usha, unsure where to direct her anger.

She tries to memorize the way Chumba looks right at this moment, to save it in her mind for later: the dappling of white along her cheeks, the orange patch on her left side that looks like the profile of a crow, the way some of her whiskers stick straight out while others have an elegant curve to them.

Mez forces herself to step in front of Chumba and look Usha full in the face, her whole body trembling.

She takes a deep breath.

"It's me, Aunt Usha. I'm the daywalker."

All the panthers freeze. Mez stares into Usha's inscrutable eyes, trying to find answers there that just won't come. Did Usha suspect this all along?

"Fine. I can't believe either of you, clearly," Aunt Usha says. "If you want to take your sister's place, I won't stop you, Mez." She turns sharply and heads out of the swampy clearing. "Good-bye. To my side, cubs."

Chumba throws herself over Mez, body shuddering. "I'm going with her!" she says.

"No, you are not," Usha says. "My last promise to my dying sister was that I would take care of her cubs. One of you has broken the sacred way of the nightwalkers, and so one of you must be exiled. But one of you must stay here so I can keep my promise. We will not drag this out any further. We go *now*."

Chumba's head hangs heavy. The corners of her eyes tip down, her lips droop away from her teeth.

"Go, Chum, before this is any worse. I'll be okay," Mez says, lowering her voice so only Chumba can hear. "I know what I'm going to do. I'll prove myself somehow and come back. Usha will have cooled off in a season or two. Just wait for me."

"I want you to stay," Chumba pleads.

"Chum, please go," Mez says, seeing Usha's glowering expression.

"Just stay in the woods for a while, and then return at dawn," Chumba whispers. "I'll convince her to accept you back in the meantime."

Usha growls. "Exile is not the worst punishment I can give. We go *now*."

"Go, Chumba. I love you. I'll be back."

"I love you too."

Tail between her legs, Chumba follows Usha and the triplets out of the clearing, glancing back over her shoulder one last time to look longingly at Mez. Mist is the last to go, with a expression in his eyes that Mez has never seen before, wonder laced with fear.

Then Mez is alone.

She plops down in the clearing, stunned. Her tail thrashes despite her efforts to keep it calm, her paws crunch the twigs and stony soil, her lips flick back from her teeth time and again.

She stares between the trees, at the movement of emerald coils.

7

As the constrictor approaches, Mez tries to keep her terror at bay by concentrating on the familiar feeling of waxy leaves under her paws, the pungent scent of the fertile soil, the tiny pops of puffball mushrooms crushing while she kneads the earth.

The emerald coils come nearer and nearer, bending and breaking branches as they go.

"Little cub," says a voice from above.

Even though Auriel's head holds motionless in the air, as if suspended from the moon, his body continues to emerge from the trees. His *very* long body. Mez fights the urge to bolt as more and more of the giant snake uncoils.

Mez holds steady, turns her tear-streaming eyes treeward. Auriel's long body has looped and looped so many times around a branch that Mez cannot tell which coils are at the front of his body and which are at the back. He slides his head closer to Mez, and as he does the emerald-and-tan patterns on his skin cross, beguiling her. Ants rain from him.

"I know I said I wouldn't come with you last time I saw you," Mez says. "But everything has changed."

"You do not need to explain," Auriel intones, "for I heard it all."

Mez stares up at the strange snake, out of words.

"You are a shadowwalker," Auriel continues in his vibrating voice. "That was all I needed to know. Joining me and the other shadowwalkers at the Ziggurat of the Sun and Moon is your destiny. I knew you would find the courage to face it."

The snake finishes arriving. His body forms wide coils under him, the raw size of it all making him look more like a tree than an animal. Now that he's talking, there's a glint to his eyes that's almost kindly. As kindly as a snake can get, of course.

"Why didn't you say anything earlier?" Mez asks.

"I didn't know how your aunt Usha would react to a constrictor," Auriel says. "It is easy to hate what you have never met. When I went to find other eclipse-born,

I've discovered young animals slain by their own kind for having the stink of day on them, or the stink of night. You know your aunt Usha better than I do. My joining the conversation might have put you in even more danger."

Mez shivers, not so much at the idea of being killed—the rainforest has reminded her every night of the many forms that death can take—but at the idea that others have died for having the same wrongness inside them that she has.

"Of course," Auriel says, as his body starts to pour onto the ground in front of her, "I would only use words of praise for a young animal of your gifts."

It's almost like he'd heard Mez's thoughts, like she'd spoken them out loud. "I'm—I'm not gifted," Mez stammers. "I've got only the weird daywalking part."

"No one has only the 'weird daywalking part,'" Auriel says, the purring sound in his voice increasing as the hint of a smile crosses his face. Undeniably serpentine and intimidating, but definitely a smile.

Mez cocks her head. "I've never met a shadowwalker before you. This is all new to me."

"You *have* met a shadowwalker," Auriel says. "Yourself. We have a long journey to make, and I will answer as many of your questions as I'm able along the way. But for now you'll have to trust me. I know that I am not mistaken in the few things that I know. Come. The columns of ants streaming toward the Ziggurat of the Sun and Moon grow thicker, which means the Ant Queen is nearing her release. Time is running short. The very fate of Caldera is at stake."

If Mez leaves this part of the jungle, she'll be even farther from Chumba. But traveling with this constrictor will still be better than being alone, and maybe she'll be able to do something special at the ziggurat thing, and come back a hero. Aunt Usha might take her back then. "Lead the way," Mez says quietly.

Auriel nods, reversing direction and slithering through the undergrowth. He's remarkably fast for such a large snake, arrowing gracefully between trunks and brambles, leaving a trail of ants behind him.

Aunt Usha always chooses the same pathways through the jungle, but Auriel has his own ways of going; though they move in a direction Mez has gone in many times, the scenery is soon unfamiliar. Here is a red flowering vine she's never encountered; here are termites with bluish carapaces, unlike the brown ones that build their mounds near the den; here is a waterfall of just a few feet, the water drumming modestly, only slightly louder than the constant patter of rainfall on leaves. Mez keeps her gaze outward, to fight off her worry about Chumba.

Mez takes a few gulps from the stream, finds herself wondering if Chumba is off doing the same somewhere, then struggles to catch up to Auriel. Panthers are supposed to be the fleetest creatures in the jungle, but Auriel's faster than she is—and he has no legs! Good thing Mist isn't there to see.

"Just because you haven't shown powers yet doesn't mean that you don't have any," Auriel explains patiently in his low and vibrating voice. "That's part of why I'm trying to bring all of the shadowwalkers together. So that you can see what your powers are, and use them. To prevent the Ant Queen from overrunning Caldera, of course, but if we're successful you can return home and help your families with your abilities, too."

"What's the Ant Queen like?" Mez asks, hopping from stone to stone across a muddy stream. Auriel easily swam across it, as if he were made of river water. She gulps. "And what could she do to us?"

"I know less than you think I do, I'm afraid," Auriel says. "I'm no older than you. Granted, I can see why you'd think I'd know more. Constrictors mature more quickly than panthers, and we are wanderers, and I am able to spy on the Ant Queen's communications with the billions of her kind, so maybe I do actually have more information than most daywalkers or nightwalkers. All I know is what you do: the last time she was free was the time of Caldera's darkest struggle."

"Do you know how far away the ziggurat is?"

"It's right at the center of Caldera," Auriel says. "Lucky for us, your aunt Usha's territory is closer to the center than most. It won't take you more than twenty days and twenty nights to make the journey."

You? Something about the way Auriel said that word sets Mez's tail to thrashing. Before she can ask about it, though, he speaks again. "You and I are not so unalike."

"I'm not so sure that's true," Mez says, pointedly looking down at her small furry body and then at Auriel's long scaly one.

"Come, this rock is still warm from the sun. Let's rest on it for a moment, so a cold-blooded creature like me can build up a little heat." Auriel doesn't seem to have been flagging, but Mez takes his word for it that he could use a rest. "That's better," he says as he arranges his coils on a mossy rock. "I was once a leathery little egg surrounded by dozens of other leathery little eggs. Then my siblings and I were born, and I would have done anything to get back into that egg and leave the outside world forever. Little snakes are food for *everyone*, and unlike you I didn't have a mother or an aunt to care for me. I was hunted by birds, insects, frogs, even my siblings. They trapped me, and attacked me, and almost killed me. But I managed to survive, and as soon as I could I left. You'll find that no one holds much affection for a top predator like a panther—but there's even less love for a constrictor, I can promise you that. But do not worry. You will find your way, like I once found mine. There are many sorts of families out there."

Maybe it's Auriel's words, or his calm and wistful manner as he says them, or the way the moonlight traces patches along the jungle paths; maybe it's the lonely call of the owls secreted away in the treetops above. Whatever the cause, the enormity of what she's undertaken comes over Mez, a sadness that's sudden and strong. She's never gone more than one night's travel from her den, and here she is speeding away from the only place she's ever known to go to some strange place called the Ziggurat of the Sun and Moon.

At least Auriel seems like an easy enough snake to talk to. "Did you ever see your family again?" Mez asks. Her mind goes to Chumba, and the thought of her is enough to make her ribs and belly seize tight.

Auriel stays quiet for so long that Mez wonders if her question might have gotten lost in the drone of the insects. It's hard to even see Auriel anymore; he is so adept at slithering through the damp leaves of the jungle floor that his heavy body merges seamlessly into the surrounding dark, making him hard to detect even with Mez's excellent darkvision.

She's about to repeat her question when finally he speaks: "My family tried to *eat* me, Mez. No, I'm never going to see them again."

"Oh, right, sorry, of course," Mez mumbles.

Silence. Then, when Auriel's voice comes again, it's controlled and tight. "That is enough conversation for one evening. Come, you must be hungry. I know I am. It is time to eat."

"We'll hunt . . . together?" Mez asks.

Auriel chuckles and opens his mouth so Mez can get a good view of his gaping fangless jaws. "This was the last gift of my childhood bullies. They pinned me down and broke off my fangs. A mean old snake trick. Hard to hunt without fangs."

"I'm sorry," Mez says.

"It feels like a long time ago," Auriel responds quietly.

"Did it hurt?"

"Another time, Mez."

"So you got to be that big size . . . by eating fruits and vegetables?" Mez presses.

"Some of them are very nutritious," Auriel says.

"It's impressive. I hope you don't mind though if I, if I . . ."

"Of course not," Auriel says, a smile in his voice. "Hunt away, Mez."

8

BEFORE THE NIGHT is through, they've gone well past the border of Mez's known world. Toward dawn, the dense jungle thins to rocky mineral mats edging a saltwater lake. Mangroves sprout around it, and Auriel eagerly twines himself into their midst to bed down. He takes a tree almost to himself, his long body spooling around the trunk and into the strongest branches, draping back down so his head nestles amid the lowest leaves. Mez never would have imagined she'd see an expression on a snake's face that could be called sweet, especially not on a snake this large and powerful, but so it is. Auriel begins to snore. Or the quiet and raspy snake version of snoring.

It's been so long since she's had a good sleep. Mez picks her way between the warm and fragrant pools, shaking out her paws, licking away the salt that stings the creases between her pads. She selects the mangrove that looks the driest, not far from Auriel. She's never been this near to one of the salty, stinky trees, and finds its bark unappealingly slimy.

Still, she locates a secure perch and spends the dawn hour licking herself clean, bringing her rough tongue directly to her fur where she can, then licking her paw and using that to groom the harder-to-reach places. Back in the den, Chumba would have been the one to lick those spots. Missing Chumba hits Mez hard enough to make her head droop. She wonders who, if anyone, is grooming Chumba now that she isn't there, and the sorrow of that thought makes her eyes scrunch shut tighter.

Come dusk, she emerges from her slumber to find Auriel still asleep in the same position, head resting on the branch. Mez watches the smooth rise and fall of the snake's green rib cage and wonders what boa constrictors dream about. Her belly growls, and even the croaks of the frogs make her hungry. Mist and Usha would consider a frog beneath a panther's dignity, but Mez has snuck one or two before and enjoyed their watery flavor.

She didn't catch much the night before, and would like to hunt again. But this salt flat is an unknown place, and Mez has only ever hunted along pathways set by Aunt Usha. She's sure Auriel wouldn't want her wandering off, so despite her hunger she holds still and watches him, willing him to wake.

Chumba, I hope you're awake now too. I hope you're thinking of me like I'm thinking of you.

Finally her hunger is too nagging to ignore. Mez climbs down from her mangrove and slinks along the ground, fearfully looking at the sky, imagining cub-stealing eagles everywhere.

Auriel's fangless mouth lolls open as he sleeps. Mez hasn't been this close to the snake before. He really is *covered* in ants. They're streaming up from the mud, climbing all over his giant body, antennae waving and forelegs tasting the air. Once they reach Auriel's head they increase in concentration, massing around his eyes. Even in Auriel's sleep his eyes remain open, only a milky membrane covering them. The ants cluster at the corners, antennae waving in perfect synchronization. As they do, Auriel's mouth moves slightly, murmuring in tones too low for Mez to hear.

She is transfixed by the dream-communication between ant and snake. Mez goes more and more still, losing track of time and place. Slowly words enter her mind as if spoken to her, though she's also distantly aware that the dusk is full only of its normal sounds.

She both hears the ants speak and knows in her deepest
heart that they cannot be speaking.

Of eclipse-born now are thirty
nineteen are found
five are dead
three will soon be
Rumi is next to find
not by snake, but by killer be
Lima is nearer
she will die next
unless
one can save her
with the magic that
is not known
Mez will—

At hearing her name spoken in her own head, Mez
startles and hears a pattering sound on the leaves around
her. Ants are cascading from her own fur like rain, from
her ears and her nose and everywhere in between.

They were crawling on her eyes.

Mez yelps, leaping and scrambling, and plunges
herself into the saltwater pond. The shock of the water
soon sets her hurtling back out and scrambling up the
bank, standing at the edge with all four legs splayed out

wide, shaking the water free.

When she catches her breath and looks at Auriel, she finds the snake is staring at her, chuckling. Ants spill from him in streams. "Decided to go for an evening dip?" he asks.

"I—I don't like a-ants on my eyes," Mez says, her shivers stuttering her words.

"Ah," Auriel says. "I see you've discovered that my ability lets others hear the ants, too, if they're at close-enough range."

"Talking to ants," Mez says. "I bet you wish you could turn that power back in and get another."

"On the contrary, my new friend," Auriel says. "I have learned much about our land through my magic. The ants of Caldera weigh more than all the other animals put together. Ants are the unsung element of our world."

"That's an element I'd prefer not to have saying my name into my eyeballs, thank you very much."

"You heard your own name?" Auriel asks, suddenly alert. "What else did you hear?"

"Nothing that made much sense."

"That's too bad," Auriel says, his head bobbing in what Mez has come to realize is the snake equivalent of a shrug. "Come, let's get moving. I'm sure you're hungry, but you can hunt along the way. Maybe I'll get you to try eating some nuts, too."

"No chance," Mez says, shaking her head in disgust.

Mez waits until their night's travel is well underway to speak up again. The moon is in a shrunken phase, so the forest is especially dark. The dim and cool scraps of light only intensify her darkvision, make any hints of movement in the brush even more evident. It's a perfect night for hunting, and her instincts bring her focus to the chase—but not so much that she can't ask Auriel a question. "Who are Rumi and Lima?"

Auriel stops moving for a moment, his back coils bunching up against the front. Then he continues his smooth glide through the night jungle. "Rumi and Lima? Why do you ask?"

"The ants mentioned those names."

"Ah," Auriel says. "So you did get something from your eavesdropping. Rumi and Lima are soon to be your new companions. We should be meeting Lima shortly, if the ants' indications are correct."

"Are Rumi and Lima . . . ants?" Mez asks.

Auriel chuckles. "No."

"Capybaras? Peccaries? Ooh—more panthers?"

"Hush. You'll find out soon enough," Auriel says.

I'd love it if there were another panther. Maybe like Chumba! I'd even take an ocelot, Mez thinks as they continue to stalk through the still night. She consoles herself that at least they're meeting this Lima at night.

The dawn's sun has begun to crack out of the horizon and Auriel still hasn't called them to a halt. "So . . . is Lima near?" Mez asks.

"I thought I asked you to be patient," Auriel replies.

"That was a *very* long time ago," Mez says.

Auriel leads them toward a gap in the hillside where rocks join unevenly, leaving a passage wide enough for a constrictor—or a young panther—to fit through. Without pausing to see whether the way forward is safe, Auriel heads right in. Apparently extra-big snakes don't have much to fear. For Mez, though, the cave entrance is tight enough to tickle the tips of her whiskers, and having walls that near both sides of her face makes her hackles stand up. It doesn't help that it's fully daylight now. "Do we *have* to go in here?" she asks.

"You're a predator, friend!" Auriel purrs back. "Time to start acting like one!"

Grumbling, Mez forces her hackles down and continues through the tunnel.

The cave is dark, at least it has that going for it. Otherwise, it's only gross. There's a bitter and stale reek, with notes of dung and fungus, nose-slapping ammonia layered on top of it. Tailless whip spiders skitter around Mez's paws, agile as scorpions, their forelegs ever poised to strike. "Who would want to live in this place?" she asks, tucking her nose in the crook of her leg.

"Look above," Auriel whispers back, "and you'll have your answer."

Mez stares up, craning her neck, eyelids wide to let as much light in as possible. Now that she's looking closely, she can see slight swaying movements. It's a carpet of bats, black fur blotting out the cave ceiling. Then Mez sees a pair of eyes glinting back. Hunting instincts take over, and she brings her body into a low crouch, creeping slowly forward, her body, nose to tail, one rigid line.

"Stop it right there," Auriel says sternly. "I did not bring you all this way to have you eat another shadow-walker."

Mez lets herself lick her chops, imagining the pleasing crunch of hollow bat bones between her jaws, then forces herself out of her hunting stance. "Is that Lima up there?" she asks, pointing her nose toward the eyes staring back at them from the ceiling.

"She's a nightwalker awake during the day, is what she is," Auriel says. "That's why we came to this cave during the daytime, so we could find her easily. I seem to remember meeting a certain young calico panther that way, too."

Mez looks up with wonder. She's seeing her first

fellow eclipse-born, after Auriel! "Is your name Lima?" she calls up softly.

The glinting green eyes blink, disappearing and then reappearing in the dark cave.

"We mean you no harm," Auriel calls up. "We only want to help."

"I know who you are," the bat says, her voice a high whisper. "The ants told me you'd be coming."

"The ants talked to you on their own?" Mez asks, strangely jealous, considering that talking to the ants also means letting them crawl all over your eyeballs.

"Part of my ability means I can send advance word through them," Auriel whispers sharply. "It would have worked on you, too, if you'd been a little more open to it. They were all over your den, trying to transmit my message. All you would've had to do was listen."

"Ants. Ugh!" Mez says. "I might have squished a bunch of your messengers. Sorry."

"Um, could you two keep it down?" Lima says. "I don't want everyone else here finding out my secret, thank you."

"Lima, please," Auriel says dryly. "We both know how impossible it is to wake an ordinary bat during the daytime."

"Still," Lima whispers. "Just in case, I'd rather not have anyone catch me dayflying, please."

"Then come with us," Mez says. "We can talk more outside of this stinky cave."

"Stinky!" Lima shrieks back, indignant. "That's rich, coming from an animal that pees on trees all night."

"That is *enough*," Mez says, growling. "You get down here right now, pip-squeak."

"Outside, ladies," Auriel says. "Both of you. Right now."

"You two leave first," Lima says. "I'll follow."

"With pleasure," Mez says icily as she pads her way across the soft stones of the cave floor—soft with bat guano, she realizes, which also explains the ammonia smell. Tailless whip spiders crackle and flail beneath her paws. She'll be glad to leave this cave, that's for sure.

She blinks into the daylight and comes to a seat on the jungle floor, facing the cave entrance. Auriel follows, his body taking a long time to finish coming through the entrance. Once he's emerged, a tiny black speck follows, flitting to the top of the rock at the entrance, then nervously stepping from one foot to another. "Oh my," Lima says in her high-pitched voice, looking at the constrictor and panther assembled below.

"Perhaps you were expecting someone . . . cuddlier?" Auriel asks.

"Yes. I think I was," Lima squeaks.

She's really, really tiny. Mez has met mice heftier than this bat. "You don't have anything to fear," she calls up to Lima. "You're much too insignificant for me to consider eating, and apparently Auriel has turned herbivore."

"Oh!" Lima says brightly. "That makes me feel *so* much better."

At first Mez figures the bat is being sarcastic, but then Lima makes a sprightly chirping sound and hops down, fearlessly perching on one of Auriel's coils. "I mean, I figured that you weren't going to eat me, because it would be so much easier to eat one of the sleeping bats, if food was all you were after. Oh my gosh, you're *so* pretty!"

Mez looks behind her, trying to see what animal might have crept up, her heart supplying all-white panther cubs for Lima to have admired. Then she realizes who she's talking about. "Wait, you mean *me*?"

Lima hops from Auriel over to Mez, her little clawed feet barely any weight on Mez's back. She picks through Mez's fur with the little hands at the ends of her wings. "All these colors! I mean, from far away you'd think it was all sort of this brown-black, like mine, but there's actually circles and lines and dots beneath, all these great golden shapes floating under the brown. Do you know how to make those kind of colors in another animal?"

"No," Mez says, whirling around to try to get a better view of her own body, to see what Lima's talking about. The patterns her mother gave her *are* kind of beautiful. At the very least they're interesting.

"That's too bad," Lima chirps. "I think I'd look good with calico spots. I mean, not as good as *you*, but good."

"I'm from a family of black panthers, but my coloring is from my mom. It's what I have to remember her by."

"Oh, that's very nice," Lima says, hugging her leathery wings tight around her own body. "I'm not sure who my mother is. Or my father."

"Wait, what?" Mez asks.

"Well, you saw how many bats there are in there!"

"But, I figure you'd always know, I mean, don't you have special calls for one another or something?"

"Well, sure, when we're *little*, but not once we're full-size. It's fine, no big deal, no bats know who their parents are, less to worry about. So, let's get going to the Ziggurat of the Sun and Moon! I've never seen a ziggurat before. I'm not even sure what one is."

Auriel clears his throat. "Allow me to properly introduce myself. I am Auriel, and I was born in an eclipse like you, which means the powers of sun and moon both—"

"—are in you, and in me. Yes, got it. I told you— your ant friends already filled me in. Let's go stop the

Ant Queen from taking over Caldera!" She shakes her little bat fist up in the direction of the queen's constellation.

"Oh, um, okay," Auriel says. "Let's head out, then."

Lima doesn't leave Mez's shoulder as they start off along the jungle pathways. The bat is so light that Mez can't even sense her on her back, but still, it does seem like Lima should have at least *asked* if she could ride her. Mez debates how best to bring it up.

"Do you think this is the first time that a panther and a bat have traveled together?" Lima asks. "I bet it is. I bet a lot of animals would be surprised to see us like this, huh? But I guess you panthers are famously good at avoiding being seen. That's sort of the whole point of being a panther, or a constrictor for that matter, so I guess no one's going to see us. Maybe panthers have been carrying bats around for all of eternity, and no one's noticed because no one can find them. Maybe!"

"Anyone can find us when we're *talking all the time*," Mez says through gritted teeth.

"Oh, right, got it, sorry," Lima says, and goes perfectly quiet. "One last thing," she whispers after a moment. "Is it always so *bright* out during the day?"

Mez is used to daywalking by now, but has forgotten that it's all new to Lima. When Auriel leads them into a bank of ferns, carefully maneuvering his body between the fronds so he's out of view, and Mez lies down beneath the broadest leaves so she, too, can sleep through the worst of the sun's heat, Lima lets out a big sigh. "There's so much to echolocate out there. So many daywalkers."

When Lima hops down from Mez's back, Mez sees that she's trembling, her eyes streaming tears. Her irritation dissipating, Mez gives the little bat a tender lick along one of her soft and fuzzy ears. Lima hops so she's closer to Mez's side, and the panther loops her front leg around her to snuggle the little bat in tight. She could almost pretend it's Chumba. They're not too dissimilar, Chumba and Lima, full of pluck and cheer.

Auriel forms a protective ring around them, the ants going about their mysterious work, crawling over him as he closes his eyes to rest. Nestling down together, the three strange traveling companions settle in to wait out the day.

◇

Come evening, Mez wakes to see Lima hopping along one of the ferns, to the tip and back. Ears and wings undulating, she's doing a dance that's both crazy and elegant. She leads with her mouth, swinging around invisible dance partners. "What are you *doing*?" Mez asks.

"Getting a meal! It's like the gnats around here have

never met a bat. They come wandering right up. I've always stuck to hunting high up in the sky before, but this, this is amazing. Tree hunting, who knew? Also amazing, look at this! Have you noticed yet?"

Lima's hopped over to where Auriel is still resting. Ants, a red-black species this time, crawl over the membranes on his eyes. Mez shudders. "Yes, I've seen it before. It's disgusting."

"No it's not, it's *fascinating*," Lima says, leaning forward so she can extend a leathery wing and use the thumb at the top to pluck an ant off of Auriel's nose. She examines it closely. It stands up on its back legs, antennae twitching as it examines her right back. "It looks like a normal ant to me. Doesn't it to you? I mean, you don't see this ant and immediately think, 'Oh yes, this is clearly an Arthropod of Prophecy,' or whatever they get called? If that's even a thing. Probably not a thing, now that I think about it. Why would the ants crawl all over Auriel like that? Ooh, maybe he's got some nectar on him somewhere." Without hesitating, Lima gives Auriel a big lick on the tip of his leathery nose. Her face wrinkles. "Nope, not sweet at all. Ugh. Kind of the opposite, actually." Her expression brightens. "Hey, have *you* ever tasted a snake before? Well, now I have! That's one for the list! Glad he didn't wake up while I was licking him, though. That would have been awkward."

With that, Lima brings the ant she's holding to her lips and daintily nibbles off its head.

Auriel snorts awake. The power of his exhale is enough to send Lima tumbling head over heels, coming to rest in a fern, wings stretched wide as if set out to dry, astonishment on her face.

"Did you just eat one of these ants?" Auriel asks, an unreadable expression on his face.

Lima looks at the wriggling half ant still on her thumb, then at Auriel, then wordlessly hides it behind her back.

A smile grows across Auriel's face. "It's fine, I'm teasing. Ants don't mourn ants, so why should we? It would be like mourning grass. There are over a million in one colony, anyway. If they stopped to have a funeral for each one, they'd never get anything done."

Her eyes never leaving Auriel's, Lima brings the body of the ant, brittle legs still flailing, up to her mouth. She chomps down. "Shmtastesgood," she explains as she swallows. She clears her throat. "Tangy. Can I have another?"

"Some other time. Let's get a move on," Auriel says. "Your next companion is near. Fleeing this way, actually. Get those sharp teeth of yours ready, Mez. According to the ants, Rumi is having a *really* bad evening."

9

WHILE THEY STEAL through the darkness, a storm comes up, night rain pelting the broad, flat leaves of the trees above. Those leaves will hold the water as long as they can, until the weight causes them to bend and give way, dousing the jungle floor below. The three companions move as fast as possible through the undergrowth, trying to avoid the occasional downpours. Auriel seems not at all bothered by the wet, but Mez finds it as unpleasant as always. Every once in a while she sprints ahead, to give herself time to pause and shake out her front paws. She feels an urge to lick Chumba dry, then it floods back that her sister isn't there.

Lima keeps her wings tented over her head as she rides on Mez's back. "Echolocation and rain are not friends," she says. "I'd rather not know the precise location of each raindrop, you know?"

Every once in a while the rain clouds part to show the moon. It has grown from its newness of the night before, and more of its light survives the trip down to the jungle floor. So far Mez has been able to avoid the worst puddles, though one especially large deluge from above catches her directly on the face, stopping her short. She sputters.

Auriel halts, and after a few long moments his head makes the journey back to where Mez is, near his tail. He listens, tasting the air with his forked tongue, then nods. "Ah yes. I detect Rumi's approach, too. Good work, Mez. Follow me." The snake starts off in a new direction, arrowing into the brush.

Mez nods vaguely. Right. She detected something. That's why she stopped.

Lima pipes up. "Oh, I don't think Mez heard anything. I think she stopped because of that massive—"

"Ready-to-go-Lima-okay-good!" Mez says rapidly before starting off after Auriel.

"Don't cut me off!" Lima cries, the rest of her retort lost to the drumming sound of the rain as Mez stalks forward.

"Quiet now," Auriel whispers. "They're coming along that path."

Mez draws back into the lightless area beside a tree.

For a long time; there's nothing for her senses to take in beyond the pounding rain and the scant moonlight scattering on the surfaces of puddles. Then Mez hears something coming along the path. Lima must have, too: "What in the world is that?" she squeaks into Mez's ear.

It's the croak of a frog, Mez is almost sure. But all the same it's unlike any other sound she's heard, all flappy and loud, like each croak is actually bursting the frog open. As it gets nearer, she pulls farther back into the shadows, suddenly wary of the possibility of a six-foot frog.

Auriel yells out. It's the first time Mez has heard him at full voice. The loudness fills the canyon between trees, and sets Lima rocketing into the air in alarm. "Rumi," Auriel booms, "we are here to help you!"

A ricocheting yellow speck appears at the far side of the tree canyon, heading right toward them. At first Mez thinks it's some hollow gourd bouncing and bounding, then she comes to realize that she's seeing an animal, a frog, only it's a frog completely out of control, its movements heedless and random. As it gets closer, Mez can see the frog's mouth is open wide in terror. It's such a small mouth, though; how could it make such a huge, croaking ruckus?

Mez has her answer when another frog launches into view, slaloming down the canyon, making a great cannonball splash each time it lands. This cane toad is as big as a thousand of the first frog, as big as Mez herself, sending up waves of rainwater with each wild leap. When it opens its mouth, Mez sees deep into its red-and-black gullet, sees the curling tongue slavering and salivating, then comes the sound, *that's* who was making it, and oh, what a sound it is! The ripping boom of the cane toad's croak sets her whiskers quivering.

The first frog whizzes past, his tiny yellow form bouncing off tree trunks, fully out of control. The giant cane toad must have seen Mez, Auriel, and Lima by now, but continues leaping after the little one, the ground thudding with each landing. "Auriel! Which one is Rumi?" Mez yells out.

"I wish I knew!" Auriel says. "I haven't met him yet!" The constrictor moves his long body so it blocks the cane toad's way, but the giant beast jumps him easily, making another fearsome croak as it lands on the far side.

The tiny yellow frog makes terrified burps, still bouncing around the far side of the clearing. The panicky sounds resolve themselves into words. "Get it away! Get it away!"

The small frog is clearly exhausted. It stumbles and rolls, splaying out along the ground, shaking all over. "Are you Rumi?" Mez asks it.

Both frogs stare at her. "Yes!" they say at once.

"Okay," Mez says, "guess I'm going to have to go with my gut here."

The bigger frog advances on the smaller, its pebbly tongue already extended. The cane toad doesn't even bother to leap anymore, just waddles forward on its jiggling meaty legs. The little frog peers back with wide, inky irises. Where it's not covered in mud, its back is a beautiful iridescent combination of yellow and brown. The cane toad advances unabated.

Until Mez pounces.

Frogs are tricky creatures. When she was very young, Mez once attacked one, but soon after her paw touched its back she fell into seizures, shaking on the ground while the frog hopped away. Other frogs have no poison at all—it's hard to predict. So when Mez pounces, she makes her body as light as possible in the air, plucking the cane toad up from the ground with the tips of her claws and flipping it. It looks like a play move more than a hunting one, but the astonished frog tumbles over and over, its tongue lolling and whipping from side to side.

When it lands, it bounces right into a patch of witch's tongue, disappearing into the fronds. When the cane toad emerges, it's to the sight of Mez standing over the tiny and exhausted yellow frog, growling, teeth bared. The larger frog takes a moment to size up Mez before hopping toward her.

Auriel curls around Mez and the tiny frog in a protective circle, his head at the front, staring glitteringly at the cane toad. He keeps his mouth closed, maybe to hide his lack of fangs. The giant frog goes pale right in front of Mez's eyes, throat wattle turning almost translucent as the blood drains. Then it hops away, disappearing into the undergrowth.

For a while, Mez, Auriel, and the exhausted frog—the real Rumi, she hopes!—lie still and catch their breath. Then Lima's voice comes from above, where Mez sees the small bat dangling upside down from a branch, her teeth bared and wings extended. "Did you see that? I scared the cane toad off!"

Mez and Auriel stare up at her. "Sorry," Mez says, "didn't even notice you up there."

Lima flutters down to her now-familiar perch on Mez's shoulder. "Well, at least that mean toad did, right?" she sniffs. "He was so intimidated by me!"

Careful, as if the small frog were a thing on fire, Mez steps away from him. The frog peers up at the three unfamiliar creatures, still hyperventilating, eyes blinking rapidly.

Auriel shifts so that he, Mez, and Lima can stare at him from the same direction, their heads all lined up in a row. "Are you Rumi?" Auriel asks.

"Yes," the frog says, his voice even smaller than before.

"Was that other frog named Rumi, too?" Mez asks.

Rumi clears his throat. "Yes. It's quite a common name among frogs. Owing to the way we name our tadpoles. According to, um, where they hatch. And thousands of eggs being in the same place. My parents glued my eggs to the inside of a leaf. And apparently, so did his. So we're both called Rumi. Different parents, though. As is, um, abundantly apparent."

His eyes are unusually large, even for a frog. It makes him look brainy. Like perception is the most important thing about him.

"Have any ants told you that we were coming?" Auriel asks.

Rumi tilts his head. "Well, I must say, that's certainly not the question I was expecting."

"What question *were* you expecting?" Lima asks.

"You can answer that one first, if you want."

"Oh, hello there, Mr. Bat. Didn't even notice you."

"I'm a girl," Lima says. "And why doesn't anyone ever notice me? It's not like you're exactly a giant yourself."

"Well, with this striking coloration, I can't help but be noticed. For good or for bad, I'm afraid. As you might have observed. In any case, I was expecting you to ask why I was being pursued by another frog. That strikes me as the most pertinent question, to be frank."

"Frogs hunt other frogs. Everyone knows that," Auriel says, giving his snake version of a shrug.

"Well, my feud with Big Rumi, as I'll call him, goes way back," Rumi says. "But yes, frogs hunt other frogs. That is the simplest explanation, and not at all untrue. Other frogs are one of the worst things about being a frog, I'm afraid." A cloud of sadness passes over his face.

"I hear you," Auriel says. "These mammals don't know how tough it is to be a reptile or an amphibian. In any case, let me be frank. I don't suppose that frog, Big Rumi, was hunting you because you were caught daywalking?"

"Daywalking?" Rumi asks. He leans in, a wily expression on his face as his voice goes down to a whisper. "Why? Has anyone *told* you that I was daywalking?"

"We all daywalk," Mez says. "We're our own little band of weirdos."

"Shh!" Rumi says through gritted teeth. Or what would be gritted teeth, if he had any on the bottom jaw. "Look around you—there are eyes everywhere."

Lima looks up, opens her mouth, and listens. She pulls her wings tight around her. "He's right. There are twenty-four other creatures nearby, spread throughout the treetops. Wait! Or, oh dear, twenty-three now. Poor little tree rat didn't stand a chance against an owl."

"Interesting," Rumi says. "Is that your magical power?"

Lima shakes her head. "No, that's echolocation. All bats can do it, as long as it's not raining."

"Ah yes, I've surmised bats had some such power from my observations. But I've never seen it in action. How fascinating. I hope you'll allow me to ask you some questions about it."

"Of course! At least something makes me special. I'm pretty sure I don't *have* any magical power," Lima says, pulling her wings even tighter around herself in the dark of the night. "I've only got the unnatural part."

"Yeah, me too," Mez whispers, her thoughts on her daywalking, which leads her to thinking of Chumba, all by herself back home. Her head hangs.

"I promise you that you've all got magic," Auriel says. "The ants have witnessed eclipses happen in previous ages, and I've learned from them. You're nocturnal creatures that are awake during the day. That makes you shadowwalkers. And all shadowwalkers have magical powers. It's a matter of discovering what they are."

Rumi croaks once, loud and sharp. Mez realizes it's the frog version of a laugh. "Shadowwalkers! Those are only legends. Like the Ant Queen."

"Oh . . . you haven't heard yet that she's real?" Mez asks.

Auriel lets out a sigh, and Mez realizes how many times he must have gone through this conversation. "You have two options: You can think of yourself as a shadowwalker, or as an unnatural mistake. The choice is up to you," Auriel says flatly. "Our enemy is awakening. I have no time for hand-wringing."

"I'm not sure how helpful 'hand-wringing' is as a term, coming from a snake," Lima whispers to Mez.

Rumi nods to Auriel, chastened. "Big Rumi hunted me out of my swamp, so going back home is no longer an option. Please allow me to travel with you."

"Why did you get chased out of your swamp?" Lima chirps.

Rumi looks down.

"Let's give him some quiet time to recover before we grill him, shall we?" Auriel says. He leads the way off into the jungle, and Mez starts the familiar work of training her gaze on his tail. It gets so narrow at the end, looks so delightfully squirmy, that she has to force back the feline urge to pounce on it. She wouldn't like to imagine the dignified constrictor's reaction to that. Once Auriel's head has gone far enough that his tail begins to move, Lima takes up her usual position on Mez's shoulder. Rumi makes a few hops, but stops up short. "I'm still tired, and even if I weren't, I'm afraid that I'm so much smaller that I'd only slow you all down. That is, unless you'd be so kind as to . . ."

Mez nods. "You can ride on my back. But are you sure you won't poison me?"

Rumi huffs in indignation. "I'm not predisposed to slaying traveling companions willy-nilly!"

"Okay, fine, hop on board."

In a flash, Rumi hops onto Mez's back. He's even lighter than Lima. A runty panther cub, a tiny bat, and a tinier tree frog. Not exactly the most impressive adventuring party. At least they have Auriel with them.

"So you know, I can only partially control the poison on my back. If I get panicky, it just starts coming out of my pores. All I can suggest is don't try to startle me or lick me or eat me," Rumi says. "That would not go well for you."

"Or for *you*," Lima points out.

"I think I'll be able to hold myself back," Mez says wryly. "I've never licked a frog before, and I don't see any reason to start now."

DAWN SURPRISES THE group. After passing through a ravine, they emerge to see that the Veil has lifted, and the sky has gone from black to charcoal. When Auriel brings them to a halt, all eyes turn to Rumi.

"What?" the frog asks, bewildered. "What did I do wrong?"

"Day is almost here. Feeling sleeeeepy?" Lima asks, scrutinizing him.

"Not particularly. I mean, we all have to rest some-time, but I don't . . . why, *should* I be sleepy?" Rumi asks.

"Ah, so you *are* one of the eclipse-born!" Mez says.

"Of course I am," Rumi says. "I thought we'd already been over all that."

"Ooh, that reminds me, do you already know your magical powers?" Lima asks. "What if you were a flying frog? That would be fun. Maybe it would be hard for you to keep on eating flies, though, because you'd feel this kinship with them. Maybe you'd be a frog with flies all over him, like Auriel with his ants."

"Don't be preposterous. I don't eat you, not because you fly, but because I do not *wish* to eat you," Rumi says. He sighs. "And no, I do not seem to have any magical powers. If I did, it would have been useful in my fight against Big Rumi."

"Okay, shadowwalkers," Auriel intones suddenly, "I'm afraid this is the end of the line."

Mez looks around, baffled. It's unbroken jungle all around them, humming with cicadas and thrumming with rain. She closes her eyes against a mosquito doggedly ramming her. What's so special about right here?

"So this is what a Ziggurat of the Sun and Moon looks like?" Lima asks, eyes darting around with interest. "Huh. If it's imprisoning the Ant Queen and everything, I figured it would be fancy. This looks like everywhere else in the rainforest!"

"No," Auriel says. "You still have farther to go to reach the ziggurat. But I have more eclipse-born to collect, and time is running out. I will tell you the route, and then I'll leave and meet you at the ziggurat. We should arrive at almost the same time, if all goes according to plan."

"You're going to leave us . . . all by ourselves?" Lima squeaks.

Mez is careful not to show worry on her face—that wouldn't be the panther way—but she too feels a tremor of dread at Auriel's words.

"The way is not difficult," Auriel says patiently. "Follow the column of ants. They're heading toward the Ant Queen, too. But in case you lose the ant trail, come, Lima, I'll show you the way."

Auriel chooses a tall tree and wraps himself around the trunk, vining around and up until he's in the highest reaches. Mez and Rumi watch as Lima soars up to join him, alighting on Auriel's head, high above the jungle floor. Mez squints her eyes; it's hard to make the pair out at such a distance.

"I'm glad to be alone with you for a moment," Rumi says.

"Why's that?" Mez asks.

"It's extraordinary, don't you think, to be led by a constrictor?"

"It's also unusual to be talking to a tree frog," Mez huffs. She feels surprisingly protective of her new snake friend.

"Granted. My kin would think it odd that I am

talking to you, too, believe me. All the same, constrictors have a reputation for being untrustworthy. I'd rather be proven wrong, of course, but we'd be wise to keep alert. Growing up safe in her cave filled with friendly bats, Lima hasn't faced much hardship, and is very apt to trust. You and I, though—we will have to use our reason to guide us, despite what our hearts may say."

"Sure, let's stay cautious," Mez says, nodding. *And that applies to mysterious frogs with common names*, she mentally adds.

"At least we can—hush, they're returning," Rumi says.

Lima is the first back, zooming down like a plummeting stone, then agilely switching course to alight on Mez's back. "It's amazing up there!" she says. "You can hear something that might be the waves at the shores of Caldera—did you know that we even had shores?—and Auriel was telling me that he's been by the coast, and the ocean goes as far as you can see, which isn't too far because there's a *lot* of jungle out there, let me tell you, so there's not much space left before the horizon. I echolocated the ziggurat, just the faintest ping of stone, because it's really far and everything and there are lots of swaying branches to get in the way, but I can tell it's really big and impressive. Well, I think it is."

Before Mez can respond, Auriel arrives. "We're all

clear, then? As I told Lima, you'll follow the ant column downhill until you reach the three ponds, then find the big beehive and continue across Agony Canyon."

"Agony Canyon?" Mez asks, swallowing.

"It's just a name," Auriel soothes. "It's not as daunting as all that, I promise."

Lima nods. "You can count on us, Auriel. We can handle any puny little Agony Canyon, I'm sure. We'll meet you at the ziggurat safe and sound."

"Be cautious," the constrictor says. "Since you are all three unfamiliar with the ways of daywalkers, you must hide when the sun is at its peak. Talk to no one, and do not ever reveal who you are or where you are going. You mustn't trust anyone you meet, do you understand?"

Mez, Lima, and Rumi nod.

"Very well, then. May fortune shine on you. If you desperately need to reach me, you can try to send a message through the ants. Otherwise, you will find me at the ziggurat."

With that, Auriel steals off into the jungle.

Is he really leaving them, just like that? Mez watches after him, dumbstruck. A panther, a frog, and a bat, each one smaller than most of their kind, heading through dangerous territory to someplace they've never been to face off with an ancient enemy.

For a long moment, all three hold still in the

undergrowth. A tree nearby releases its wild garlic scent, spicing the air. From the top of an ironwood comes the strident call of a macaw. Mez is starting to become used to those daywalker birds, so pretty to the eye and harsh to the ear. A saddleback tamarind monkey sits on a branch above, peering down at the three companions, its tail swinging in the open space as it calmly stares at them. Mez has no idea what to expect from daywalker monkeys, and now she doesn't have Auriel to ask.

When Mez cranes her neck to look at the companions on her back, trying to see what they think they should do, she finds them staring at her. Expectantly.

Waiting for her to decide. She's . . . the leader? "Look, just because I'm the biggest—" Mez starts.

"I was thinking I'd be best as navigator," Lima says.

"And I suppose my gift is strategy," Rumi says, "but I need time to think whenever anything comes up, so for the moment-to-moment decisions I'd rather cede to someone else—well, some *panther* else for our general leadership needs."

Mez doesn't know what to say, and the tamarind monkey keeps staring down at them—maybe it's *laughing* at them, who knows how monkeys laugh; Mez doesn't want to look closer and find out—so she just takes one step and then another. Rumi and Lima assume their positions, one on each shoulder.

"You'd think if we were so important," Lima says cheerfully, "Auriel would want to make sure we weren't eaten by daywalkers on our way to the ziggurat."

"I considered that," Rumi says, "but then I realized it's a cost-benefit decision. There are other eclipse-born to pick up, and increasing our risk of, um, early mortality must have been outweighed by setting them on their way to the ziggurat. If the n-number of surviving eclipse-born is ten, say, then bringing us from ninety percent to sixty percent survival rates will be worth it if and only if Auriel plans to pick up at least 0.9 new eclipse-born. Which seems likely. Fractions of eclipse-born are impossible, of course—well, fractions of *surviving* eclipse-born are impossible—so if he brings even one more back it's fine . . . unless all three of us are eaten, which isn't actually that hard to imagine—"

"Hush," Mez says. "You remember what Auriel said. We are three night animals, walking by day. We need to be as quiet as possible." It might not be the *exact* reason she wants Rumi to stop talking, but it'll do.

The small voices on Mez's back silence. She slinks along the furrows of deepest shadow between the trees, stepping only where the broad leaves provide most darkness.

Becoming invisible: it's always been her greatest instinct. Once, when she was a nursling and got distracted chasing a moth and found herself suddenly alone outside the den, even then she knew to set her ears back and narrow her eyes to slits and lower her head to the ground, making herself as inconspicuous as possible until she got home. Her family hadn't even spotted her coming in, Chumba falling right over in surprise when Mez materialized in front of her.

Instincts set Mez's body the same way now. Only this time there is no den to escape back to. There is no Aunt Usha for protection. There's not even Auriel.

Mez frequently looks back, and whenever she does she finds that same tamarind monkey has followed them through the canopy, is lounging on a sunlit branch and swinging its tail. It doesn't move while Mez is looking at it, except for its eyes: those are always staring right at the three unnatural night animals walking by day. Mez shivers and presses forward. As soon as they're out of view of that monkey, as soon as they're in a new section of jungle where not every creature around has witnessed their conversation with a mystical constrictor, Mez pulls off to one side, making herself as small as possible in the mossy shadows of a fig tree. "Auriel's right, it's too dangerous to travel during the brightest part of the day. We'll stand guard here," she announces. "You two rest first, then I'll wake you up, Lima, so I can rest a bit. Then Lima, you can wake Rumi. How does that sound? Guys?"

From her back, the sounds of two snoring creatures. "Okay, terrific," Mez says, settling her head down on her paws. "Just terrific."

As her companions doze, Mez watches the dayworld and tries to learn as much as she can. She grew up in a world of shapes, of the faint glimmers that her darkvision can pick up around the edges of anything that moves. In the dayworld there is so much light that shapes are less useful; instead it is color that rules. The yellow-orange beak of a songbird against the blue-black of its body, the blue-gray of the sky behind it; the alluring purple vee of a fly-eating plant; the shock of green mealy parrots against slick brown bark. She doesn't know how daywalkers can do it, survive under the onslaught of information. The world Mez knows is one where information is sought out, not simply received.

The ants are the one constant thing, streaming toward their queen. But even though Mez is familiar with them from the nightworld, they're becoming the most mysterious creatures of all. If they are loyal to the Ant Queen, wouldn't they be more careful about who gets to hear about her preparing to emerge? Maybe the ants have no idea that Auriel can eavesdrop on them. But surely they're reporting back about the eclipse-born coming together, which means the Ant Queen's minions might be plotting their own counterattack.

Mez stays alert as best she can to any incoming dangers. It's exhausting work, figuring out what's important and what's not, and she's relieved when she feels Rumi stir on her back. "I'm afraid this active mind of mine has woken me early," he says softly. "Once it starts spinning, there's no going back to sleep. So let me take my turn now."

"Yes, that's fine," Mez says sleepily. "I'd love . . . to close my eyes . . . for a bit." With that, she shuts out the strange world of color.

◇

She dreams of snuggling next to Chumba, feeling her sister's soft fur alongside her. Then she wakes to screaming, to something leathery slapping her face. "—Mez Mez Mez!"

"Lima? What is it?" Mez asks, getting to all fours and whirling about. Sudden daylight fills her eyes and sets her mind to spinning. There are moving shapes, but Mez can't quite make them out. Lima's screaming continues, her constant wail further fracturing Mez's thoughts.

Then her vision clears enough to see what's got Lima upset: In front of them are three monkeys—not elegant golden tamarinds like the one she saw earlier, but hulking howler monkeys, muscular and long-toothed. Their black mouths open wide as they scream at Lima, who is darting in their faces, doing her best to keep them off-balance. They paw at her, sharp nails outstretched, but she's able to dart away from each strike just in time. As Mez watches, still too groggy and stunned to act, one of the howler monkeys lunges at Lima mouth-first, jaws open wide. Lima dodges, but the movement brings her right into the clutches of the next howler monkey, who swipes at her, sending the little bat hurtling into a nearby trunk. She hits it with a thump, then slides to the ground.

Fury brings Mez lunging at the howler monkeys, claws outstretched. She bowls into the one who swatted Lima from the air and rolls with it, holding on to the monkey's shoulders with her front claws while her rear legs rake its soft flesh. The moment they come to rest Mez lunges off the monkey and whirls on the remaining two.

"Unnaturals!" the one nearest shouts. "We won't let you destroy Caldera."

Mez rears back in surprise, as if she's been splashed with water. "What?!"

"Look!" says the other one. "She doesn't deny it!"

The monkey that Mez mauled isn't getting up anytime soon. All the same, Mez knows that, as an ambush hunter, a panther's odds of succeeding in a fight get lower the longer it goes. These monkeys are nearly as big as she is, and there are two of them flanking her. Mez takes a step backward, though she can already feel the trees close behind. There's not much room left to maneuver. "Rumi?" she says. "Are you there?"

"Yes," comes a trembling voice at Mez's back.

"Okay, hold on!" The one thing Mez knows she has going for her is speed. She leaps, not away from the monkeys, but *toward* them—right over their heads. The howlers are caught off guard, falling into defensive positions as Mez whips through the air, twisting a full rotation to land elegantly on four paws behind them.

The monkeys whirl, but by then Mez has reached Lima's still body—stunned or dead, she doesn't know. Mez tries to pick Lima up by her scruff, but the little bat is too delicate. Instead Mez shovels Lima's whole body into her mouth, keeping her jaws ajar so as not to accidently chew her new friend. Then, the deafening hoots of the enraged howler monkeys behind her, Mez takes to the air again, leaping into nearby brambles, dry berries scattering as she hurtles her way through vines and thorns.

"Keef tholding on, Rumi!" she says as best as she can around Lima's body. The words come out a garble, but she can feel tugs on her hackles where Rumi's fingers grip.

Mez scrambles her way forward, claws digging into

thorns and mushrooms and small scurrying insects. She's blinded by the dense vegetation, but she knows that darkness is an ally of hers and not the daywalker monkeys, so she presses deeper into the undergrowth, until there is no light anymore. Finally, she allows herself to pause. "Rumi, shoo okay?" she mumbles around Lima.

"Yes. A little scratched, but yes."

"Think itsh safe enough?"

"Safe enough to what?"

Phteww. Mez opens her mouth and spits Lima to the ground, like she would a furball. The bat is curled up and motionless, impossibly tiny, and covered in panther slobber.

"Oh, now I see what you meant," Rumi says. He hops down beside Lima. "I didn't realize that's how you were carrying her body," he says. "Alas, poor Lima. You can't blame yourself, Mez, you tried your best. If anyone could have saved her life, it would have been you."

The bat stirs.

Her little round ears start wiggling first, then her fingers. Finally she unfurls her long wings and her eyes open, inky glimmers in the dark undergrowth. She shakes off some of Mez's slobber. "What. Just. Happened. To. Me."

"Well, um, maybe I . . ." Mez waffles.

"She carried you in her mouth. But at least she didn't swallow you!" Rumi says matter-of-factly.

"Oh my gosh," Lima says, staring at her saliva-wet wings. She pauses for a long moment. "How *cool*!"

Just what Chumba would have said, Mez thinks. She shakes her head to clear it. They're going to need to make a plan, and fast. "Quiet, you two," Mez says, ears cocked as best she can in the tight thicket of thorny vines. "I'm trying to listen and make sure those howler monkeys have gone."

"Why would they *do* that to us?" Lima asks, indignant. "What did we ever do to them?"

"I think it's not so much what we *do* as who we *are*," Rumi explains. "You know, since the ants are the only other shadowwalkers and their queen once almost destroyed Caldera. Even so, it seems a little overboard to chase us down and murder us."

"It's so *rude*," Lima sniffs.

"I agree!" Rumi says, nodding. "I want to keep an open mind, but it just confirms all the worst stereotypes about daywalkers."

"Quiet!" Mez says, listening. There are constant rustles in the thicket, and she keeps getting sharp pains along her tail—there's probably a stream of ants crossing over her body, biting her as they go. But at least there are no signs of any more howler monkey vigilantes.

"Do you think any *nightwalkers* would band together and try to kill us?" Lima presses. "I can't imagine it. It's not a very nightwalker thing to do. I'm not trying to say we're *better* than the daywalkers, but . . . I guess I'm trying to say we're better."

"Mez," Rumi says, "I think it's past dusk, so the Veil is down. I bet those monkeys are asleep by now."

Mez nods. "Good. We have a lot of ground to cover. Let's get moving."

11

WHAT A JOY to travel at nighttime, when travel
should happen! With the daywalkers all at rest,
Mez feels her hackles lower, her ears perk, her fur go
smooth and flat along her back. The mood of her companions improves too: Lima spends long periods in
flight, plucking gnats from the air, making sounds of
bat glee as she darts across Mez's view; Rumi can't leave
Mez's back, as he would soon fall behind on his small
legs, but takes advantage of the ride to shoot his tongue
out to catch any flying bugs he spots as they go. Mez
can't see any of it, of course, and only knows when he's
caught a bug because of the cry of delight he makes.

"I've been thinking. How come we name flies for what they do, but not other insects?" Rumi asks.

"Hmm," Mez says. "I've never thought about it."

"I mean, we could call a beetle a 'walk,' but we don't, do we?"

"We should call flies 'tasties' instead," Lima says, hovering before Mez and Rumi with a mouthful of gnats. "Oh look, caviar!"

Lima points out a mat of mosquito eggs floating in the watery hollow of a stump, glinting in the moonlight. She takes a mouthful, and Rumi shoots out his tongue to take some of his own. "You should try these," Lima says. "They're *so* good."

"Why not?" Mez says, and takes a good lick of the black quivering eggs. They burst across her teeth. "I think I'll stick to meat, but it's not bad," she admits, before taking another lick. "Mmm. Salty aftertaste."

"What's tonight's course, Lima?" Rumi asks between snaps of his tongue.

"Well, we've already had the fresh gnat snack, then the appetizer of mosquito eggs. Perhaps an entrée of moonlit figs, and for dessert a mousse of flying termites."

"Not that kind of 'course.' Our *route*."

"Oh, sorry! Yes. See where the moon rose? We're heading for that smudge between it and the tallest tree.

The ants are still heading there too, like Auriel said they would."

"You've got the best view from up there," Mez says. "Just let me know if I ever need to shift direction."

"Will do, OOH!" Lima says, her words lost as she makes a gleeful swoop. "Twenty-two in one blow!" she says around a full mouth.

"That's the most fascinating thing about bats," Rumi says. "They can count gnats in the dark, in an instant. They make us frogs seem imprecise by comparison."

The night is moist and heavy, the air liquidy and dark. Mez slinks as she goes, eyes alert to the creatures all around her. Virtually everywhere she looks are the glowing red discs of nightwalker eyes reflecting back at her. Most are unaware of her presence, but a few look right at her, swiveling to follow as she moves along. Owls. It seems even a panther can't move quietly enough to avoid their notice. They make no move toward the group, only watch, but Mez is on edge after the howler monkey attack.

"Rumi, are you watching behind in case we're followed?"

Rumi makes an affirmative croak. "Yes. I'm looking out for one unusually large cane toad in particular, as you can imagine."

"No enemies up ahead," Mez says quietly, though

her gaze keeps returning to the owls above, the red orbs of their eyes blurring slightly whenever they shift on their perches.

The companions have been tracing the edge of the ant stream, and as the night continues Mez uses the moonlight glinting on insect bodies to catch a few meals. The anteaters scurrying along the ant column are too appealing. "Hey," she says, mouth full, "I tried the bug eggs. Now it's your turn. Anyone want to try some anteater? I saved you the brains and eyes, best parts."

"Ugh," Rumi says. "Are you kidding? Even the smell is setting off my stomach."

"Yeah. Eating anteaters? Seriously gross, Mez," Lima calls down from above. Then: "Ooh, a scorpion!" Crunching sounds from above as Lima chows down, followed by a rain of arachnid legs.

Once the clatter of Lima's scorpion-eating dies down, Mez hears a distant rumble. "What is that?"

"That? There's a waterfall up ahead," Lima says. "Didn't I mention that?"

"No," Mez says. "You did not mention that."

"Waterfalls are no problem, of course," Lima says. "You just fly right over—ooh. Right."

"Maybe someone else should take over navigation duties," Rumi says dryly.

"It's not my fault!" Lima says. "I spent my whole life around bats until yesternight. It's taking me a while to catch up, okay?"

"Is there any way around?" Mez asks.

Lima soars out of sight, then returns. "Not really, I'm afraid. We're much higher than the land ahead, and there are cliffs on either side of the waterfall. Finding another way around would take us many nights out of our way."

"Auriel is expecting us much sooner than that," Mez says. "We could be far away when the Ant Queen finally breaks out and overruns Caldera."

"Being away for that moment doesn't sound like the *worst* thing in the world," Lima says. "But I see what you mean."

"Can you swim, Mez?" Rumi asks.

"Yes, I can swim," Mez says. "It's the sheer drop I'm worried about."

"Yeah," Lima says. "This is not a training waterfall. Not that training waterfalls are a thing."

They pass alongside a stream that joins with another, and then another, widening into a river as the roaring sound up ahead increases. Wary of falling in now that the waterfall is near, Mez steers Lima and Rumi deeper into the brush near the edge. The ground becomes rocky and the trees farther between, until the companions find themselves on a promontory overlooking the waterfall.

As she looks down, Mez's stomach drops away. The dense jungle opens into a wide nighttime expanse, hot winds—the sole remnants of the day—gusting up from vast open space. As she scouts, Lima is dragged high into the sky, her little winged body disappearing for long moments before it's outlined by the moon. She arrows down to alight on Mez's shoulder. Down below—*way down below*—is a lagoon, its surface a mirror beneath the silver moonlight.

Mez watches a floating branch go over the edge. It tumbles for many seconds of freefall before striking the lagoon below.

"So, any ideas?" Mez asks.

"I've got nothing," Lima says sadly. "I wish I was bigger, I'd carry you guys."

"I might have a possible plan," Rumi says, leaping into the brush before calling back: "Hold tight for a few minutes. And, um, come rescue me if you hear any screaming."

Mez and Lima stare into the froth and spray of the waterfall. Now that she knows she's not going to be instantly bounding into it, Mez is calmer about the tumbling water. She enjoys its nighttime beauty, the warm mist wetting her nose.

Perched on the rock beside Mez, Lima has her mouth open, echolocating. She does a slow turn around, then faces forward, stock-still. "Hey, Mez," she whispers. "Don't look now, but there's something a little unusual back there, that—"

Mez looks back. The owls from earlier have lined up on a low-hanging branch. A half dozen of them, staring right at Mez and Lima.

"I said *don't* look now!" Lima squeaks.

"Yes, it's eerie," Mez says. "But don't worry, I won't let them hunt you."

"Over here, guys!" Rumi calls excitedly from within the bushes. "I think I have it figured out!"

"Coming!" Mez says, relieved to get off the exposed stretch of cliff. She tucks Lima safely under her chin as she goes.

Mez wades through a cluster of water lilies by the river's edge to find Rumi perched in the center of a wide fallen log. He's a bright yellow dot right in the middle of sodden wood, and looking very proud of himself. "What is it?" Mez asks.

"A log!"

"I can see that. What do you want me to do with it?"

Rumi gets up on his back legs and mimes surfing the log, teetering, little arms out for balance, holding his nose and waving his frog fingers to mimic sprays of water.

Mez shakes her head. "No. Not going to happen. Uh-uh. No way."

"Come on," Rumi says. "It will be fun!"

"Of course you'd think it would be fun. You're an *amphibian*."

Lima wriggles her way through Mez's fur until she's perched between her ears, holding on to the thicker hair over her eyes. "Do-you-think-I-could-stay-here-instead-okay-thanks."

"What's the matter?" Mez asks, struggling to stare up at the little bat, going cross-eyed and dizzy in the process.

"Up there," Lima whispers. "The owls are *right there*."

Mez looks back to the branch where the owls last were, and sees nothing. Then she looks up to see four sets of eyes staring down at her—*whoosh*—now five. They line up silently, shifting from one talon to the other, glaring at the companions.

"Hello?" Lima calls out, all bravery now that she's deep in Mez's fur. "Do you nice birds need something?"

"It's them," one owl says to another, voice hollow and resonant.

"Yes, indisputably," says the second owl.

"'Indisputably,'" Rumi notes. "Fascinating. It appears that owls know good words."

"It is true," says a third owl. "These are shadow-walkers. Traitors to their own kind. The stink of day is on them."

"That's not true!" Mez calls up. "We're trying to *help* the nightwalkers."

"Ants are the only animals to walk night and day," calls down the first owl. "And we owls know the stories of times past, when the Ant Queen rampaged her ants across Caldera, eating birds and eggs alike. Shadow-walking is a sign of wrongness."

"Evil has returned, and these three are its harbingers," says the fourth owl. "The end is near."

"Now hold on a second," Mez says hotly. "Just who do you think you're calling evil!"

"Enough!" shrieks the first owl. "Listen no more to them, owlkind! They will try to twist our minds with their lies."

The owl lets out a loud hoot, and Mez can feel Lima go rigid with fear, seizing up as any small creatures will do, trembling in her hiding spot. She's not the owl's target, though. It soars straight for Rumi, who leaps, plunking into the river and disappearing. That leaves Mez and Lima. Mez whirls, snarling with teeth bared, facing off against the rest.

Rumi's attacker returns to the branch, but the other three start their swoops, wings terrifyingly wide, talons outstretched. Their heads are perfect pale circles framing sharp beaks, backlit by the Ant Queen's constellation.

Though it must be nothing like the fear paralyzing Lima, Mez feels tremors of tension ripple up and down her body. The owls would struggle to lift her, but those talons could do plenty of damage.

"Why are you doing this?" Mez pleads, darting along the ground, zigging and zagging as best she can by the riverbank, trying to make herself a more difficult target. The owls come chillingly close each time they swoop, their talons gnashing open air inches from Mez's neck.

"Do not listen to her!" hoots one of the owls, before launching another death swoop.

This time the owl predicts where Mez is going. As she sprints toward the cover of the lilies, the owl manages to close its talons on her tail, sending a bolt of pain up her spine. Mez whirls. She's able to sink her claws into the owl's thick feathers, ripping out as many as she can, until the owl releases her in a flurry of down. In the midst of the fray, Mez's fight instincts make her vaguely aware of two more shapes leaving the branch, blasting out low and resonant hoots as they prepare to attack.

Mez lunges again, too panicked to choose a direction, and is surprised to feel her paws touch wet wood: the flat log that Rumi found. "Okay, Lima, here we go!" she calls.

"Here we go *what*?" Lima shrieks, still hidden away in Mez's fur, voice trembling.

Mez leaps onto the log and sinks all four sets of claws into the soft waterlogged wood. The force of her landing is enough to set the log skidding along the mud and into the water, Mez's body thumping smartly as it bounces into the stream. The current picks the log up, pulling it into the center of the river and then downstream— toward the rushing sound.

"My body . . . still full of batfear . . . can't fly . . ." Lima squeaks.

"Then hold on!" Mez says. She can hear the powerful wingbeats of the owls overhead as they try to get a bead on the bobbing log. Mez keeps her head down, tightening all of her muscles, trying to dig her claws ever deeper into the wood. A fat orb spider darts along the log in front of her, soon lost in the flood. The rushing sound is closer and closer, and Mez can see the spot ahead where the water ends, the river catching the light of the rising dawn as it curves over into the abyss. It's like she's going to tumble right up into the sky.

As the log drags ever faster toward the edge of the waterfall, Mez sees two little yellow hands appear at its edge, then a head, black eyes twinkling. "I see you came around to my idea," Rumi says.

"Rumi! It's not like I had any—"

An enormous hoot interrupts her. Mez looks up to see beating wings, outstretched claws coming right for her face—

And then they're over the falls.

The log tips and tilts, pitching heavily as it tumbles. Mez's stomach drops away, and for a moment all looks peaceful in the world, despite the tumult she feels inside her. There are stars everywhere, the pale green-yellow of the horizon dawn, sprays of mist catching the early sun. Distantly below, she sees the trees at the lagoon's bank, so tiny from this height. Trees are twigs, the monkey at the water's edge a mite. There's so much space between her and where she will soon be.

Then she's aware only of falling.

Mez scrunches her eyes shut, tries to blot out the tumbling world around her, tries to keep her anteater meal from rising up into her throat. The flat log kites on the wind, and when fear brings Mez's eyes springing back open, the log mercifully blots out the view below. But then the log starts to spin, and it's all she can do to hold on. She feels her claws tearing, the muscles in her legs burning. The log spins more and more, threatening to fling her free, then it steadies again and she's beneath it, wind streaming at her back, fur whipping in her eyes. She sees Rumi managing to hold on with his gooey hands, his yellow-spotted body flapping against the side of the log, then there's a tremendous thud against the back of Mez's head as she splashes down.

The force of the impact sends Mez's claws raking free of the wood, and she's hurled deep into the lagoon water. Tumbling and spinning, she can't tell which way is which, wouldn't know how to reach the surface even if she could get her shocked muscles to move well enough to swim.

The air emptied out of her when she hit the surface, and her lungs instinctively inflate, sucking in a big mouthful of water. The cold surprise of it sets Mez's mind to spinning, and she only just stops herself from breathing more water right into her lungs. Then she sees a little yellow shape in front of her, a kind face that she recognizes. Rumi starts swimming, and Mez manages to follow him. She paddles as hard as she can, following him to the surface where finally, sputtering, she emerges.

Paws churning the water, Mez casts her head this way and that, trying to free it of enough muck so that she can see. As soon as she does, she casts desperately about for Rumi and Lima. She can't see them, though, can see only chill dawn light illuminating the waterfall, the quiet banks of the lagoon. She starts paddling toward the nearest shore, but as she does she hears another horrible rush of wings, and ducks below water only a moment before a talon would have slashed her head.

Mez spends as long as she can stroking below water, coming up stealthily only when she absolutely must breathe more air. She takes in a long breath, swimming a quiet circle, knowing she has only moments before the owls, with their uncanny hearing, locate her and attack again.

She hears a piercing scream. She can't place it at first, but then she realizes: It's her name, stretched over one long, high-pitched call. Rumi is croaking at her. Heedless of the noise she's making, knowing only that she needs to help her friends, Mez paddles ferociously through the water, heading straight for the sound of Rumi: "Mezzz!"

She hears the horror of owl wingbeats again, but Mez is almost at the shore this time. She zigs to the side, then as soon as her claws find purchase on the bank she twists so she's on her back, facing up to attack, claws waving wildly in the air. She clubs talons away right before they would have raked her belly; though she's trying only to defend, her claws sink into feathers and flesh, seizing and ripping into the scaly skin on the owl's ankle. It screeches in anguish and takes to the air.

Mez hasn't had a chance to free her claws. For a moment she's aloft, carried into the air by the shrieking bird. It flails and dips, crashing back to the ground. Mez works another paw into the owl's chest in her attempt to leverage the first one free, digging in deeper than she means to, though the thick plumage on the bird's front blunts the worst of her attack. "Leave me and my friends alone!" Mez bellows as loudly as possible, right into the owl's sensitive ear.

It screeches, apparently in even greater pain from the sound than from the panther claws digging into its chest. Mez's instincts tell her to hold on and lock her teeth around the owl's neck, to make this into a meal instead of a warning, but she knows that the other owls are still out there, and she has the safety of her tiny friends to worry about. Better to leave this one alive to warn off the others. So she forces her claws to release, steals away from the owl flopping on the muddy bank. Rumi has kept up his chirping call, leading Mez straight into the concealment of the jungle line.

She hears more wingbeats, but they seem to be converging on the floundering owl behind her. Mez can't afford a moment to look, can only barrel forward into the safety of darkness.

Then she's in a patch of thick reeds, stepping between their slick stalks as she heads into the trees. Rumi is there, hidden within some ferns and still chirping away, and once Mez is near enough he leaps so he's on top of her back. He's shivering and panicked, croaking without words, until he's calm enough to speak. "Can I tell you how glad I am that *that's* over?" he asks.

"Agreed," Mez says.

"Where's Lima?" Rumi asks.

A quiet rustle, then Mez feels a slight weight on her ear. "I'm here, I've been on your head the whole time, and all I can say is *wow*," Lima says. "And that you're injured."

"I am?" Mez asks, flicking one ear and then the other. She doesn't feel any pain, but maybe that's because of the adrenaline of their escape. There *is* something warm trickling down the fur on her brow and into her eyes. Ah, now that she's thinking about it, there's the pain: one of the owls must have gashed her with its talons.

"You've got two big cuts up here," Lima says, tenderly picking through Mez's fur with her delicate fingers. "Hold on, this won't take a sec."

Lima goes quiet, and Mez can't feel the top of her head anymore. No pain, not even the weight of the little bat. "Lima? What's going on?" she asks.

There's no response for a long while. Then comes

Lima's muffled voice. "Sorry, all done. I can't quite talk while I'm doing that."

Rumi hops to Mez's head so he can join Lima. "Doing *what*?" he asks. "Oh, wow. Fascinating."

"Guys, I can't see you on top of my head," Mez says, aware of how ridiculous she must look. "What's going on up there?"

"Healing," Lima says. "All it takes is a little saliva."

Rumi chuckles. "Did you hear that, Mez? A bat licked your head better."

"It feels kind of amazing," Mez says dreamily. It's like the top of her head is in a cheery little moonbeam.

"So," Rumi says, "healing is your magic! Fascinating. And here I thought you didn't know what your power was yet."

"All bats can heal," Lima scoffs. "It's not that special."

"No," Rumi says flatly, "I am certain that all bats can*not* heal."

"I'm pretty sure I would . . ." Lima's voice trails off. "Oh. Huh!"

"Have you ever *seen* another bat heal?" Rumi asks.

"Now that you mention it," Lima says, "I guess I haven't!"

"A healing bat," Rumi says in awe. "I wonder if these powers come with a random distribution, or if this is a reflection of your internal state, of the bat inside the bat, so to speak."

"What did you say?" asks Lima. "I'm sorry, I don't speak Frog."

Rumi sighs. "No one finds the same things interesting that I do."

"I'm hungry," says Mez.

"Yes, well, let's get going, then," Rumi says with a sigh.

"Looks like we took the shortcut after all," Mez says as she shakes more water and mud off her fur.

12

M EZ, RUMI, AND Lima move steadily through the
night, trying to stay as inconspicuous as possible
as they make their way through the rainforest. As often
as not, Rumi and Lima are perched on Mez, clutching
her fur as she creeps along. Though back home Aunt
Usha often led the family over the shadowed jungle
floor, Mez has taken to moving through the safety of
the treetops. Jumping from branch to branch is slower,
but she feels safer with the cover of the greenery and the
surrounding leaves to hush any missteps—and Lima's
running commentary.

"If having magical powers didn't inspire murderous
fury in every animal we met, I'd tell *everyone* that I can

heal. Bats have this image, you know, of, well, draining blood, but that's only really *rude* bats. I would never do that, of course, and I keep thinking that maybe, I don't know, I could be an ambassador for the bats who keep getting their reputations slimed by—oh, is that a toucan? Hi, toucan!—these animals who don't really know the first thing about bats ohwaitwhatis*that*?"

Well used to Lima's running commentary, Mez doesn't even look up to see what's caught her attention. This time, though, Rumi tugs on her ear fur and points. "Mez, stop. Look down!"

Mez is on the farthest edge of a branch high up in a fig tree when she halts and peers down, the jungle floor spreading out far beneath her. The lifting Veil casts the scene in the golds of dawn: dewy rain-soaked palms, the twisting arc of a river, mist shrouding it all. "It looks like everywhere else in Caldera," Mez says.

"Wait for the breezes to change again," Rumi says.

As Mez stares down, perfectly still on the branch swaying over the scene far below, her thoughts go to her family. She's traveled through scenes like this with them many a time. *I hope you're okay, Chumba.*

Then the mists part and Mez sees what Rumi and Lima were so excited about. There, on the edge of the horizon, is what can only be the Ziggurat of the Sun and

Moon: a giant stone formation washed in the golden light of early day, dew edging it in dazzling silver. The structure is wide at the base, each layer narrowing until the top layer is half as wide as the bottom, and taller than the tallest nearby tree. Mez has never seen anything like it, and can't shake the feeling that this ancient unexplainable thing was meant to be hidden away.

"We're almost there!" Mez says, trying to sound eager for her friends' sake.

"Yes we are," Lima whispers, her voice low and hushed.

"Auriel is probably waiting for us," Rumi says.

Mez isn't sure, but she thinks she can see movement on the ziggurat's top level, can see figures peering out at the edge. Strange blue lights glow and wink along the stone surfaces. It's too far away to know exactly what she's seeing. "I guess we should head there," Mez says.

"Yes," Rumi says.

"Uh-huh," Lima says.

None of them moves.

As if to make the decision for them, the branch Mez is standing on rattles and shakes. "What the—" Mez blurts, wrapping her paws as tightly as she can around the branch. It shakes again, and from the jungle far below comes a deep rumbling sound.

The rumble seems to be centered on the ziggurat itself. Clouds of dust and dirt rise from the earth around it, and the stones themselves seem to breathe, grinding against one another before settling back down. There are screeches of monkeys and birds over the ruckus, and Mez's vision blurs and shifts as the tree shakes more wildly. She's remotely aware of Rumi yelling in her ear, "Back to the trunk, back to the trunk!" and she retreats as best she can along the tremoring branch. Once her tail strikes bark, she scrambles down the tree, claws making ragged slashes in the trunk, seeds and dirt raining around her.

The rumbling stops just as Mez reaches the ground. She nervously kneads the soil with her paws. "Did you see her blow the stones of the ziggurat around?" she asks. "Can the Ant Queen really produce that much force?"

"Oh, sure she can," Lima says. "Every bat knows that. We have a rhyme we sing to little batlings about her, to scare the living moonlight out of them: *'Little wings, little wings, go see the Ant Queen! Little wings, little wings, lead her back home. Little wings, little wings, what have you done? Little wings, little wings, now we're all chewed up and dead.'"*

"That's . . . a beautiful song, Lima," Rumi says.

"All I'm saying," Lima says, "is that if the Ant Queen can take down a whole bat colony at once, we'd better be *really* sure her prison holds."

They pause on the now-quiet jungle floor, each of them waiting for one of the others to start forward. "Well, I guess we—" Mez begins to say.

Just then, the fig tree begins to creak. Mez watches it curiously, trying to figure out how such a sound could come from deep in its trunk. "Um, I—I do believe this tree has become unstable," Rumi stammers. "We should, if we're being prudent—"

"Flee!" Lima yells.

The bat takes off flying, whirling haphazardly through the air. Mez hurtles after her, two little yellow hands at the edge of her vision as Rumi holds on to her brow fur for dear life.

The tree's creaking becomes rumbling, and then suddenly it's back into view, the massive trunk cracking and plummeting, its buttresses ripping up from the soil, taking more trees down with it. Mez darts this way and that, narrowly avoiding a sapling brought whipping down by the larger tree. The earth shakes with each strike, and Mez waits to feel clobbering death at her back, to be smashed into the jungle floor.

Darting around debris, Mez just manages to clear the falling tree. As the ringing in her ears fades, she can sense the new stillness of the surrounding jungle, becomes more aware of where her panicked flight has led them. They're deep in the forested hollow in front of the ziggurat.

"So do we camp for the day," Mez says, looking nervously up at the sun, "or do we press on?"

"We press on," Rumi says resolutely.

"Yes," Lima says, alighting on Mez's shoulder. "Just Agony Canyon to cross, and then we're there."

"Oh right," Mez says. "Agony Canyon."

The bottom of Agony Canyon is so far below that it's hard to tell anything more about it than that it's filled with raging white water. If Mez tumbled, and were somehow lucky enough to survive the journey, there is no bank on either side of the river—to fall in here would be to drown. Agony Canyon, indeed.

The ziggurat awaits on the far side. Ominous and silent. Even the surrounding trees have no motion to them, as if they're fixed in time.

Crossing the canyon is a swaying length of vines, intricately tied together and fixed to posts on either side. The fibers are green-black with age, some of them broken clean away and dangling far above the raging white water.

"Who could have built something like this?" Mez asks.

Rumi considers it, tapping his lips. "Monkeys, I suppose. They have those agile hands, you know?"

"But why would they *want* to build it?" Lima asks.

"To get to the other side, of course," Rumi says.

"But why would they want to get to the other side?" Lima presses, a look of triumph on her face.

"Ah, what is life at all but a sequence of crossings to 'other sides'?"

"You're speaking Frog again, I can't understand you."

Mez tunes out her companions as she edges toward the vine bridge. It's brightly illuminated in the harsh sun, utterly exposed. Still, it's not overly long; if all goes well she'll be across and into the foliage on the other side after a few long strides. If all goes well.

Mez can hear the hum of bees and wasps nearby, watches fat flies sip on nutrients in the soil. Ants stream along the ground, and she wonders what Auriel could glean from them, if he were here to listen. Then she remembers Chumba, and the threat of the Ant Queen, and that if she returns victorious then Usha will *have* to come around to Mez's daywalking and accept her back. It gives her courage. She tests the first vine under her paw.

A vole appears out from underneath, a mother with two little baby voles trailing after her. She scampers about, looking for seeds, then goes motionless once she notices Mez. "A panther!" she exclaims.

"And a bat!" Lima says.

"And a frog!" Rumi says.

"Please don't hurt me," the vole says.

"I'm not in the hunting frame of mind," Mez says. "You don't need to worry."

"Three nightwalkers!" the vole says, looking at them quizzically. "Why are you up and about?"

"We do not mean to be," Mez says hurriedly. "We'll be on our way now, actually." Then, hoping to distract the vole, in case she's off to inform any other daywalkers about them: "Tell me, does this bridge belong to anyone?"

"Oh no," the vole says. "Maybe it once did, but now it's free for anyone to use."

"Mama," says one of her kids, jaw wide-open in amazement, "are these really nightwalkers?" His wondrous expression makes Mez feel bad that she's ever eaten voles at all. And she's eaten a *lot* of voles.

"Hush," the mother vole says. "Let them go about their business without gawking at them. It's what we'd hope for if the roles were reversed." She nods at Mez and gestures toward the bridge with her tiny claw. "I'm sorry. We don't want you to feel unwelcome. Please, go ahead."

"Thank you for your help," Mez says.

"Good luck!" the mother vole says.

Mez takes another tentative step onto the vines.

"How does it feel?" Rumi asks, peering down nervously from his spot on her back.

"Not too bad," Mez says. "I think it will hold our weight."

She places her paws on the knots where vines meet vines. There's less give there, and she hopes she can spring and snag her claws into other vines if part of the bridge gives way. She's a panther, after all, and panthers are *made* to leap and grasp. Mez picks up speed.

The morning is hot. The buzzing of the bees gets louder.

"Oh, hello, Miss Vole," Mez hears Lima call. "Have you decided to come along with us after all?"

Mez whirls to see the vole darting along the bridge's bottom vines, so fast she's a blur of brown. She disappears underneath, and the buzzing increases.

Suddenly bees—enough bees to be a cloud, enough bees to make gusts and flurries—emerge from beneath the vine bridge. They fill the air, their droning beating out all the other sounds of the jungle. As they whiz around them, batting against Mez's face, wriggling their way into her fur, she realizes that they are not bees: They are wasps. Very aggressive wasps.

So this is Agony Canyon.

The stings start. Fiery stabbings on her face, behind her ears, along her ribs, even in her tail. Rumi cries out in pain, and Lima takes to the air, but the wasps are harrying her, too, arrowing into her wings and belly, plump stingers stabbing.

They've only gotten halfway across. Mez balks, unsure whether it's safer to continue or return. She staggers forward, her steps haphazard, her view blocked by the clouds of insects. One of her paws passes right through the bridge, and she hits the vines hard, the lengths giving way so that she's straddling open space, staring into the white water churning far below. Mez scrambles back up, more vines shredding and tumbling away around her. She's gripping only one vine now, clutching it like a branch. Despite her best attempts, her sharp claws begin to shred the fiber.

The vole blurs by, back to where her babies are waiting on her side of the bridge. "Death to the shadowwalkers!" she screeches. "You will not bring back the Ant Queen!"

"Please!" Mez calls out. "You've got it wrong! We're trying to *stop* the Ant Queen."

"You cannot help what you will do," the vole calls out. Her words continue, but they're soon lost beneath the angry buzzing of the wasp swarm.

The air is black with them now, and as more and more sting her Mez can no longer see the way forward, flailing blindly through open space as often as she's gripping vines. Already she's finding it hard to feel her limbs, can sense numbness spreading over her. And if she's this bad, with her protective fur and larger body, she can't imagine what's happening to Lima and Rumi. She calls out their names, but there is no answer.

"No!" comes a thin voice Mez doesn't recognize, from the far end of the bridge. "You won't have them!"

She tries to see who this stranger is, but as her vision blurs even more it's all Mez can do to keep holding on. She hears a crackling sound, then the air is full of red light. An arc of fire whooshes by, then another. The wispy flames are soon extinguished, but they smoke the air, leaving trails in the morning sky. The wasps relent, clouds of them dropping away. Mez chokes, wrinkling her nose, but feels a surge of relief that at least the wasps are no longer attacking.

Moving forward by feel alone, Mez continues to the far end, gripping shreds of vine, waiting to hear a rip and begin the plummet to the river below. Mind floating above her body, she finally reaches the far side. Once she feels solid ground beneath her, she lets her muscles give way, laying herself out flat.

"Ow, ow, ow!" says the voice she heard earlier. Mez looks up to see a monkey hopping from one foot to the other, sucking on his fingers. His tan tail curls and uncurls as he howls in pain. He shakes his fingers out, tendrils of smoke rising from them. "A smarter monkey would have figured this out by now," he says.

Mez stares at him in shock. A flame-throwing monkey! But she can't muster the energy to run away. The poison in her veins makes her want to sleep, sleep, sleep.

There's a whizzing sound in the air, and a little black shape falls from the sky to land in front of her. It's Lima. She's on her back, clawed thumbs moving weakly. Two angry red welts rise on her belly, growing in front of Mez's eyes.

Lima raises her head enough to lick one of the red welts. The strange monkey squats on his haunches and watches as she runs her little tongue over the swelling. It shrinks. With a little more energy now, Lima licks the other welt. Like the first, it melts away.

"Rumi," Mez manages to gasp. "I haven't heard a word from him since the attack began. Find him. Help him next. Please!"

Lima hops to Mez's head. Mez can only hope she's helping Rumi, but the poison in her system is making her so sleepy. Each time she closes her eyes it takes longer for them to reopen. Whenever she does, she sees the strange monkey with the smoking fingers, expression inscrutable as he stares at her with his shining black eyes.

13

MEZ DREAMS OF day. She is not a panther, could not be a panther to love the daytime like this. For now she is a creature of sunlight. No slinking, no ambushing—she is a ball of energy, unabashed and fearless. She romps through a meadow, leaps into banks of wildflowers, bats at songbirds. She lifts her face, whiskers quivering, to receive a shower of sun.

Her sister is there. Chumba clings to the shadows, peering fearfully from beneath rocks and within trees, her eyes set deep in calico fur. "Mez," she whispers. "Mez, I need your help!"

"What is it? Chumba, I've missed you."

"It's Mist. Without you here, he's been picking on

me, nipping my tail, trying to lose me on the hunts. I need you, Mez. How could you leave me when I needed you most?"

Mez noses into the pocket of shadow. It feels like she's crying, though in the dream all she senses is an aching emptiness in her throat. "I'm here, Chumba."

But Chumba retreats farther into the shadows, terror in her eyes. "Mez! Why are you awake in the day?"

Chumba's shocked tone stills her. Mez cocks her head, stares at her sister.

"What kind of panther *are* you?" Chumba scolds.

What kind of panther is *she?*

Then Mez is awake. Ambush instinct causes her to stay still and open her eyes only to narrow slits. If there are enemies around, or prey, best to be motionless. Even as she fills with fear about what might surround her, Mez's heart aches at the memory of Chumba. What if she really is in trouble? Is anything—even protecting the rainforest itself—really more important than being at her sister's side?

Fur fills her vision, wiry and straight, a mix of brown and tan. She's not sure what part of what creature she's seeing, but it becomes clear when a finger reaches back and scratches, a tail flicking in response. She's staring at a monkey butt.

Mez shifts back so her nose isn't right against it, and

at that very movement the monkey turns around and eyes her. It's the same one she saw right before she lost consciousness, the one who had singed paws. The one who threw fire.

For a moment panther and monkey stare at each other.

Then the monkey howls in fright, jowls and chin hair quivering. Wondering what he's seen, Mez yowls in return, staggering to all fours, hackles raised. She whirls around, until she sees that the monkey is staring right at *her*.

"Oh, calm down. I don't like the taste of monkey," Mez growls.

"That's good to hear," the monkey says. "I know I'm not really the one who gets to decide, but considering how I saved your life and all, it does seem the least you could do is not eat me."

"You . . . made that smoke," Mez says.

"Yes," the monkey says. "And the fire behind it, too. Gogi the Seventeenth, at your pleasure."

"There are seventeen Gogis here?" Mez asks, looking around. They seem alone.

"No. I'm the only one named Gogi. But, well, I don't know how much you know about monkeys, but we're sort of obsessed with who's on top, and everyone's got a ranking. Seventeen's . . . not too good. But I was eighteen last dry season, so at least I'm improving, right?"

Mez stares back at him.

Gogi taps his lips. "I know what you're thinking now—what is a posh panther doing talking to a lowly seventeenth monkey? I can't blame you if you stop right now. Though come to think of it, I've been away from my troop for a while, and who knows what's happened while I've been gone. So maybe I've dropped down. Maybe there's another seventeenth. Or maybe . . . maybe I'm sixteenth now! Wow. That would be nice."

"Rumi, Lima," Mez says groggily, looking around for her friends.

Gogi's face brightens. "Your friends are *so nice*. Maybe they'll be my friends someday. Rumi's off catching flies. That's sort of a cliché for a frog, right, but who am I to judge? Lima's tired. She spent all night healing those wasp bites you had. Tuckered her all out. She deserves some rest, sweet little thing."

Mez runs a paw over the top of her head. The wasps! But her fur is smooth and flat over her skin. She's healed.

"It's that horrible little vole mom," Gogi says, shuddering. "She's fooled a lot of us as we approached. Never quite as well as she did you three, though. The animals around here are amping up their defenses. Good thing

I was there standing guard in case she got up to her tricks." His face falls. "I don't understand why all the normal animals dislike us so much. I mean, look at you. You're a *panther*. How cool is that?"

"I want to see Rumi and Lima," Mez says resolutely, taking a step in one direction and then another, unsteady on her paws.

Gogi prattles along. "I mean, I guess there have always been taboos against shadowwalking, and the only animals that usually do it are the *ants*, and the animals remember when they ran amok ages ago, and their *queen* is awakening, which can't make anyone feel too good about it, I mean, I get all that. But still, riling up a bunch of wasps to do your dirty work? That's *pretttttty* low, right? I guess everyone has their reasons, though, who's a seventeenth to judge anyone."

Mez blinks rapidly as she tries to process Gogi's words. "Do all daywalkers talk this fast?"

"Me? Oh, I don't talk fast. You should try talking to a tamarind monkey. I mean, *they* talk fast sortoflike thisit'ssofastthatyoudon'tknowwhenonewordstopsand thenextbegins."

"My head hurts," Mez says.

"Yes, wasp stings will do that," Gogi says, nodding wisely.

"Yes, wasp stings . . . that must be it," Mez says. "Still, I'd like to know my friends are safe. Would you take me to them?"

Gogi's face softens. "Of course. I understand the urge. I'd feel the same way myself. If I had friends, of course. Seventeens generally don't. I mean, it would be weird if a monkey *did* have friends with any rank worse than twelve or so. I don't deserve friends, so I don't really feel bad about it. All the same, once we locate your friends maybe I could hang out with you guys? Don't answer yet, give me a chance first, okay? Anyway, come on!"

One moment Gogi's in front of Mez, and then suddenly he's leaped into the air. She looks up and sees him on top of the thin stone battlement that traces the edge of the ziggurat, swinging his legs over the edge as he smiles down at her. Her eyes widen as she finally has a moment to look at where she is.

Mez is surrounded by old sun-warmed stone crossed by light misty breezes, the tops of the trees at eye level all around her. The massive hewn rocks of the step pyramid have been pocked and worn by eons of tropical storms, and so many varieties of plush moss have grown to cover the scoured surface that the stone is as soft as skin under Mez's paws. *The ziggurat. She's on top of the ziggurat.*

Mez sees movement on the edges of her vision, creatures scampering and hiding, but she can't spare a moment to see what sorts of animals they are. All she can think about is how exposed she is. Head and tail low, she slinks toward the nearest shadows. There are ants under her paws, streams of them slipping into the cracks between the rough stones, disappearing somewhere below. Mez steps around them as best she can.

Gogi heads in the same direction, scampering along the stones, hands and feet never losing grip as he darts along. Limbs trembling, Mez tails him, body tensed in case any of the nearby animals pounce or lunge or bite.

Under a dusky sky, the ziggurat's flat top is full of life. Mez is nearest a huddle of daywalkers: she first sees a bird, a nervous trogon that flits to a branch before darting back to the stones and then back to the branch, then what Auriel once described to her as "a three-toed sloth" clutching the stone edge, its blank eyes staring out at the infinite steam rising from the surrounding jungle. Standing in front of them is what must be a uakari monkey, her bald red face glowering at Gogi. When she spies Mez, her eyes widen. "Hey, maggot," she calls to Gogi, "you didn't tell us your little nightwalker buddy was awake!"

Gogi cowers at the sound of the uakari's voice. "Come on, Mez," he says. "Let's not bother Sorella."

"That's right," the uakari says, her arms crossing over her chest. "'Let's not bother Sorella.'"

"This way," Gogi says. "I'll bring you over to where your kind stay."

Intimidated and a little grossed out by the uakari monkey's bright red face, by those intense black eyes that are like two pits in the middle of cracked red skin, Mez slinks behind Gogi as he crosses the ziggurat.

A long seam runs along it, as if the whole roof is a set of doors that open down. If that's true, they don't appear to have been opened in years and years, as moss and weeds fill the seam in tight. Even the ants don't seem able to find a way in, tapping their antennae at the green line before turning in other directions. Gogi pays the seam no mind, happily scampering across, but Mez hops the line when she gets to it, imagining the doors parting beneath her at any moment, opening like the brambles that obstructed the entrance to her old den.

"They're over here!" Gogi calls from the far side of the ziggurat's roof.

Mez prizes her attention from the seam and the ants. On the opposite side of the ziggurat's top, huddled together where Gogi is wildly pointing, are the night-walkers, keeping as best they can to the narrow shadows that border the ziggurat's low wall. Mez first sees a kinkajou with a trembling nose, little rodent hands covering huge eyes adapted to the blackest nights, then a dwarf caiman, eyes closed in deep sleep. There are no other panthers, but Mez does see an ocelot sitting regally on the stone, taking in the scene. He looks at Mez for a moment, then looks away, as if he is too important to notice a panther. Despite the family resemblance, ocelots and panthers do not generally communicate. Usha has always claimed it's because ocelots are insecure that they're so much smaller.

Gogi has stopped short of the hodgepodge of nightwalkers, twisting his fingers together. "Lots of monkey-eaters here," he says, his tail curling and uncurling around the crown of his head. "Auriel has very strict rules about not eating one another, and so far no one has attacked anyone else, but I still, I mean, I get a good vibe from *you*, but maybe not that ocelot . . . he gives me what we capuchin monkeys would call a 'ripe fig' look. I might wait here and let you go talk to them on your own, if you don't mind."

"You've been kind to me. I won't let any of them hurt you," Mez says.

Gogi's face brightens. "Really? Maybe I'll stick with you, then. Monkeys *do* hate being alone, and I've had no one to talk to since I got here. Once a seventeen, always a seventeen. I wish Sorella hadn't let everyone know." He lets out a long breath. "I guess I was naive to hope my status back home wouldn't matter here."

Just then, Mez sees a yellow blip hopping along in her vision, and Rumi bounces before her. "Mez!"

"Rumi," Mez says, a smile breaking over her face. "I was so worried about you."

"You've recovered. I'm so happy to see that. It's fascinating here!" Rumi says. "Have you seen the carvings on the stones? They're ancient sigils! And some of them near the bottom are glowing! There's so much to study."

"Is Auriel here?" Mez asks, casting her gaze over the edge of the ziggurat, into the darkening jungle all around them. She'll look at the carvings Rumi's so excited about later.

"Yes," Rumi says. "He's off making preparations most of the time, but he swings by sometimes to check in on us. Tonight is when it all begins, anyway."

"When all what begins?" Mez asks.

"When we finally figure out how to use our powers, and what Auriel's plan is to combat the Ant Queen," Gogi says. He's crept nearer, though he still keeps a healthy space between himself and the nightwalkers.

"Who's this?" Rumi asks, drawing back from the unfamiliar daywalker, his throat pouch trembling.

"Gogi the Seventeenth, at your service. Well, Gogi

the Maybe Seventeenth. Maybe Sixteenth! A guy can dream."

"He's very friendly for a daywalker," Mez whispers to Rumi.

Apparently Gogi has good hearing. "Most daywalkers are friendly!" he protests. "It's *nightwalkers* that have the reputation for lurking and sneaking and all that."

"I'm most curious to learn more about your kind," Rumi says. "Though I don't admire your nicknaming habits, I must say."

"I've been watching both sides for a few days, and let me tell you, turns out we're not so different from you nightwalkers," Gogi replies, arms across his chest. Then he gets self-conscious again, and his arms drop. "Though I could be wrong. I probably am wrong, come to think of it."

"Okay, okay," Mez says soothingly. "Let's all take a deep breath. Now, Rumi, how's Lima? Where is she?"

"It's not good, Mez." Rumi hangs his head for a moment, then hops over to a pile of fern fronds at a corner of the wall. He parts one gingerly to reveal the small form of a bat huddled beneath. Lima is usually such a bundle of motion; she looks so small when she's still.

"Is she—" Mez says, not able to make herself finish the question.

She lets out a sigh of relief, though, when Lima weakly raises her head. "Mez?"

Mez lowers herself to the ground, placing even her chin on the stone so that her eyes are on a level with Lima's. "Hi there. I hear I have you to thank for being whole and healthy."

Lima scrunches her eyes shut, unable to keep a satisfied smile from spreading across her face. "Oh, I don't know about *that*."

"A healing bat," Gogi says admiringly. "That's like the reverse of a vampire bat."

"I don't know who you are, strange monkey, but you'll make no more vampire comments around me, if you please. We normal bats do *not* approve of those guys," Lima says, before nodding back to sleep.

"Very sorry about that," Gogi says, wringing his hands. He turns to Mez and Rumi, eyes suddenly glowing with excitement. "I know my power, and I know hers now, but what is *your* power?"

Mez shrugs. "I don't really know. I don't think I have one."

He pokes her in the chest. "Oh, you have one in there somewhere. Otherwise you wouldn't be here. What about you, Rumi?"

The frog stares furiously into the mossy stones. "I don't know."

Gogi looks sadly at his own hands, covered in calluses. "I make fire. It's really a shame. Monkeys *hate* fire."

Mez lays a paw on his shoulder. "Well, *I* appreciate your fire, I can tell you that. You saved my life."

Gogi's face brightens. "Well, it's like my people always say: 'If you're going to make poop anyway, you might as well throw it around.'"

Mez and Rumi stare back at him.

"I'm starting to learn that maybe you have to be a monkey to really appreciate our expressions," Gogi says.

"Yes. Perhaps you're onto something," Rumi says, nodding politely.

Gogi is about to say something else, but his mouth snaps shut as the ziggurat tremors, the ancient stones grinding below their feet. With her usual agility, Mez stays on her paws, and Gogi goes to standing on two feet, arms outstretched, as if surfing the shifting stones. The massive seam along the length of the ziggurat's roof cracks and then closes, as if exhaling, releasing as it does a gust of frigid and stale-smelling air. Mez hears a dull echoing roar from beneath, whether from creature or stones, she can't be sure.

Is this the Ant Queen?

Then, as suddenly as the vibration began, it stills. The ants along the roof have scattered in all directions, covering the ziggurat in frantic shining movement.

"Was that . . . her?" Mez asks.

Gogi and even Rumi seem to have taken it in stride. Gogi's back to all fours, picking through his hair, finding a particularly plump ant and eating it. "So," he starts, chewing on the ant's still-squirming legs. "The Ant Queen is . . . sorry, this beast is putting up a *fight*, okay, there, I've swallowed most of it now, the Ant Queen is . . . one second." Gogi pulls out a wad of half-chewed ant and examines it. "Surely you're not still alive? Go down!"

"It is the Ant Queen," Rumi finishes hurriedly. "As her bonds weaken, she moves more and more down there."

"This is what the carvings have told you?" Mez asks.

Rumi shakes his head. "Not exactly. I haven't been able to make much sense of them yet. There wasn't any teaching of ancient languages in the swamp where I grew up, I'm afraid."

"Don't be too hard on yourself," Gogi says, finally swallowing down the last morsel of ant. "Not everyone can be as sophisticated and worldly as the capuchin monkeys of the north."

"Once you're ready I'll show you, Mez. Some of the carvings down near the bottom are glowing in blue," Rumi continues. "The kinkajou grew up near here, and

says they all used to glow, lighting up the entire ziggurat, but since the eclipse they've been winking out one
by one, and Auriel thinks once the last has extinguished
the Ant Queen will burst through—"

"And we must all be ready," comes a purring voice
that Mez recognizes.

Mez looks up to see the branches of a mighty tree
shake, then long coils of emerald and tan pour off. All
the animals go quiet as Auriel arrives, dropping headfirst to the ziggurat's roof. Daywalker and nightwalker
alike stay at full attention as the giant constrictor traces
across the warm stones. "I see you're feeling better," he
tells Mez as he approaches.

"Auriel!" Mez says. "You've retrieved the last of us?"

"Nearly," he says, lengthening and twisting as he
coils himself along the ground. It takes Mez a long second to trace his body to the end. "I found the sorubim
named Niko, but there's one eclipse-born left to fetch.
I'm sure there are more than that out there, actually, but
I'm limited to what the ants have happened to mention
in their communications. As Rumi said, the sigils are
winking out, and we can spare no more time. We must
be ready for the Ant Queen."

Mez can imagine they're all thinking what she's
thinking: they seem like a pretty small force to combat
an evil that was once strong enough to dominate all of

Caldera. The shadowwalkers stay silent. Well, except for one. "Count me in," Gogi says, scratching at an armpit.

"And me," comes a small voice as Lima crawls out of the fern fronds to join them, head sagging but eyes full of cheer.

"Very well," Auriel says, nodding in gratitude. "We will need everyone's help. Come close. It is time I explained our plan."

14

W E'RE NOT MUCH *to look at.*

The word "shadowwalkers" made Mez
assume they'd come together as some impressive warrior
force, but as she looks around at the assembled young
animals, she sees Sorella the uakari monkey yanking
cruelly on Gogi's tail, the sloth staring apprehensively
at the dwarf caiman and ocelot. The caiman looks hungry, but the ocelot actually looks bored, yawning widely
while Auriel addresses the group.

Worst of all is that the trogon won't shut up. The
little multicolored bird hops from spot to spot, chirping
his unending *caow*s, flashing his yellow underbelly and

iridescent flight feathers. It's hard to hear Auriel's words over the ruckus he's making.

"You have all sacrificed much to be here," Auriel says. He's facing them in the middle of the ziggurat, unafraid to lay his body along the seam, head drawn up high so all can see him. He gives Mez the same feeling he always has. There is something both regal and approachable about the constrictor, like his life has passed more quickly than the rest of theirs in his short time on Caldera. Maybe he was worn out by his journey to the panthers the last time Mez saw him; he radiates health now. More colored scales glitter around his neck.

Night has fallen—Mez is relieved to at least be in *her* element now, rather than that of the daywalkers—and the Ant Queen's constellation glitters magnificently behind the snake, making him look almost otherworldly. Mez sits at attention, tail motionless and spine bolt upright, as she would if Aunt Usha were addressing her, alert to any information that will help defeat the Ant Queen and get her back to Chumba. Rumi is similarly rapt. Lima and Gogi, though, are so involved in a gossip session that they haven't noticed that Auriel has started addressing them.

"Did you hear that the new guy, Niko, fathered babies when he was only a few months old . . . but then he *ate* them?" Lima says.

"I didn't, but I'm hearing *you*, batgirl, that's so crazy. Wait, I haven't met a Niko—which one is he?"

"Shh!" Mez whispers sharply, baring her teeth at them.

". . . and I thank you for that sacrifice," Auriel continues. "But much more will be required of you than leaving your families behind."

As if responding, the roof below them breathes, the stones shifting and grinding. Under it all is a strange and grating voice, making words that are too muffled to understand. Gogi yelps when his tail nearly gets caught between two shivering stones.

Auriel's expression gets sterner. "Even now, she prepares to rise," he says. "Even now, we may be too late."

Mez clears her throat. "Auriel, if the Ant Queen *does* break out, wouldn't it be safer not to be right above her?"

"Yes," Sorella says gruffly, picking bullet ants off her fur. "Wouldn't we all be more comfortable in the jungle rather than up here on the ziggurat?" Gogi jerks at the sound of her voice, then relaxes once he realizes that for once she's not bullying him.

Auriel nods. "We'll all be more comfortable in the trees than on this structure. I wanted to convene up here so the daywalkers and nightwalkers wouldn't instantly hide from one another, but once we're done with our discussion it would be wise to move to the surrounding rainforest. We can keep an eye on the ziggurat from the canopy. We will have to be cautious. As I was arriving here, I narrowly avoided a patrol of coatimundis, and then a group of coral snakes. There are howler monkeys and owls, too. They've set up a perimeter around the ziggurat."

"I've been hearing those howler monkeys every morning," Gogi whispers to Mez. "Horrible racket. They're embarrassments to monkeys everywhere."

"Do you have any new information about the Ant Queen?" the caiman asks. Despite her many teeth, the caiman has a serene face, and always seems to be chewing something. It makes Mez calm just to look at her. Even though she's a reptile, maybe they can become friends. As long as the caiman doesn't find out that Mez has, um, eaten a few caimans in her time.

"Yes, why is she here, *caow*, what is she, *caow*, what can we do about her, *caow*, what is her name, even, *caow*?" chirps the trogon, who never quite seems to know how to finish a question.

"I wish I had answers for you," Auriel says sadly. "But I've never seen the Ant Queen, and anyone who has seen her is long dead."

Lima audibly gulps. Mez places a paw around her and gives her head an encouraging lick, like she would to Chumba.

"If the Ziggurat of the Sun and Moon is a prison, the sigils carved into it might have something to say about how it works," Rumi offers.

The eyes of all the assembled animals, daywalker and nightwalker alike, turn to the little yellow tree frog. He expands and releases his throat pouch, steeling himself before he continues. "I'd like to go back to studying them after we finish talking. Maybe someone here will help me. Two minds are better than one."

Silence floods the ziggurat. Rumi's head hangs, his big black eyes wetter than usual.

"I'll come with you," Mez offers.

Rumi raises his head again, gratitude flooding his face.

"A panther and toad sleuth team? That's a first," says an unfamiliar voice. A bright red macaw soars through the humid air of the night, coming to land on Auriel's neck.

"Sky," Auriel says. "Thank you for joining us."

"Of course, Master," Sky says.

Mez raises an eyebrow. *Master?* That's a new one. Sure, maybe Auriel acts older than the other animals, but that doesn't make the rest of them servants.

"That reminds me—I should do a few introductions," Auriel says. "Sky is the first eclipse-born I was able to track down. He has come the furthest of any of you in harnessing his abilities, so if you have questions when I'm not here, consider him my second-in-command."

Sky nods solemnly and grudgingly, as if he is truly too humble a creature to accept such a tremendous honor.

"I didn't realize we had picked a *first*-in-command," Sorella says, getting into a threat position, on all fours with shoulders puffed up and teeth bared.

"Forgive me for presuming," Auriel says, showing no sign of being intimidated by the uakari monkey. "I don't have to be in charge here. If you have better ideas of how to go forward, please feel free to suggest them."

Sorella doesn't appear to have any ideas. She looks around, waiting for someone else to pick up the fight, then when nothing is doing she closes her mouth and sits back down.

"Except for me and Sky, no one here has a power that's developed past its infancy," Auriel says. "But some of you don't know your power at all. Who does that describe?"

After a nervous look around, Mez edges forward. She allows herself a glance to see who has followed. From the daywalkers, the sloth and the trogon. From the nightwalkers, the caiman and kinkajou. She realizes that Rumi hasn't joined them.

"Rumi," Mez says out of the corner of her mouth, "come *on*."

He shakes his head, staring down at his webbed feet. "No."

Mez looks forward again, stung. Rumi must already know his power. He just hasn't told her.

Sky stares down each of the animals who volunteered. With eyes on opposite sides of his head, he has to look at them with his beak turned, which gives him an imperious look. "Look at me! I'm so amazing! I've got feathers growing out of my butt!" Lima mutters out of the side of her mouth. Mez can't help but smile.

"I will assist you in discovering your abilities," Sky says gruffly. "But it takes some time, and I can only do it one by one. Don't try to rush me at once for my favors."

"The eclipse gifted Sky with powers of divination," Auriel says. "Spend a few hours with him, and you'll know what you can do."

Mez can think of nothing less appealing than spending a few hours with this self-impressed parrot. But then again, to know what she has to offer the world, how she might help here and then return home victorious . . . maybe for that she could put up with Sky.

She's about to raise a paw to volunteer herself when Léon, the kinkajou, squeaks up. "I'd like to go first," he says, looking around worriedly at all the predators around him. "A magical power seems like it would be . . . useful."

"What a wise little morsel you are," the ocelot says, eyes glittering.

"That reminds me," Auriel says. "This should go without saying, but let me be perfectly clear: There will be absolutely no eating of your fellow eclipse-born. You may hunt in the immediate vicinity, as long as you are wary of the patrols out there. But you may only hunt those creatures who are not eclipse-born."

The ocelot and caiman groan. Mez fixes them a withering look. *Come on, did you really think I was going to let you eat my friends?*

"I will help you, Léon," Sky caws to the kinkajou. "You will be my first subject. We'll begin as soon as possible."

"And with that, I must head back out. There's one last shadowwalker to fetch," Auriel says.

"Meanwhile, you and I will go figure out the mystery of the sigils!" Rumi says to Mez. He turns hopefully to Lima and Gogi. "Unless you two want to come help too?"

"I, um, have some gnats to eat," Lima says, looking away.

"And, uh, I'm *way* behind on my grooming," Gogi

says. "I've got this tick in my armpit I've been trying to pull out for ages."

"Okay, no problem," Rumi says. "As long as I have Mez helping! Mez, looks like it's you and me. How fun!"

Mez nods, wondering just why it is that no one else wants to come along.

◇

The little tree frog bounces excitedly down the steps of the ziggurat, soon disappearing from view. He makes his high-pitched chirps as he goes, so Mez can keep track of him. He also keeps talking, but the words become a little harder to make out. "Sealing ritual . . . the two-legged animals . . . last eclipse . . . runes . . . chants!"

"Uh-huh," Mez calls as she pads down the steps. "You know you're going to have to repeat all this once I've made it down there, right?"

". . . so excited that you're willing! Everyone else has gotten bored and stopped wanting to help. . . ." His words fade away again as he turns a corner on the ziggurat, then come back in when Mez catches up to him. "Scholarship is important, right? As if ancient engravings could be anything but fascinating. Okay, here we are!"

Mez slinks down from the last layer of stones to the mud of the forest floor. Rumi is holding on to the tip of a skinny branch, brushing the ziggurat and then gliding away as night breezes sway his perch. He's got a click beetle pinned between his lips. The bug is frantically trying to fly away, its abdomen glowing as it does. Rumi squints, reading the stone's carvings by its ruddy light.

Mez leans in so she can see the carvings too. "Oh, wow," she breathes.

She'd thought the stone block had been scraped up, but what she'd taken for accidental gouges are actually intentional markings. "Start in the top left corner," Rumi says. "That's where the markings have the most erosion and moss growth, which makes me think they're the first ones carved."

Mez stands up on her hind legs, front paws against the stone, craning her neck to view the markings. Rumi hops to the top, leaning down with the click beetle in his lips so that Mez can see more easily. The engraving shows strange two-legged animals, sort of like tall monkeys, arms around one another, looking to the horizon. The next image shows them running, chased by swarms of ants. Mez looks to the next panel over, but it shows only grasses. "I don't understand. These weird tailless monkeys . . . turned into a field?"

"The panels aren't in order," Rumi explains. "Look in the corner of each—there's a number of notches. *That's* the order. This has one notch, so it's the first panel. Now we have to read the one with two notches in the corner . . . and that panel is over here. . . ."

Rumi leaps into the night. Mez follows the glowing trail of the click beetle, eventually finding Rumi a long way down the ziggurat.

This panel makes Mez wince: the ants are overrunning the two-legs, the tailless monkeys writhing as they succumb to the swarm. Mandibles slash into arms and legs.

"What's interesting in this panel," Rumi says, "is that it's not just the two-legged animals that are being eaten. Trees, snakes, other insects, birds. Look—even other ants!"

"Yes, I see," Mez says before turning away. "It's all very gruesome."

"Now for the panel with three notches. Time to go up a level!" Rumi says, before leaping away.

Mez hauls herself back up the ziggurat to reach him. Huffing with exertion, she's starting to understand why the others claimed to be too busy to help Rumi research. "Here's where it gets *really* interesting!" Rumi says.

The ants cover almost the entirety of this panel. Gnashing mandibles and teeming antennae fill the scene from horizon to horizon, except for a huddle of desperate two-legs pressed into the middle. They cower and shield their faces from the onslaught. "Look at *this* crazy tailless monkey, though," Rumi says. "He's pointing to the sky. See? There's the moon on one side, and the sun on the other. And the arrows? They're pointing toward each other! Next panel!"

Rumi springs away.

"Couldn't you . . . just . . . tell me what's on it?" Mez asks, still breathless.

In the next scene, some of the two-legs are trying to fight off the ants with their bare hands while the others are hard at work, cutting stones and arranging them into a pyramid shape. One of the two-legs is pointing to the sky—the sun and moon are almost on top of each other. "Next panel!" Rumi calls out.

"I was worried you were going to say that," Mez says, taking a deep breath before following Rumi back up the ziggurat.

This panel shows more and more ants amassing, the two-legs huddling on the top of the ziggurat as the insects scale its levels. At the front of the ant horde is one that's far bigger than the rest, the size of a buffalo. She rears back, her many legs tapping the air. "The Ant Queen," Mez says.

"Yes," Rumi says, nodding. "Look at those huge mandibles the artist gave her. And all those sliced-up two-leg bodies littering the ground—look, there's a severed leg hanging out of her mouth! I'm hoping the artist was exaggerating."

Mez is speechless. They're going to fight this giant armored murderer?

"Um, if you can peel your eyes from the Ant Queen, take a look at the sky," Rumi urges. "The sun and moon have nearly joined, see?"

"So where's the next scene?" Mez asks.

Rumi spits out the click beetle. It chirps in outrage before zooming off into the night. "That's the problem. It should be the one with six notches. But there *isn't* one with six notches. Or seven, or eight. Those panels are missing."

"Oh," Mez says, looking around. The ziggurat is made of hundreds and hundreds of stones.

"I've looked everywhere," Rumi says. "Nothing. All the other stones are either blank, or have carvings that seem to be just decorative."

"Hmm," Mez says.

"Whatever secret the two-legs had to defeat the Ant Queen is probably in those last panels," Rumi says glumly.

"Well, at least show me those glowing blue sigils you were talking about," Mez says.

Rumi leads her to the far bottom corner of the ziggurat. The rainforest hems in closely here, the night sounds of chirping frogs and creaking branches tight at

their backs. Remembering Auriel's warning about enemies patrolling the forest, Mez draws near to Rumi.

Four of the stones have large runes carved into them,
glowing faintly in blue. Mez tries to see if the shapes will
tell her anything, but they're abstract figures, lines and
squiggles and circles gouged deep in the rock. Maybe
those symbols meant something to the two-legs, but
they say nothing to her. "They've been winking out,
and now it's down to these four. It was five when we
arrived," Rumi says.

"And if they correspond with the magic the two-
legs once used to restrain the Ant Queen . . ." Mez says
grimly.

". . . then it's not good. Not good at all."

One of the runes is right at ground level. Mez noses
it, and finds the glowing sigil isn't warm; it's as cold as
the rest of the night-chilled stone. "Look at this," she
says. "This rune is like the one above it, but only half
is here. And these blocks on the bottom level are much
shorter than those above them."

"I guess the two-legs were in a rush," Rumi says. 🐾

"I don't think it's that they were in a rush," Mez
says, a smile growing across her face. "I think the ziggurat has sunk."

"What do you mean?"

"There's a mudflat near my den," Mez says. "When we leave an animal skeleton there after a hunt, each night less and less of it is visible. It's not because more mud appears—it's because the weight of the skeleton itself makes it sink."

"So you're saying that we're seeing only the top part of the ziggurat?"

"It's clearly been around a very long time," Mez says. "You yourself pointed out all the moss and erosion. And the ground here is soft and muddy."

"So the panel that explains the magical ritual that the two-legs used to seal away the Ant Queen . . ."

". . . might be below us," Mez says.

"Finally we're getting somewhere," Rumi says.

Mez stares down at the grass and soil beneath her paws, wondering what mysteries and marvels—and dangers—might be trapped beneath.

15

IN THE CHILLY dawn, a panther, a frog, a bat, and a monkey stare down at the creature before them. They stare at it for a long time.

"So. That's Niko," Lima finally says.

"I wouldn't have thought . . ." Mez starts, her voice trailing off.

"I *know*," Gogi finishes.

"Well, he must have hatched when the sun's and moon's powers were combined, like any of the rest of us," Rumi says, tapping his lips with a webbed finger. "I wonder if any vertebrate at all has the potential to be a shadowwalker. Or even if there could be a shadow-walker slug! The possibilities are—"

"—fascinating, we know," Lima says.

"I was going to say 'endless,' actually," Rumi sniffs.

"I mean, how do we go scouting underground with . . ." Mez starts again.

". . . something that has gills?" Gogi finishes, his hands on his hips.

Niko is floating in a hollowed-out gourd set on the ground before them. The kinkajou rigged it up with his nimble fingers, eating the fleshy insides of the gourd as he went. The caiman helped fill it with water, and now they're using it to transport Niko. He's a sorubim catfish, and not a big one at that, his body small and spiny, not much bigger than a minnow's. He seems able to sense their voices, swimming to whichever part of the gourd is closest to whoever is talking. But whenever he tries to speak, all they hear is a gurgle.

"How did he even *get* here?" Lima asks. "It seems very difficult for a catfish to travel to a ziggurat."

"I know the answer to that, would you believe it?" Gogi says. "So nice to be helpful sometimes. You remember that river at the bottom of Agony Canyon? He traveled down that. Auriel found him in a far-off estuary, and directed him here to come live in the pond behind the ziggurat."

"Don't worry, my new little fish friend, I'm not going to hurt you," Gogi continues as he reaches in, gets his fingers around the fish, and dexterously lifts it out of the water.

"—not my fault," Niko is saying, his voice clear now that he's in open air. "I'm just a fish! Besides, you need my power over the earth." Mez wouldn't have thought that a fish could look indignant, but here it is: the barbels on either side of Niko's mouth are quivering in outrage.

"It's, um, unexpected that a fish would have power over the earth. Because fish, uh, live in the *water*," Lima says, her voice starting to rush. "Which you obviously already know, *being* a fish and all." She ends with an awkward chirping sound.

"Are you kidding? Having earth powers is amazing! I can bring all sorts of mud up from below the water, mud that has plenty of little eggs and insects and worms in it to eat. There's as much earth beneath the water as there is beneath the open air, after all." Niko's gills begin to pump more and more wildly. "Umpleaseput-mebackinthewaterrightnowplease."

With a startled gasp, Gogi drops Niko back in. The fish flits around and around the hollowed gourd, frantically running water over his gills.

"This is hopeless," Mez says mournfully. "How are we even going to be able to communicate with a catfish?"

"Now I begin my new career—translator!" Rumi

announces, before plopping into the gourd.

He swims for a while before popping back up. "That was a joke, by the way. I guess I'm not so good at jokes. Have to study up on them. Anyway. Niko has a *lot* to say," he reports. He promptly hops back in, his yellow body swimming circles around the catfish, arms and legs kicking.

"And I should put my nest-making skills to use on a new project," Gogi says. "Here, Mez, help me find some nice strong vines."

Together, they root through the brush, Mez biting off vines and Gogi using them to rig a makeshift harness for the gourd. Carefully, Gogi lifts the sloshing gourd onto Mez's side, strapping it on tight. It's as big as her rib cage and takes away all of her stealth, but by staying low to the ground Mez is able to walk without sloshing any of Niko's water over the side.

"Okay, team," Rumi says. "There's a whole world beneath us. Here's the plan: We look for a small cave or crevice that will bring us as far as we can go under the ziggurat. Then we use Niko's power to move the earth from the underground stones, exposing their carvings. Gogi's fire will light them up so I can study them. That's how we'll learn how the two-legs imprisoned the Ant Queen in the first place."

"What am *I* going to do?" Lima asks.

"Someone needs to eat any gnats we encounter," Gogi offers.

Lima nods, satisfied with herself. "Mission accepted."

Rumi travels on the edge of the gourd, his arms flung over the side, as if he's luxuriating at the edge of a hot spring. Occasionally he'll dunk down below, communicate with Niko, then pop back up. "He senses the ground opening up off to the left," he'll report, then: "Quicksand up ahead!"

They quickly change direction.

Around the base of the ziggurat the ground is marshy and swampy, given to broad brown mosquito-clogged pools of standing water. The bloodsuckers seem to go straight for Mez's sensitive nose, and Gogi is constantly scratching at bites, but Rumi and Lima and even Niko soon have full bellies and satisfied expressions on their faces.

Lima cocks her head at one point, as if listening to something far away. "What is it, Lima?" Mez asks.

She shakes her head. "Nothing, I don't think. But let's be alert."

The weight of the ziggurat puckers the ground. They travel around its broad perimeter, through the thick ferns and mosses that have grown up along its edges, looking for any openings.

They've gone only a short way before Lima stops them with a sharp clicking sound. The rest of the companions hold still while she pivots her head, wide ears craned. "It's that sound again. The howler monkeys," she says softly.

With a shiver of dread, Mez looks to the treetops.

At first she can see nothing but swaying branches and misty vines. But then she sees them in the distance, black shadows among the branches, tails wrapping around their faces or whipping through the air as they make their way from tree to tree, toward the eclipse-born below. One begins to hoot, and then the others start in.

"Are they saying words?" Mez asks.

"Something like 'Health to the ant pearls!'" Lima says. "But that doesn't sound right. Oh wait, I got it! 'Left by the unnamed girls!' That doesn't sound right, either. Oh, now I hear it. 'Death to the unnaturals!'"

"Um, guys, I know I'm just a seventeenth, but I have to say it seems like those howler monkeys are about to—" Gogi says.

The howler monkeys attack.

They surge down from the treetops with sudden ferocity, making their guttural howls and baring long teeth as they plummet. More and more join the attack, emerging from the trees all around, crying and shrieking, their deafening roar enough to rattle Mez's thoughts. She hops this way and that, whirling to face each new sound, Niko's water splashing each time she startles.

"Death to the unnaturals!" shrieks one of the howler monkeys again, before it drops right on top of Gogi, teeth gnashing toward his exposed neck. As she sprints toward the stricken capuchin, Mez catches sight of movement from the direction of the ziggurat. At first she senses only a massive force, as if a tree is falling on top of them, but in the split second it takes Mez to spring away she realizes it's Auriel, streaking through the companions and toward the nearest howler monkeys.

He bellows, using all the force of his cavernous lungs, the power of it enough to set Mez's whiskers quivering. The howler monkeys pause their attack and go silent. The one that was about to sink its teeth into Gogi's neck backflips away, a fear grin plastered over its features. The diamond-colored scale on the side of Auriel's head glows.

When the howler monkeys start a retreat, Auriel wastes no time pursuing them, whirling and slaloming through the clearing, whacking monkeys off their feet, sending those that are still able to flee staggering headlong into the trees. Clearly the howler monkeys have decided that it would be futile to fight back against the powerful constrictor.

"I'll chase them farther off on my way out!" Auriel shouts, not even sparing a glance at the eclipse-born as he scans the treetops for any remaining attackers. "I'll be back as soon as I can. Now, go find the underground entrance before they return!"

He doesn't need to ask twice.

Mez turns and stalks through the undergrowth, away from Auriel and the howler monkeys. She feels Lima and Rumi on her back, and sees Gogi beside her, his skin visibly pale even under his fur. "Are you okay?" Mez asks as they rush along.

The capuchin nods, gray-lipped. "Just a little rattled."

Auriel's furious roars fade at their backs as the group presses deep into the foliage. "My echolocation is showing some hollowness to the ground," Lima says. "Wait—turn left!"

Under Lima's direction, Mez darts through an arch in the brambles, tracking the rotting trunk of a fallen tree until she comes to a clearing where the standing swamp water becomes a sluggish stream that disappears underground, a tight, airy passage above it. Thick tendrils of ants stream along the edges.

"I think we should keep looking," Gogi says,

worrying his hands. "No way am I going down there."

"Yes, maybe that's wise," Mez says, eyeing the dark and narrow passage.

"I'll investigate. I'm sure I'll be fine!" Lima chirps. Before they can stop her, she's flown into the narrow pitch-black passage and disappeared.

"It's lovely in here!" she calls. "As long as you don't mind the constant ants. Plenty of room. Well, plenty of room for a bat. I think you guys will be okay, though. Probably."

"What a rousing endorsement," Mez says dryly.

"I'll go next," Gogi says. "If one of us gets eaten right away, better a seventeen like me than someone important."

"That's ridiculous," Mez says. "Stop talking like that."

"Look at it this way, then: I'm slightly smaller, Mez. I can test it out--if it's tight for me, then it'll be too tight for you."

Mez starts to realize that Gogi's apparent insecurity might be more of a way to put everyone else at ease. "That, I can go along with. Thanks, Gogi. Be careful," she says.

Gogi steps up onto his two legs, arms high in the air, and wades into the stream, making nervous little grunts as he goes, his tan face scrunched up. He switches to all fours as the passage pitches down, and soon he's stepped into the underground stream and disappeared from view. Mez hears traces of words. "Whoa, it's dark in here. . . . Lima, help a monkey out. . . . I'm just a daywalker, please help! . . . Okay, up and then over? . . . Yes, I'm sure it's very beautiful, if you can *see in the dark*, I'm sure you're loving it, and I'm happy for you, don't get me wrong. . . . Mez, can you hear me back there? I think you're good to go!"

"Coming!" Mez calls as she slinks into the water and heads through the opening. Soon she's craning her neck upward to keep her nose above the surface, and then she's swimming.

The gourd floats beside her. "We're doing fine in here," Rumi reports.

Mez's eyes take some time to adjust to the darkness, and for a while she's swimming blind. Drowning ants pepper the water. Strange, unknowable things slip past her paws.

Then her eyes pull in more scraps of light, and she snorts in astonishment.

The ceiling is glowing like the night sky. Swirls of stars and constellations—only these are underground, and right above her head! If Mez didn't have to swim, she'd be able to reach up and stroke the nearest ones with her paw. As it is, she sees Lima's black form cutting out bat-shaped swathes of the cavern's stars as she flits among them, making admiring sounds.

Then Mez hears scrambling up ahead, and a monkey grunt. "The ground rises up here, Mez!" Gogi calls. "We can climb out. Sheesh. And none too soon!"

"These are glowworms," Rumi says from Mez's side. She hears a suckering sound as Rumi's tongue lashes out, and one of the stars disappears. "Ugh," Rumi reports. "They look better than they taste!"

"You ate one of those?" Lima asks from above. "I wasn't going to, but then I figured it would make my belly glow. Actually, I wonder how they look when they come out the other—"

"Okay, let's keep moving," Mez says. "Remember— we're looking for the carvings, and then we're getting out of here. Keep alert." She swims toward where she last heard Gogi, and sure enough, she feels the ground rise beneath her so she can stand. The cavern floor goes up at a steep pitch, so she has to scramble, digging her claws deep in, scraping painfully against shards of stone within the mud.

Once she's fully out of the water, Mez shakes off her fur. She forgot about Niko at her side, and hears a splash and the fish's voice clear out of the water before he splooshes back in: "Hey, careful with the waves!"

"Sorry! Tell him I didn't mean to scare him!" Mez says to Rumi.

The tree frog splashes into the gourd and then returns. "Niko has decided that he will accept your apology."

"Some catfish are way too sensitive," Mez grumbles as she edges forward. She calls out to Lima. "Do you want to take lead? Your echolocation works better than my darkvision."

"And *definitely* better than my dayvision," Gogi adds. "It's feeling pretty useless to even *have* eyes at this point."

"All right, guys," Lima says, flitting ahead. "The passageway continues until . . ." She pauses. "Until . . . well, darn."

"What is it?" Mez calls.

"We're going to need Niko's help. It's a wall of hardened mud up here. I was hoping it was a ziggurat stone, but it's not."

"Rumi, you hear that?" Mez asks. Suddenly she's deeply aware of the tons of earth around her, *above* her, earth that in any moment could fall and entomb them. "Make sure Niko thinks it's safe before he goes using his power, though."

"And that there is no Ant Queen nearby!" Gogi adds.

"On it," Rumi says, making only the hint of a splash as he disappears into the gourd's water.

With a great rumbling sound, the hardened mud ahead shifts and falls. Gogi yelps in surprise, and Mez feels loosened mud swirl around her paws, panic filling her as the cold slurry rises up to her belly. Then the sound stops, and the mud stills.

For a while she and Gogi and Rumi hold motionless, waiting for the worst, the only sound their own breathing and the dripping of cave water. Gogi shivers. "I wish Auriel were here with us."

"Way's clear up here!" Lima finally calls.

"Remind me why we agreed to this mission again?" Gogi grumbles as he creeps forward, a hand on Mez's head so she can help the nightblind monkey find his way.

"*You're* the one who said 'me, me, me,' the moment Rumi and I asked," Mez reminds him.

"Yes, but when you asked me to come along we were out in the open air, sunbathing on a tree branch. It was easy to be brave up *there*."

Niko might have opened a passage, but it's a narrow one, dripping cold globs of mud along its length. Mez squishes her way forward with her friends, the walls narrowing so that one shoulder or the other is always grazing stone. Once she nearly wedges fast, and her breathing goes rapid, fear making her head light. But then the passage widens again, finally opening out into a cavern. Mez's darkvision only goes so far, and she can't see the roof, or the far edge. But she can hear the ants teeming along.

The Ant Queen is somewhere down here. Sealed away, of course, but not for long. Mez can't get out of these caverns soon enough. "Any sign of carvings?"

"It's big," Lima reports, her voice sounding far away indeed. "The echoes I'm getting from above are dulled by something very dense. I think we must be underneath the ziggurat now. It's hard to imagine all that stone is *above* us. Yikes."

"I'd rather not have that particular mental image in my mind, please!" Gogi says.

"Okay, sorry," Lima calls down. "Maybe you'd like to imagine a giant and all-powerful Ant Queen entombed somewhere nearby instead?"

"Everyone's a comedian," Gogi grumbles.

"Hold!" Rumi says, adding a few sharp croaks. "Everyone hold perfectly still."

Mez doesn't dare even risk the noise of asking Rumi why. She goes as motionless as if she's spied quarry while hunting. She thought Rumi was communicating with Niko, but realizes he must have left the gourd when his voice comes again, from a ways in front of her.

"That voice . . ." he says. "So beautiful. I wish I could make the words out better.'"

"I don't hear anything," Gogi says. "But maybe that's because I don't clean out my ears often enough."

"A singing ant?" Mez says. "Do you think it could be the queen?"

"I don't know," Rumi says. "The sound is muffled and far away. But so beautiful." He clears his throat. "Hello! Are there any singing ants down here?!" he croak-yells.

"Rumi!" Mez says curtly. "Keep your voice down!"

They all go silent again, the only sound the hushed lapping of water and the skittering of ant legs. Mez watches a nearby stretch of water, glimmering with the reflected light of the glowworms. The waves finally stop and it goes still.

Then it vibrates.

"Oh no, oh no, oh no!" Lima cries.

"What is it?" Mez calls.

"I'm picking up tremors with my echolocation," Lima says. "They're getting stronger. Oh no. It's here!"

16

"WHAT'S HERE?" MEZ screeches. But it's too late for discussion. She crouches as if to spring, eyes wide and staring. She curls her body around the gourd slung at her side, to prevent the water—and Niko—from sloshing out. With a splash, Rumi leaps back inside.

The ground rumbles, great vibrations passing up from beneath their feet. As it does, Mez feels mud pressing against her mouth and nose, and she's worried that a cave-in has started, that the end has come, but then the pressing mud cries out in fear, and she realizes it's Gogi, plastered in mud, wrapping himself around her head.

"Gogi," Mez says as best she can around the

quivering monkeyflesh covering her nose and mouth. "Get off me. . . . Can't breathe . . ."

Another tremor comes, making Gogi wrap himself even tighter. Mez's got monkey hands in her ears, monkey feet pressing into her throat. Then the ground beneath her slides, and mud splatters her vision. She shuts her eyes as soon as she can, but even so bits of gravel press painfully into her eyelids. "Lima," she calls. "I can't see—which way can we go?"

The bat chirps from ahead and to the right. "This way, this way, hurry!"

Mez desperately slams her way through the shifting mud. There's a thud in front of her, and before she can change direction she's bashed into a falling rock, nearly rolling under it as it plummets. She staggers, the pain bringing stars to the insides of her eyelids. The gourd pitches in her struggle, and as Mez thrashes free she can feel the vines that bind it tearing and pulling.

Is all this tumult caused by the Ant Queen? Four sigils on the ziggurat above are still lit—but have the eclipse-born been foolish to assume that meant Caldera's ancient enemy couldn't yet escape her bonds?

Lima trills her voice constantly, and Mez uses the staccato chirps to guide herself. Gogi's hand is no longer on her, and she can only hope that the nightblind monkey is also following the sound of the bat, that they'll all find one another on the other side of the cave-in.

Mez is beyond thought, has become a creature of only reflexes, slaloming down twisting dark canyons of shifting rock. She tumbles into a pit of swirling mud, and is dragged under. It closes over her head, sealing her in, and her world becomes even darker than before, impossibly dark, mud filling her nose, her mouth, her ears. In desperation, she leaps as hard as she can with her back legs, flailing through the thick muck until she strikes a surface solid enough for her to gain purchase and spring, up and out of the mire.

As she scrambles onto a rocky ledge, Mez's reflexes are about to bring her exhausted body leaping forward again when she realizes two things: the awful grinding sound of the cave-in has stopped, and she's in another glowworm cavern, the bugs' light too weak this time to give her more than the feeblest outline of her surroundings.

There is no more danger, at least not for the moment. For a long while, Mez lies there panting, waiting for her breath to return to normal. Any time she breathes deeply, her body is consumed by racking coughs, the last one producing a large glob of mud. She instantly feels better, and breathes in deep, clean breaths. She's filthy, and her instincts tell her to lick herself clean, but there's too much muck. Mez shakes as much off as she can, then sits upright and listens.

Nothing but drips and distant creaking. No sound of her companions.

"Lima?" she calls. Of all of them, the bat has the best chance of having survived a mudfall in these dark caverns.

No answer.

"Rumi?

"Gogi?"

She checks the gourd at her side. But it hangs upside down, its contents long since turned out. "Niko?" she calls.

Nothing.

For the first time since she left her den, Mez is fully alone. There are fewer glowworms here than in the previous cavern, and their light is too scant to outline much more than the occasional mossy stone covered in ants, the flat surface of dank cave water. Mez has no idea where to go, and the wrong decision could mean the end of her. She shivers in the chill currents of air.

One thought overrides all others: *I want Chumba.* She imagines her sister beside her, the warmth, the unending cheer. Maybe she wishes for Chumba for the same reason she called for Lima first when she was in trouble. Chumba or Lima wouldn't know what to do any more than Mez, but they would do something to stop this despair that's threatening to creep over her and make Mez do *nothing* in the face of her helplessness.

So. What would Chumba do? Mez sits up as tall as possible, tenses her muscles, ready to act the moment opportunity arises. But there is only darkness, unwinking glowworms, lapping waves. She steps one way, nearly slips on a cold, slick surface, then steps in the opposite direction, stopping short with a gasp when her paw enters chill water strewn with drowned ants.

This is hopeless. Mez's future unspools in front of her: she's completely blocked in, and she'll wander farther and farther until she runs out of energy, curls up, and perishes.

Mez lies down, places her head between her front paws, and closes her eyes. Why didn't she stay near Chumba, even if it meant risking death by disobeying Usha? Why did she believe the word of a snake and leave her home to come to a strange ziggurat, then travel underground blindly, disregarding her own safety all the while? Maybe her instincts are duds. Maybe she is a faulty panther.

She imagines Chumba roaming around this dark cavern, sniffing every corner. She'd be disappointed that her sister had given up.

Of course. That's what Chumba would do. She'd explore, in case there's an exit that she'd overlooked.

When Mez opens her eyes again, they've adjusted enough to the dim lighting that she can make out more of her surroundings. There's a jagged wall of rock on three sides of her, and a smooth wall behind.

Smooth.

Mez backs toward it to investigate. The wall is perfectly flat, with shallow markings up and down it.

Carvings.

She runs her paws over them, but her rough pads aren't as sensitive as monkey or frog fingers. Touch won't be enough to figure out what the image is. She'll need her vision, but the glowworm light in the cavern is too diffuse.

Unless she brings a lot of them together. Mez bounds across to a rough wall and scoops up as much glowing silk as she can with her paw. Soon it's covered with the gooey bright filaments, enough to light whatever's directly in front of it in a chilly glow.

When she returns to the flat rock, her breath catches in her throat.

Six notches in the corner. It's the next panel!

Mez cranes her neck to study it. The ziggurat is front

and center. The land around it, though, looks raw—all the nearby trees have been cut down to stumps. The two-legged animals are on top of the structure, only a handful of them left, the ants swarming up the sides. At the front of their teeming mass is one ant far larger than the others, larger even than the two-legged animals. The Ant Queen.

Mez shudders. The Ant Queen has the head of one of the two-legs in her powerful mandibles. Its face is one of tortured agony as the queen's sharp jaws dig in.

That's it. No real answers. She'll need to find the next panel.

Mez continues searching. She swims the length of the cavern, then back, replenishing the supply of glow-worms on her paw when the first batch washes off. She gets more and more tired with each stroke, her muscles burning even in the chill water. At the far end of the cavern, she finds an outcropping. She plops onto it to rest, pressing her back against smooth stone. Smooth!

It's the panel with seven notches. Partially submerged, the image is hard to discern in the dim glow, but Mez is just able to make it out. The two-legs are on top of the ziggurat, holding aloft two pieces of carved stone. One is an icon of the sun, stone tendrils of rays streaming from it, and the other is of a crescent moon. On the ziggurat below are two empty spaces, one of the sun and one of the moon.

Two of the ziggurat's carvings can be removed.

The panel with eight notches is right nearby. It shows the two-legs raising the carvings high in the air, the real sun on one horizon and the moon on the other. Strange, curving magics have emanated from the carvings, surrounding the Ant Queen. The rest of the ants have begun to retreat.

The carvings are the key. Raising them at the moment the Veil lifts or descends appears to activate the ziggurat's magic.

There's hope! Hope that they can do the same thing and renew the Ant Queen's bonds. Hope that they'll be able to return home as heroes. Hope that Mez will be reunited with Chumba. It could all come together.

If she ever makes it out of this cave alive.

Splash.

Mez pricks her ears, keeping the rest of her body still in case she's in danger.

Splash.

Mez holds motionless. Could it be the Ant Queen?

Splash. Then high-pitched croaking and a voice she recognizes: "Hello? Any of you guys there?"

Rumi.

"Yes!" Mez cries. "I'm over here! Come see!"

"Where are you?" the frog says, his voice muffled.

"Oh. Now I get it. We're in separate caves."

"Oh," Mez says, voice falling.

"I'm in a tight space here, and the only passage goes in the other direction," Rumi says.

"The last panel is here, Rumi!" Mez says. "I think I know how we can renew the Ant Queen's bonds. But not if we're trapped down here."

"That's great news, Mez," Rumi says. "And terrible news, too, I guess."

Mez sits in the darkness, staring up at the glow-worms while she shivers. The cave is still scary, but not nearly as terrifying as it once was, now that there's Rumi to talk to. But the swimming has tired her out; her body can't seem to get itself warm.

"It's the carvings," she says, teeth chattering. "We have to hold them up while the sun and moon are both in the sky."

"We'll get out of this somehow," Rumi says. "Niko's alive, and has been scouting. And he's off again already, trying to locate the others. It's tricky, because there are strong currents passing through the cave system, so any way he goes could turn into a one-way downhill. But he's a smart fish, and those barbels he has on the front of his nose are pretty sensitive to danger."

"That's . . . good," Mez says, teeth chattering harder. "Keep talking . . . makes me . . . less lonely."

"Oh, okay," Rumi says. "Let's see. I've never really tried to talk to a fish before. Frogs always claim that fish have nothing useful to say, but it's really not true. I can't wait to report back about what I've discovered once this is all over." He pauses. "I'm sorry, that sounds insensitive. I talk about unimportant things when I'm worried."

"No . . . it's good. . . ." Mez says. Even though she's not intentionally moving her paws, Mez's nails clatter against the stone. At first she thinks it's her shivering getting worse, but then she hears another rumble. "Rumi," she warns, "I think it's about to happen again. Another cave-in."

This time it's not just a rumble coming from below. Mez hears an even deeper sound, too—singing. It's lower than any vocalization Mez has ever heard, and sounds more like a resonant rattling than a voice. Whatever's making this song must be huge to create a pitch that low. "Is that . . . ?" Mez asks.

"The Ant Queen?" Rumi finishes. "What do we do if she's coming for us?"

They leave Rumi's thought unanswered. Mez wonders why the Ant Queen would be singing that eerie humming song, whether she's excited because she found Gogi or Lima, if even now they're trapped between her horrible sharp mandibles, being sliced open between musical notes. At least the shaking isn't increasing—the roaring might be horrifying, but the cavern's not about to fall on their heads.

Little pips of sound come from Rumi's direction. "I think I hear Niko, hold on. . . . Oh no."

"What is it?" Mez asks, darting to all fours. But Rumi must have his head below water.

Finally he responds. "Are you ready to swim?" he asks urgently.

"What?"

"ARE YOU READY TO SWIM?"

"Yes," Mez says, biting her lip. It's true—she *is* a good swimmer. For very short distances.

"The chambers connect, but only far below. I'll guide you. Dive into the water, as deep as you can go!"

"What's gone wrong?" Mez yells as she runs pell-mell toward the water's edge. Before she knows it, she's tumbled in. It's cold enough to seize her muscles, forcing all the breath out of her lungs.

Against the cramping that immediately sets into her legs, Mez manages to force herself to start swimming. Water covers her head and ears, surrounding her in cold blackness. Rumi's speaking underwater now, his voice louder and clearer than it was in the air: "Down, down, now a little to the left. Closer, closer. It's Niko. He's figured out where the caverns connect, but as he was telling me he was attacked. Straight ahead. Now come back up!"

Mez surges upward, before promptly cracking her head on a stone outcropping. She sees stars and her body jerks in panic, taking in a mouthful of cave water. She resists the urge to gulp in more and instead descends again, currents shivering her whiskers as the wall of rock opens up in front of her. Mez swims forward, traveling along a watery dark passage stroke by stroke, then rises. Rumi is saying something, but she can't hear him within the roar of the current and the song of the Ant Queen vibrating the water. Her lungs begin to burn against her ribs, insisting: *Inhale. Inhale. Inhale.*

Mez continues upward, though, her vision turning from the black of the passage to the red of blood. She courses upward despite the urge to give in and let herself sink. She can once again make out Rumi's insistent voice. "Almost there! I can see you. Rise carefully, though—the Ant Queen—!"

But rising carefully is no option. Mez's desperate need for air has taken over everything else, fueling her legs as she kicks frantically through the water, only slackening once she's broken the surface and gasped air into her lungs. She nearly gags; the air here is ancient, full of staleness and the smell of stone. But even though it's fetid, it's *air.* The best she's ever tasted.

Drowned ant carcasses glint everywhere Mez looks, and though she's able to stand where she is, it's only because the rock she's crawled onto is close below the surface—the water still rises up to her chest. If it comes to combat here, she will be at a severe disadvantage.

At first this new cavern seems calm, but then she hears a popping sound as a flare of light rises to the jagged stalactites of the roof. She's dazzled, vision stained bright purple, until the fire on her retinas fades and she can make out a familiar shaggy head, just above the waterline on the other side of the cavern. Gogi. Gogi sent up the flare.

Mez gets to all fours, ready to leap to the defense of her friend. But where is the enemy? Her panther instincts tell her to stay still until she can figure it out. Gogi's head bobs, and even from her distance Mez can hear that he's panting heavily as he faces off against some invisible foe. The air is filled with the smell of burning dust, the sweet tang of singed hair. The hand that released the small bolt of flame is shaking; Gogi must be exhausted. But there don't seem to be any immediate attacks, either—maybe he and the Ant Queen have reached some sort of stalemate. If that's who he's facing.

Mez wishes she could see Gogi's enemy, but it's on the far side of him. The capuchin monkey hasn't made any sign of noticing her: he's either too distracted by the fight to realize she's arrived or he's trying to keep Mez out of his enemy's view. Either way, she figures she should keep quiet for now.

Rumi clings to Mez's ear. "What's Gogi facing off against?" she whispers. "And where's Lima?"

"I don't know," Rumi whispers back. "I haven't been over there yet. And Niko should be in here somewhere, but he's not responding."

The water at Mez's chest begins to lap, and she feels currents tug her ankles. They're pulling toward the far side of the cavern, gently at first and then with increasing power.

Splaying her paws and bracing herself lets Mez resist the current for now, but it's clearly stronger where Gogi is; he's having a much harder time of it. He shrieks and flings his arms above his head, uncontrolled tendrils of fire snaking up from his hands toward the ceiling, illuminating the cavern with popping bursts of light. "It's attacking again!" Gogi screams. Maybe he knows his friends are there, or maybe he's desperately calling out to anyone who's around and might be able to save him.

I'm coming, Gogi. But even though she wants to, Mez can't leap to the attack yet: she's still far away, and the moment she gives up the element of surprise, she loses her best chance of saving him.

Once she sees where he's looking, Mez gasps.

In the sudden illumination of Gogi's fire, Mez sees that a whirlpool has formed at the far end of the cavern, the dark water swirling into white water as it spins faster and faster. The force of it has dragged Gogi off his feet, sucked him in so he's splashing and flailing, the flames from his palms fizzling before they can even start. His shaggy head disappears below water.

"No!" she cries, leaping into the water despite her terror, despite her impulse to stay invisible, despite her exhausted muscles. She immediately realizes her mistake, foundering in the current, only barely able to drag herself back into shallows.

With a splash, Rumi has leaped off her and into the water. In her darkvision she catches sight of him swimming toward where Gogi last was, then his tiny yellow form, too, disappears.

"Rumi? Gogi? Niko? Lima?" Mez cries.

There is no answer in the cavern, nothing beyond the roar of the whirlpool.

Then there's an entirely different roar, a roar more like the wind that whistled over the edge of that waterfall many nights ago, and Gogi is suddenly floating above the water, his body wet and limp, hands and feet dangling toward the surface. Mez strains her eyes and blinks rapidly, struggling to understand what she's seeing. Rumi hovers above the whirlpool, not steadily but bobbing in the air, shooting this way and that as gusts emerge from his mouth. He struggles to point those gusts at Gogi, and the force of wind emerging from the tiny frog hits him often enough to keep him airborne.

Rumi screams at the exertion, his body pitching this way and that in the air, until he loses control and plummets headfirst into the whirlpool. In one last burst of effort, he emits an earsplitting croak, and Gogi flies through the air, landing in the shallows beside Mez. She gets her teeth around the scruff of his neck, lifting the capuchin monkey's white furry head out of the water so he can breathe. She's relieved to feel his lungs rise and lower, once and then again.

"Gogi, you're alive!" Mez says, after settling him into a sitting position beside her. Immediately she's looking about, trying to see what happened to Rumi, and whether she can spy Lima. But she can't see either of them anywhere.

The monkey is too dazed to answer, but Mez hears another voice come from up high. "Mez, is that you?" Lima calls.

"Yes—I've got Gogi and we're okay. But Rumi, find Rumi!" Mez yells into the blackness.

Without prompting, Gogi lets out a weak burst of flame, enough to illuminate the whirlpool. Though Mez tries, even with the benefit of the extra light she can't see Rumi.

"I've echolocated him!" Lima says, her voice trailing off as she arrows toward the very center of the whirlpool.

Then there is no more sign of her.

"What's happening?" Gogi asks, his exhausted voice little more than a whisper.

"I don't know," Mez says, growling in frustration.

Flashes of movement. Then more. Mez makes out the wings of a bat, rising above the maelstrom on the far side of the cavern. Rumi is gripped in Lima's feet. Though she's struggling mightily, Lima's barely able to make headway against the winds surrounding the vortex and floats unmoving in midair, flapping away as hard as she can. Then Rumi must have given her a burst of wind, because they're whizzing through the air toward Mez and Gogi. "Whee!" Lima calls.

"The Ant Queen," Mez hears Rumi say. "I've seen her, and she's terrible—her minions have Niko, and they're, they're eating him! We're running out of time. We have to save him!"

Lima launches back toward the vortex. "No!" Mez calls after her. "We can't lose you all."

Then Mez hears it. A piercing scream, rising up from the whirlpool. Niko's voice collects into words.

"She's not alone. He's here with her! Run!"

"I can't hold Rumi in the air any longer," Lima gasps, before crash-landing on top of Gogi's head. The exhausted monkey barely reacts as frog and bat tangle into his hair.

Niko's cries continue, until his voice cuts off in a strangled, anguished gasp, followed by the unmistakable crunching of bones.

17

NO SOONER HAS Niko cried out his last breath than a massive rumbling sounds above their heads. Mez scrunches her eyes shut as pebbles pelt her head and pock the water's surface. When Lima and Rumi move to her underside for safety, Mez huddles over them. Only once she's sure they're secure does she risk a look up, and sees that scraps of daylight now can make it down, lining the edges of the cavern. As she peers about in confusion, more debris strikes Mez's head and paws.

The rocks get bigger, and as Mez peers into the light above she sees the ceiling is fraying and falling, larger and larger chunks of rock dropping.

"It's all collapsing!" Gogi screams, adrenaline

making his exhausted body spring into action.

Whether it was Niko's last act to rend the cavern open with his earth magic or some power of the Ant Queen that started the fall, gravity is now taking care of the rest. The gaping hole broadens, chunks and boulders dropping into the watery cavern. Mez is stunned by the shuddering earth all around her, the plummeting rocks that are each many times her own weight. One hits the surface right beside her, dousing her in a wave of black water.

Under it all is a voice, low and throaty and garbled by surging water, singing words whose meanings Mez can't make out. The Ant Queen.

The ancient horror of the sound, and the memory of the dismembered two-legs in the carvings, jolts Mez into action. As she surges forward, she realizes that Gogi is bounding ahead of her, jumping from fallen rock to fallen rock, twisting in the air to make each landing, using the accumulating debris as a ladder to make his way up toward the daylight.

"Fly, Lima! Follow Gogi!" Mez cries, and then she surges forward. She's relieved to spy the black bat streaking toward the daylight above. Mez knows she's responsible for getting her and Rumi safely through, but at least Lima is likely to survive.

Mez takes off after Gogi, trying to land his same

leaps. As the cavern's ceiling continues to crumble, the field constantly shifts, boulders sliding into new formations or dropping into the deeps. Gogi can scramble up the rock faces with his grasping hands and feet and tail, but Mez will have to find some other way up.

She springs to one of the shifting boulders, and almost as soon as she lands is dipping and sliding, soon slipping off entirely into the churning water. She flounders, swimming desperately, trying to find a rock to grip her claws into. The moment her back paws hit a hard surface she springs, launching herself into the air.

It's been many nights since she's been able to give her leaping legs play, and Mez now comes fully alive, twisting like a grappling snake, front half and back half moving almost independently, rotating and whipping her through space so she can go even farther with each jump.

Mez's legs take over as they scramble and claw and hurtle her ever higher. The rocks fall in cascades, and Mez is able to trace each flow, Rumi giving shocked croaks as Mez launches herself off the individually falling boulders before they've hit the cavern floor. Moving by instinct alone, she's climbing through the air itself.

Finally, only one rapidly expanding open space awaits her. There's no time to hesitate—if Mez doesn't leap now, she'll fall with the rocks down below, crushed or trapped underground forever. Even though she doesn't think she'll make it, she leaps anyway, paws flailing wildly, stretching for the rocky edge of the jungle floor. She concentrates on Gogi's friendly face, gripping the edge of the earth with his tail and one hand as he reaches the other to catch her and pull her in.

Mez doesn't make it that far.

The tip of a claw scratches the rock at the soil's edge, but grinds right through, and suddenly she's falling, belly up, limbs flailing as the sun shrinks at the edge of her vision, while the noise of roaring water below—and the terrifying song of the Ant Queen- -calls to her, calls her to come close, calls for her death.

Feline instinct brings Mez to face the bottom, limbs outstretched so she can kite in the air. She slows, air resistance dragging her face and belly upward even as her body continues to fall.

"No!" Rumi yells from his spot buried in her fur, and then Mez feels herself slowing further. Her spine wrenches as wind gusts out of Rumi, slowing their fall even more so they are hovering in the air instead.

They're stuck in open space, Rumi trembling with the exertion as wind gusts from his mouth, causing them both to wobble this way and that.

All Mez's attention is on what's below her. The whirlpool is clogged with ants, the ones who are still alive swimming frantically in the water, clumping into great clods and rafts of teeming dying insects. Below them, at the center of the whirlpool, is a blurred sphere of softly glowing blue. The whirlpool of ants and water scatters as it hits the barrier, nearly hiding the creature trapped in its center. Nearly.

Within the sphere is a giant ant, larger even than Usha, her many legs pressed against the glowing blue barrier as she sings her song, staring up at Mez and Rumi. The barrier wavers and bends under the pressure of her sharp limbs, as if it might at any moment puncture and release her into the outside world. Her slavering mandibles, grotesquely large and gleaming like obsidian, open and close while emotionless black orbs stare out from within the broad plane of her head.

Mez hears more low humming words. She wonders what the Ant Queen is saying, but it's either an unknown language or its sound is too muffled by the magic barrier of the blue sphere to come through clearly.

Then the surviving ants in the whirlpool start singing too, clambering over their dead brethren to raise their voices. There are tones to the song, but it's not quite music. The hum is otherworldly, serene, eerie, beautiful. Horrifying.

Now there are words Mez can understand.

Rumi, greetings

. . . Mez, you finally appear

This prison is not

. . . justice

It is

. . . cruelty

I have been held for

. . . so long

You who shadowwalk

. . . should know one of your kind

"Mez, are you hearing this too?" Rumi asks, their bodies dropping the moment he uses his mouth to speak instead of produce wind. He struggles to raise them back up in the air, and when his voice comes again it's ragged and harsh. "I can't . . . keep this up."

Mez looks around in desperation. The rockfall is over—the boulders have all settled under the water's surface. Once Rumi tires out they'll pitch down into the waiting froth of ants and dark water. Whether they'll drown or be picked apart by millions of mandibles, Mez doesn't know.

The era of the ants was the most peaceful

. . . Caldera has ever known

Let me be released, for this wrong

> *. . . can be fixed*

Free me and you will survive

> *. . . to rule with the ants*

While she tries to understand the strange song, Mez locks eyes with the Ant Queen. The interlocking plates of her exoskeleton gleam in the pale bluish light, her giant heart-shaped head curving in brutal lines unbroken by any blemish other than thick yellow bristles. Her song is niggling into Mez's mind. How has the Ant Queen not gone mad, entombed for ages? *Isn't* it unfair to have imprisoned a thinking, feeling creature for so long?

"—last chance . . . now . . . get ready," Rumi gasps.

Startled, Mez realizes he's been speaking to her, but she was too transported by the queen's gaze to hear him. "Wait, Rumi, get ready for what?" Mez asks.

Then they're rising, Rumi croaking at the exertion as they pick up speed. Mez looks up and sees Gogi and Lima at the edge, peering down, Gogi's arm still out-stretched. Rumi is rising too fast, though, and quickly losing control. They're starting to pitch, heading for the side of the earth instead of the open exit.

"Rumi, more to the right!" Mez cries.

The frog desperately overcorrects. They career back

toward Gogi, then they're hurtling past his hands, and then they're above him, above the jungle itself.

They've gone way too far. They're soaring high above the ground now, the daylit world shrinking away. "Rumi, that's enough!" Mez yells, even though her voice is lost in the violent wind.

Rumi stops gusting, but their momentum keeps them flying, sideways now, then arcing toward the ground. Terrified that they'll wind up falling back into the gaping hole in the earth, back into the ants teeming in the dark water, Mez swims through the air, legs paddling uselessly as she tries to head toward Gogi.

As Mez and Rumi rocket toward him, Gogi beams and claps. Then, as he sees their speed and trajectory, the monkey's eyes widen in shock and he throws his arms over his face. Mez tries to swim backward, but though the movement turns her around it doesn't alter her course—she slams into Gogi tail-first. They're one shrieking mass rolling through the jungle, limbs entangling. Finally a dense clump of ferns slows them and they come to rest, katydids bounding away as Mez sits up, looking at Gogi worriedly. "Are you okay?"

Rumi hops to one side, lies gasping in the middle of a fern. Lima flits down from a tree above, lands beside him, and begins to inspect him for wounds.

Gogi sits up, examining each arm and leg. It's all

intact—though a wisp of gray smoke is coming up from his tail.

"Your tail is smoldering," Mez points out.

"It does that when I get upset," Gogi says, eyes crossing as he concentrates. The ribbon of gray smoke subsides.

Suddenly Mez is breaking into laughter, great peals of mirth, more from relief than anything else, relief that she's alive, that her friends are alive after she so nearly lost them.

Except for Niko.

Mez stops laughing, her gaze dropping toward the ground. Her friends don't need to ask why. Their expressions grow serious too.

There's a roar from the area of the pit, and then the soft muddy earth begins to fill it in. They huddle at a safe distance, panther, monkey, frog, and bat, all growing silent as they watch the land slope and pour. Gradually, the sounds of the jungle recommence around them, the calls of the insects and birds and mammals that have lived in Caldera for eons, that have seen endless cycles of birth and death.

"So that was the Ant Queen," Mez says. "The dark whirlpool was full of her ants, drowning just to be near her. She asked Rumi and me to help her get free. Because we're all shadowwalkers."

"Well, *that* certainly sounds like a bad idea," Lima chirps.

Gogi nods. "Even a mere seventeenth can see she was imprisoned for a reason. And we saw what lengths those two-legged animals went to trap her away. After what happened to them on those panels? Yeesh. I'd have thought it would be harder to carve such vivid gore in a stone block."

"Yes, you guys are right," Mez mumbles. Rumi is quiet, and Mez can imagine why. Maybe he was as transfixed as she was by the Ant Queen's eternal eyes, by the sound of her song.

Mez eases toward the rockfall, testing the ground on each step. As she gets close she sees that it's not really a hole anymore; it's more like a wound that's healed messily. The falling rock and mud have come together to seal the underground lair tight, making a broad gash of brown and black within the rich greens of the rest of the jungle. There is no returning the way they came.

"At least the Ant Queen can't follow us out this way anytime soon," Lima says.

"*Probably*," Rumi says darkly. "Although you'd be surprised what a few billion ants can do when they put their minds to it."

"Poor Niko," Gogi says. "Eaten by a horde of ants."

"He said something odd as he was dying," Mez says.

"Something about the Ant Queen not being alone. He could have meant the other ants, but it was still strange."

"At least we know what to do now," Lima says as she examines Rumi's fingers for injuries, bending and flexing each one while the little tree frog whimpers. "Find the sun and moon carvings that can be removed, and hold them up at dawn. Or maybe dusk. Whenever the Veil is coming or going."

They all linger unmoving in the clearing, girding themselves. Then Rumi makes a hop in the ziggurat's direction. Gogi steps the same way, followed by Lima and finally Mez. As one, they make their way back.

◇

"Only *two* sigils are lit now?" Lima asks, her voice squeaking at the end.

The other eclipse-born nod grimly. They are lined up in front of the bottom level of the ziggurat, where there used to be four winking blue lights. Now there are only two glowing squiggles left—and even they are looking feeble.

"No wonder the sphere was puckering around her, and no wonder the ants were swarming. Their queen is almost free," Mez says.

"I wish Auriel were back already," Sky says.

"The Ant Queen asked us not to interfere, because we're fellow shadowwalkers," Rumi says, chin jutting.

"That's what she said to try to convince Mez and me. I want you all to know in case she tries any similar tricks again."

"Well, of *course* she would want us to help her go free," Sorella says. The burly uakari monkey has none of her usual bravado, is hunched down and staring intently at her fellow exhausted companions, her beady black eyes glinting in the glow of the remaining blue sigils. She and the rest of the young eclipse-born have been hanging off every word of Mez and her friends' adventure.

"I didn't get to see her up close, but apparently she was surrounded by something like a whirlpool," Gogi says, looking at Sorella with wide, hopeful eyes, grateful to finally have her attention. He clears his throat. "Well, I guess it really *was* a whirlpool, but made of ants with the water. So not sure that still counts."

"I'd call it a vortex," Rumi says. "My thinking is the swarms of ants coming to visit their emerging queen opened up passages, causing cave water to drain to lower and lower levels. Or the Ant Queen's emerging power drew everything toward her, including underground water."

Mez cuts a glance at Rumi. He hasn't mentioned his power over the wind, and she hasn't had a chance to ask him about it in private. She assumes he has good reasons for keeping it secret, and will follow his lead for now.

"Poor Niko certainly got a good view of it all," Lima says.

"Ghastly," says the sloth, shaking his pretty head.

Rumi glances at the sloth quizzically, opens and then closes his mouth. Mez is grateful that he doesn't say what he's so clearly thinking: *I didn't think a sloth would know a word like that!*

Then she winces, her mind going back to the sound of Niko's crunching bones.

"Auriel definitely can't get back soon enough," the ocelot says. He's kept up his cool expression, but Mez can tell how agitated he is by the thrashing of the tip of his tail.

"Agreed," Rumi says, blinking one frog eye and then the other as he takes it all in.

"It's a wonder the rest of you made it out unscathed, since Mez and Rumi don't even know their powers yet," Sky says, tilting his head to one side so he can fix an eye on Rumi.

"Yes," Rumi says, avoiding Sky's penetrating gaze. He steals a look at Mez, the message on his face clear: *He might be onto me. Please keep my secret.* "We got very lucky."

Sky stretches his red wings out wide and begins to preen, working his beak between his thick feathers, spreading the oil from his glands. "Well, there's no way we're going to figure this out on our own," he says when he comes up for air. "Auriel will be back soon with the last eclipse-born. I wish you'd figured out something more useful down there, so I'd have more to report to him than that you got Niko killed."

The gathered eclipse-born go silent, aghast.

"Excuse me," Mez says, her voice coming out as a low and threatening growl despite her efforts to remain calm, not to pounce and make a meal of this cocky red parrot. "*More useful?* We found out how to conduct the ceremony! All we have to do is wait for this night to be through, find the symbols, and bring them together at dawn. And we *all* nearly died down there. I didn't see you so eager to come with us."

"There was enough to handle here," Sky sniffs.

"What does *that* mean?" Gogi asks, hands on his furry hips.

"You're so concerned with what happened to *you* that you haven't noticed what happened to *us*. Look around you," Sky says. "Notice anyone missing?"

Gogi looks at the assembled group. He tries to count them on his fingers, getting halfway through one hand before the fingers he's put down begin to wander back up, the first hand entirely unticked by the time he finishes with the second. "Sixteen?" he says, shrugging.

Then his eyes scrunch. "No, that doesn't make any sense. I think I meant six."

Sky tut-tuts. "Monkeys and arithmetic. Not a pretty combination."

"Whereas macaws can count to fifty," Rumi says admiringly.

Rumi, Mez thinks, *no complimenting the bully!*

"That's right," Sky says, literally preening as he speaks, "and since I *can* count, I can tell you that there are nine of us."

"Three fewer than before!" Gogi gasps.

"No," Sky says, shaking his head. "Nine is eleven take away *two.*"

"Sheesh. Okay, two fewer! I'm just a monkey! You don't have to rub it in," Gogi says.

"Did the ants get them?" Lima squeaks, turning a shade paler than her usual black.

"No," Sorella says darkly. "After Auriel sent you out after the Ant Queen, the caiman and the kinkajou got spooked and escaped into the jungle. I saw them go."

"I did too, *caow!*" says the trogon in its singsong voice. Mez barely noticed he was there, he was standing so still. "Well, I didn't *leave* too, but I *saw* it too, *caow!*"

"They are cowards, if you ask me," Sky says. "Auriel will not be pleased."

"This is an extraordinary situation," Rumi says. "I

think it's perfectly reasonable for self-preservation to win out."

"Yes," Sorella says, eyeing Sky. "I ran into a howler-monkey patrol last time I was off foraging. There are more and more each time. If more animals come to join them, we'll wind up totally trapped. Easy targets."

"Auriel will keep them at bay," Sky says defiantly. "I know it. We have to survive this night, then conduct the ceremony at dawn. Auriel will definitely be back by then."

"Why are you so faithful to that constrictor?" Sorella asks him, poking hard enough at the macaw's chest that he falls right over. "He's just another animal, no better than any of the rest of us."

"I don't need to explain myself to you," Sky sniffs.

"Niko is dead," Sorella says, "and two more of us have decided to risk the border guardians rather than stay here. It seems a lot to ask that the rest of us remain because a smelly bird and a *boa constrictor* have told us to."

"At least there's some good news. Sky did figure out my ability, *caow, caow, caow*," says the trogon. The beautiful little songbird falls into his usual trogon vocal-izations, and if he goes on to say what his ability is, Mez doesn't hear it.

To prove what he's discovered, though, the trogon

concentrates, and one of the stones beneath his foot lights up, eventually turning as bright as a firefly before he opens his eyes again. The stone returns to its normal stony color.

"Ooh, that's *way* pretty," Lima says.

Sky nods proudly. "One more magical power figured out. We're making progress."

"I wish my ability were more useful, *caow*," the trogon says mournfully. "But I guess we can't all make fire. *Caow*."

Gogi blushes. "I'm sure your ability will come in handy, don't worry."

"So who wants to be next to discover their power, *caow*?" asks the trogon.

Sky's head swivels to take in the group, then he opens his mouth to speak.

Mez's voice comes before he can say anything. "I am. Please. Let me go next."

18

ALL MEZ CAN do now is wait for the Veil to lift. And figure out her power in the meantime.

While Gogi and Rumi and the ocelot go off to search out the removable sun and moon sigils, Mez steals to a quiet corner of the ziggurat and stares out, waiting for Sky to come find her. She extends and retracts her claws, scraping into the stone.

Sky flaps through the night air to land in front of her, long tail fluttering as he settles in and starts preening. After keeping Mez waiting for a long moment, he looks up dramatically from his feathers and fixes her with his penetrating stare. "I hope you're ready to find your power."

"Yep, we're ready!" Lima says from under Mez's chin.

"Agh!" Mez exclaims, startled. She hadn't realized Lima was with her. She peers down the length of her nose and is just able to see the fuzz on top of Lima's head as the bat hangs upside down from Mez's chin fur.

Sky clacks his beak disdainfully at Lima. "You know she has to do this alone. That's part of the rules."

"Oh," Lima says. "I didn't know there *were* rules. Sorry! Good luck, Mez!"

Mez watches Lima fly off, wishing that she could keep her friend with her. But Léon the kinkajou didn't need a friend with him, so she doesn't push the point. All the same, Mez wistfully follows Lima's departing form, waiting until she's disappeared from view before nodding to Sky.

He stares at her for a long moment, an unknowable expression on his face, before he uses his beak to grasp a vine and lower himself, claw by beak, down to a lower level of the ziggurat, out of view of the other eclipse-born.

Mez pads down to follow him. They're below the level of the treetops that surround the ziggurat now, and are cast further in shadows.

Sky shifts from claw to claw, staring at Mez with one eye and then the other. Mez catches herself being intimidated by it, then says *panthers eat macaws* twice to herself, until she's able to rise up to her full height and stare back.

"I expect you already know what your power is," Sky says. "I think you've already *used* it, in fact."

"I don't know what you're talking about," Mez says.

"I believe that, too," Sky says, his eyes smiling. "Let's get started."

"Let's get started doing *what*?" Mez says.

Sky wraps his beak around his foot and tugs, something Mez has come to recognize as a nervous gesture of his. "You don't trust me, do you?"

Mez considers how to answer. "I . . . don't have a reason not to trust you."

"But you don't trust me all the same. You're not the first to feel that way toward me. It's the problem of being put in a position of power."

"No, I don't think that's it," Mez says. She considers saying *You just seem shifty* but keeps her mouth closed.

Sky holds perfectly still, staring at her. "Interesting reaction. Keep track of that feeling. It might help us to reveal the Mez that lives within."

"Hoo boy," Mez says, rolling her eyes.

"Have you had trouble trusting anyone else in your life?" Sky asks.

"Are you kidding me?" Mez scoffs. But her mind

says *Mist, Mist, Mist.* She hopes it doesn't show.

Sky's eye travels over Mez's face. Like he's reading her. "Mez," he finally says. "I'm trying to help you. Do you *want* to know what your power is?"

Of course she does. She felt invisible in that den for way too long, and now the Ant Queen is right below them, ready to emerge at any moment. Mez nods.

"I've found that the eclipse-born who have already discovered their power on their own are those who have, let's say, fewer defenses built up inside them. But you have plenty of defenses, don't you?"

"If this is a way of trying to put me at ease, it's definitely not working," Mez says.

Sky winces. "Okay, okay, I see your point. But I do think it's useful to look at any reasons you might have *not* to know your power. That could be what's blocking it."

"Okay, I'll try," Mez says. Though she quickly knows she won't tell Sky, her mind goes to Aunt Usha bearing down on the mewling kitten, teeth bared. *Unnatural!* Mez's imagination provides her aunt's teeth around its little neck, dragging it out into the dark, returning alone. Somewhere deeper in, more complicated, are the sense memories of Mez's own mother, gone too soon because of the childbirth brought on by the shock of the eclipse. "It's dangerous to be different," she whispers.

"*I'm* dangerous because I'm different. That's why I didn't deserve to stay."

"Yes," Sky says, his voice unreadable. "That makes sense."

Mez stares down at her paws, trembling. Much as she has tried to clean it all off, the muck and staleness of the belowground cavern are still on her. Facing the Ant Queen didn't scare her as much as this interrogation. Is she going to let Sky undo her with a few questions? She raises her head and steels her eyes.

Pushed by some macaw instinct, Sky makes a strident call, the sound harsh and unlovely. "Here's how I see it," he says, returning an eye to Mez. "Right here, right now, would it be so bad if you revealed yourself? We're all eclipse-born. Do you think any of us would call you unnatural?"

"No . . ." Mez says. Her voice trails off. It's true: she doesn't think any of them would. But all the same, it doesn't *feel* that way.

"For what it's worth, I'd like to share something I've learned talking to the other eclipse-born," Sky says. Despite herself, Mez can't help but open her eyes and perk her ears. "Each of you has come to me hoping to become powerful despite your weaknesses. But the very place I find the root of power, each and every time, is at the very source of that weakness."

Mez shakes her head in confusion. What does that even mean? Maybe macaws are smarter than panthers.

Sky opens his mouth wide and cocks his head, as if Mez's words were a food to devour. "You know, Sky," Mez says. "That look in your eyes? It doesn't really make me want to get all vulnerable with you."

Sky snaps his beak shut. Then he tries again. "So we could say that the same thing that gave you your magic also led to your mother's death, and your sister's missing paw."

"Oh, come on, Sky."

"It just seems to me that you felt outside of your 'family' from the start," Sky continues. "I could see why you wouldn't want to make it any worse by uncovering something different about yourself."

"That's not true! I had Chumba," Mez says.

"She's still back home at your den?" Sky asks.

Keeping her eyes scrunched shut, Mez nods, only one thought in her mind: *I left her behind.* "Did you leave someone back home, too?" she asks Sky.

"This isn't about me."

"Why isn't it?"

Mez's questions seem to surprise Sky. He seizes up, then shifts from one foot to another. "Fine. As you may have noticed, macaws are very . . . noisy. All of us try to talk over everyone else, and as a result the loudest macaws are the most powerful. For a long time I tried to keep up with the rest of my flock, but I couldn't. I shrank farther and farther away, and was always at the back, last to get to the fruit tree or the clay lick. I stopped trying to fight the way I was, and instead started to do what comes most naturally to me: I watched. I listened."

"And now your power is to see," Mez says.

Sky's feathers ruffle. "I am a seer, yes, but maybe I will be able to do more than that. Already I suspect my visions might someday work in both directions, that I will be able to send them as well as receive them. My power is in its infancy, too." Sky shifts from claw to claw.

Then Mez understands it: Sky sounds self-assured, but he's a young animal taken from his home, like the rest of them. His seeming confidence has been put on deliberately, like any other armor. "You were ready for Auriel when he came. You couldn't wait to leave your family."

Sky startles, his neck feathers ruffling so they stick straight out. He preens them back down. "It's different. My family was worth leaving."

"What does *that* mean?" Mez asks, bloodlust rising when she sees the cocky macaw on the defensive.

Sky stands his ground, looking at Mez shrewdly. "Fine. Let the truth set me free. Macaws lay up to four eggs. Only the first two are fed, and the rest are left to die. I was the third to hatch. It's simple math, and I was on the wrong side of it. My parents didn't feed me once, not once. I watched my siblings grow stronger, while I was left with scraps. If Auriel hadn't heard about my nightflying from the ants, if he hadn't come to take me away, I would be dead right now. So don't look at me like I'm Auriel's toady. I owe him everything."

"I'm sorry, Sky," Mez says. "I had no idea."

"I was the one of my brood who happened to be born at the moment of the eclipse. So my powers have *saved* me," Sky continues.

"Do you ever think about—"

"We won't talk about this anymore."

Sky nods, again shifting from claw to claw. His eyes are wet. Mez wishes she could ease the pain she sees in him, but she also understands why he doesn't want to talk about it. "I get it," Mez says softly. "Maybe later. Whenever you want to talk. Do you think you'd be willing to keep helping me for now?"

Sky sniffs, clacks his beak shut, then turns so that one of his eyes is directly in front of Mez's face. "Let us begin."

"What do I do?" Mez asks, eyes darting around.

"Nothing. You've already started," Sky says, edging ever closer, the hint of a smile back into his voice.

Mez is about to answer, but the words die in her

throat. Sky's eye has begun to swirl with black and gray, the grays twisting in and the blacks twisting out, fast enough that it's impossible to follow any one of the currents. The eye expands until it fills Mez's vision, becomes the only thing she can see.

In the center of his pupil the black and gray open up into stars, then the stars become glowworms. She's back in the cavern below the ziggurat, where she'd been alone and no one had been able to see her. The glowworms pulse at her, as if trying to communicate something in their glowwormy language, then Mez is soaring toward them, as if she's a bat like Lima, then she's through and out the other side, where the points of light become the spaces between leaves in her den, where she once stared out at the beautiful blue sky and wondered about the daywalker world, where she snuggled next to Chumba while Usha's newest litter frolicked together.

I've made a huge mistake. I should have insisted on staying, whatever the risk. I should be with my sister.

Mez is on the hunt now, a tiny cub among muscular cats, a ghost that can thread through vines that never move at her touch, scamper over nests of branches that never creak. She quickly dispatches the eagle that had taken Chumba, the eagle that didn't even seem to know where to find her while she was attacking. Then the ground squirms with delicious animals, each one the size of a bite, each one furry and each one plump. They scatter on the approach of the other panthers, but they don't even sense Mez near them, and she can hunt freely, eating until her belly is full. Mez simply can't be seen, and on this hunt she's able to catch more animals than all the rest of the panthers combined.

There's a scream, a horrible, rending scream, loud enough to split the bones of the creature that makes it, and Mez whirls to see Chumba flailing on the ground, calico limbs uncoordinated as she struggles against her attacker, and the eagle is already dead so it's Mist that's attacking her, Mist with his jaws locked around Chumba's neck and pressing her against the ground, Mist crushing Chumba until she's still, Mez paralyzed and unable to help, no sound coming out of her open mouth, as much as she tries to scream. What good is being tiny and weightless now, when it means she's powerless to help her sister?

Then the squirming prey are gone, Chumba and Mist are gone, the den with its points of light is gone, the glowworms are gone, the stars are gone, and the macaw pupil is back, the whole eye is back, the red feathers are back, Sky's head is back, Sky's wide-open beak is back. He's yelling at her. "Wake up, Mez, wake up!"

Mez startles and leaps in the air, whirling, looking for enemies. But she's still on the shadowed step of the ziggurat, still alone with Sky, only he's looking at her like *she's* the monster from below. "What? What is it?" Mez manages to sputter.

Sky cocks his head. Like that, the distress melts from him, and he's back in full control of himself. "You. You were yelling a name."

Mez looks away from him, eyes downcast.

"It was 'Chumba,'" he says.

Mez stares at him, chest heaving. *Do not dare say my sister's name.*

"Do you have any better sense of what your power is now?" Sky asks.

Mez looks at him, feelings at war within her: relief that the terrible vision is over, embarrassment at what she might have said aloud during it.

Her mind races over what she's seen: feeling invisible in the den; the eagle, unable to see or find her; Auriel, startled by her sudden appearance, even though Mez had been there the whole time; the Ant Queen's strange words: *Mez, you finally appear.*

"I think I know what my power is," Mez says softly.

Sky nods. "I just saw it happen. Mez, while you were in your trance—"

The macaw is interrupted by a clamor coming from the top of the ziggurat, animals yelling and screeching. Mez can hear Lima's high-pitched voice above it all, yelling, "And Mez, where's Mez?"

She leaps into action, bounding up the steps of the ziggurat, pace unfaltering until she's reached the top. Mez hears buffeting wings as Sky flies over. "Invisible, Sky," she cries up to him. "I can turn *invisible!*"

And then Mez is up on the moonlit roof of the ziggurat. Into chaos.

19

SORELLA'S VOICE IS the loudest. The uakari shrieks and jumps, ripping up moss and hurling it directionlessly, deafening sounds coming from her bright red mouth. The sloth makes gasping, squeaky grunts, his broad nostrils wide with fear. The rest of the animals are in the center of the ziggurat's top level, clustering around something Mez cannot yet see.

From high up in the sky, Lima calls out, "She's here, Mez is okay!" and then she's arrowing through the night, landing gracefully on the nape of Mez's neck and wrapping wings around her even as the panther bounds forward. "Thank goodness," Lima says, her voice barely audible, muffled by fur and wind as Mez presses forward. "We thought that we lost you, too."

"Too?" Mez asks, dread slowing her as she approaches the group.

Gogi must have heard Lima. He bounds to Mez as she nears, hugging her tightly. "I'm so glad you're okay."

Mez is close enough now to see what's in the center of the circle. There's a body there—no, two bodies. The caiman and the kinkajou. The corpses are emptied out. Husks, like a cicada's molt casing. Only these are animals that do not molt. Their withered flesh dimples over crushed bones.

"What happened to them?" Mez breathes.

"No one knows," Rumi says. He's at the far side of the group, next to the trogon and sloth. The small animals are sticking together, away from the larger eclipse-born.

The sloth cocks his head. "Uh, it was me who found them. I was off foraging leaves in the swamplands down below. There was this, uh, this large frond in the way, so I pushed it to one side, and there down below I saw, like—these! All hidden away, sorta."

"You don't know the bodies were intentionally hidden away," Sky says.

"You're trying to claim these two animals happened to die in the same place?" Rumi asks. "And in this same weird way?"

"The truth is clear! We're being hunted! *Caow!*" says the trogon, his voice sharpening into a tinny squeak at the end.

"The evidence would point to that," Rumi says. "We allowed these two to go off on their own, and now they're dead."

"What we *all* should do is leave," Sorella says. "Auriel didn't say anything this bad might happen when he took us from everything we knew to bring us here. We should all go home and pretend none of this ever happened."

Chumba, Mez thinks. *Maybe then I could be with Chumba again.*

"Auriel never promised we would be safe," Sky protests.

"Just because you're so deep under his spell doesn't mean the rest of us have to be," Sorella says. "We don't owe him anything."

"You're suggesting we fight through the owls and howler monkeys patrolling the forest around here?" Gogi asks, shuddering. "Maybe you haven't met them yet."

"Where *is* Auriel?" Mez asks.

"He wouldn't be away this long without good reason," Sky says. "I know that."

"Do you guys think he'll be back before dawn?" Lima asks, head tilted up. "I mean, we won't have to do the ceremony without him, right?"

"If he's not back in time we'll do the ceremony ourselves, don't worry," Mez says softly, giving the bat a reassuring lick.

"It's the Ant Queen who killed these two," Sorella spits. She considers her own words for a moment, nudging the kinkajou's body with a toe. "At least I think so."

"The Ant Queen was sealed in by the rockfall," Mez says, "and though she's certainly powerful enough to kill any one of us, it's hard to believe something as big as she is could escape without any of us noticing. And the last sigils are still lit on the ziggurat."

Sorella bares her teeth. "You have a better theory, panther?"

"Maybe the Ant Queen found some other, quieter way out," Rumi proposes.

"She could be watching us right now," snuffles the sloth.

They all go still, looking worriedly at the treetops sighing in the jungle breezes, branches waving at them in the deep night.

"We've been brought here and then ignored," Sorella says, her voice rising. "Doesn't that seem odd to any of the rest of you? Even before two of us were found dead?"

The chill inside Mez deepens. The answer to all this is in front of her. She needs quiet time to put all the threads together.

The trogon gives a tittering cry. "It's like we've been herded up here, *caow*! And now we're being picked off one by one, *caow*! Like we're being, like we're being . . ."

". . . penned up and then slaughtered?" Gogi supplies helpfully.

They all fall quiet again. Though the stones beneath them are still warm, as the night progresses the heat of the day seeps away, and their moonlit silhouettes are lengthening over the ziggurat's mossy surface. The dread of something great and terrible and unnameable comes over Mez, the feeling that she is at the summit of an immense wrongness that she does not yet understand. That she's here because she's been so dutiful, and that maybe dutiful has not been the right way to be.

She needs space to think! But the night is winding down, and with the lifting of the Veil will come the imprisoning ceremony—if the Ant Queen hasn't already escaped by then. Mez can't get her thoughts to settle under the pressure of it all.

"We need Auriel to return. He'll know what to do," Lima says, hopping into the air and coming back down, opening and closing her leathery wings as she presses tight to Mez's fur for comfort.

"What we need to do is leave. Right now," comes a purring voice. It's the ocelot. Mez has been avoiding him, but sees that he's looking directly at her for the first time. As if he's appealing to her because she's a panther, that being a cat should automatically make Mez the best option to listen to reason. Not that he's paid her any attention before.

"We're hemmed in by the enemy. Or haven't you noticed?" Mez says. It makes her hackles raise, that the ocelot always acts so superior because he's a feline. It's the thing she's come to like least about her own kind.

"We've all been obeying orders, trusting to how things should be, and now look what's happening!" Sorella says. "Two of us are dead!"

"Three of us, *caow*," the trogon chirps.

"Three?" Mez asks.

In response, the ocelot noses the body of the dwarf caiman onto its side. Underneath is the husk of a fish.

It's Niko.

"Now how did he get up here?" Rumi asks, surprised.

"I don't understand," Mez says, shaking her head. "Niko was eaten by the Ant Queen. And even if his body still existed, it should be sealed under the earth. Not hidden away in the swamp."

"Are you sure?" Rumi asks. "Did you witness the Ant Queen eat him?"

Niko's last words come back to her. Is it possible that it wasn't the Ant Queen but someone else who produced that horrible sound of his crunching bones?

"The simplest explanation," Sorella says sourly, "is that the Ant Queen has gotten free. That she killed Niko down below, then picked off these other two once they were separated from the group and vulnerable."

"Two sigils are still lit," Rumi offers. "So it seems like the Ant Queen's imprisonment still holds. That's a hole in your argument, if I may say so."

"We know too little to assume we know *anything* for certain," Mez says. "Since leaving isn't an option, we'll set watches and stay close together. No one leaves sight of the rest of the group until Auriel returns or morning comes, and we can figure out our next steps."

"We won't have to wait long," Sky says. "I'm sure Auriel will be back before we know it." He doesn't sound too convinced by his own words. From the weary looks of the group, no one else is, either. Everyone slinks back to their favored positions on the ziggurat, casting wary eyes on the outside world—and one another.

I figured out my power. I can turn invisible, Mez reminds herself. But that news has been so quickly overshadowed. She turns a slow circle, looking for someone to tell, but all the animals look shell-shocked by the deaths of the kinkajou and caiman. Mez hangs her head. Being invisible seems all too appropriate at the moment.

Then there's a flutter of wings, and a bat lands in front of her. "Mez, I forgot in all this—how did your time with Sky go?" Lima asks.

A patter on the stone as a tree frog hops over. "Yes, I'm very curious!" Rumi says.

The creak of a branch as Gogi drops to the stone from an overhanging tree. "Let's see it!"

Gratitude flattens Mez's whiskers. "Here it is: I can turn invisible."

"Wow!" Lima says.

"That's a great one," Gogi says.

"Can you show us now?" Rumi says.

"I don't know how," Mez says. "I guess I've been doing it for a while! But I'm not sure how to turn it on."

"Don't worry. A smart panther like you? You'll figure it out," Gogi says, stroking her between the ears. There was a time Mez would never have allowed a monkey near her, much less to *pet* her, but tonight it feels nice.

"Yeah, you'll have the hang of it soon," Lima says.

"In the meantime," Gogi says, "take a look at these!" Hand still on Mez's head, he leads her to a corner of the ziggurat, where there are two stone discs. One is decorated with a crescent moon, the other with a blazing sun. Each has a pinprick hole in the center.

"We tried to hold them up already, but nothing doing," Rumi says. "The moon one hums a bit, but not the sun one. My working theory is that beams of moonlight and sunlight will have to mingle at dawn to renew the eclipse magic."

"A little while more, and we'll be able to try it out," Mez says. She looks down at the seam in the rock, which at any moment could open and release the Ant Queen—if she's not out already. She looks, too, at the bodies of the kinkajou and caiman and poor Niko. "In the meantime, while we're hanging around waiting, let's go hide in the trees."

MEZ.

At first she thinks her own name must be coming to her through a dream, that she's back in the open blackness of her mental hunting grounds. Maybe the air itself is speaking to her, calling her forward toward the plumpest quarry.

Mez.

Or maybe it's Chumba, calling for help. Mez's limbs pull hard through the open air as she dozes, trying to gain traction on ground that isn't there.

Mez.

This time her heart tells her she's hearing her mother search for her. She can't remember what her mother's face looked like, but this warmth, this looming loving presence, is definitely her.

"Mez."

Now the voice is right in her own ear. She startles awake. Her name was not coming to her from a dream. It was coming from the creature in front of her, in glittering darkness on this half-moon night. A forked tongue tickles the inside of her ear.

"Auriel!" Mez says.

The outlines of the snake's head shift in Mez's darkvision as he nods.

Groggily, Mez gets to her paws. "You're back," she says, shaking her head to clear it.

"And you managed to fall asleep—and at night, even," Auriel says, winking. "Very un-panther-like of you."

Mez shrugs. "I didn't think I was going to. I just needed a rest. Everything gets a little mixed up around here. Auriel, let me wake the others so we can tell you about what happened belowground. We discovered so much! I want them to be able to tell you their part in their own words. And . . . something terrible happened to the caiman and the kinkajou, and to Niko."

"No, don't rouse them," Auriel whispers. "I've been filled in on what happened."

"Sky told you?" Mez asks.

"I had no idea you'd reach the Ant Queen herself down below—I assumed she could only be reached through the ziggurat's doors," Auriel says, his triangular head rising into the sky. The moonlight catches his diamond scale, his glossy charcoal one, and two new ones, too, topaz- and ruby-colored. With the other two they form a sort of necklace under his head. He's so quiet when he moves—none of the other dozing animals have even stirred. "You discovered the final panels, I understand. And you know how to conduct the ceremony now?"

Mez nods, her mind still half-asleep. "The removable sigils—Gogi's got them. Did you find the last eclipse-born?"

Auriel nods. "I did. I will introduce you soon enough; he's still tired from his journey. In other good news, I also understand that you have discovered that you can turn invisible."

Mez nods. Not that she knows how to turn it on or anything. "Why don't we bring everyone together?" she asks. "We need to be in place when the Veil lifts, before the last sigil goes out."

Auriel shakes his head sadly. "We need to get ready for the ceremony, I agree. But we can't make a plan with all of the eclipse-born present."

"Why not?" Mez asks.

"I'm surprised you haven't figured this out yet," Auriel says, his voice dropping to a whisper so low that if his head weren't right in Mez's ear she wouldn't be able to hear him. "One of you is a traitor."

"What?" Mez says, springing to all fours. "How do you know?" Her mind goes to the slain eclipse-born, dispatched so efficiently the moment they left the ziggurat.

"It's too dangerous to discuss this here," Auriel says. "The traitor might overhear us. Come with me, away from this thicket. You and I can figure this out."

"Why me?" Mez asks.

"Because you're the one I can trust the most."

"You can trust Lima and Rumi and Gogi, too," Mez says, hackles rising. "There's no question about it."

"I don't doubt that," Auriel says. "And I admire your loyalty. Once you and I have settled on our plan I'll count on you to fill them in. But for now, pulling all four of you to the side would be noticed. Come now, we're already risking discovery by talking here."

Auriel soundlessly rears back and, coiling and then uncoiling, sloughs off the tree branch and into the darkness. Within moments, even with her excellent darkvision, Mez can discern only the slightest suggestion of his long body looping its way into the forest.

Somewhere nearby, Gogi, Rumi, and Lima are on

watch. If Mez were anything but a panther, she wouldn't be able to sneak off without their knowing it. But Mez has always been able to go her own way without disturbing others. Like she once did when she daywalked from her den, she gets up silently and flows like liquid, her calico fur seamless with the starry night. Undetectable.

She can't sense Auriel anymore, can only move blindly into the darkness, hoping she's going in the same direction as the constrictor. A soft rain has begun, the misty droplets making their own hushed sounds against the leaves of the surrounding trees. There is the occasional hoot of an owl, the off-silence of a swooping bat, but more than anything there is the patter of soft rain, over the smell of baked moisture rising from the mossy stones of the ziggurat at her back, the heat of day dying into night.

Where is he? Mez goes motionless, listening and watching.

"Mez." When he speaks, Auriel's voice is right beside her. She startles, cringing away in the darkness. He was able to come right up to her without her noticing. "Sorry to scare you," Auriel continues. "This whole experience has been an exercise in fear, hasn't it? At least it will be over soon."

"That's . . . okay," Mez says, eyes wide as she concentrates on the vague outline of Auriel's head, only a breath's distance away. There's something about his tone that unsettles her, but she can't quite get to the bottom of it. She wants to ask for Gogi, Rumi, and Lima again, but the words die in her throat. He knows so much. It's hard to refuse him.

"I know it can't be easy to have been taken so far from your home, to be reviled, brought into a group of strangers and adversaries."

"No," Mez says. "Of course not. But . . . this is to stop the Ant Queen, right? So it's for the good of everyone. You don't need to worry about me, Auriel."

"Oh, you misunderstand me. I'm not worried about you," he says, voice low and vibrating. "I'm not worried about you at all."

"Okay . . ." Mez says, her voice trailing off. She senses motion around her, rustling leaves and cracking branches. "Auriel, do you hear that?"

"No," he purrs. "I hear nothing beyond the sounds of the night. You should be used to those sounds, nightwalker."

"I guess I am," Mez says, getting to all fours and making slow turns in the darkness so no one else can sneak up on her the way Auriel did. Why *did* he sneak up on her? She's not the enemy. Does he think *she's* the traitor? Mez feels her thoughts scrambling, blood rushing to her face, saliva flooding her teeth. Her intuition is preparing her for combat. As if it knows an enemy is nearby. But there *is* no enemy nearby. "What do you want to tell me?" she asks Auriel, voice quavering. "How will we figure out the traitor?"

"The traitor. Yes," Auriel says. "Let's talk about the traitor. I have something to tell you about that. Where do I begin? Earlier than you might expect."

"Really?" Mez asks, confused, heart racing without clear reason.

"Yes. As I told you before, I spent my childhood avoiding being tortured by my siblings. Snakes deserve some of their reputation for cruelty, I'm afraid. I don't know if you've ever witnessed a defanging, but it's nothing you'd soon forget, believe me."

"I'm sure it was very painful," Mez says. This conversation is only heightening her confusion. Why are they talking about Auriel's missing fangs when the Ant Queen could emerge at any moment?

"Yes, and this was by my *siblings*. Sky and I understand each other this way. We both learned early on that the ones closest to you might be your worst enemies. But I showed my evil siblings, I showed them all."

"What happened?" Mez asks, dread tingling her claws.

"The thing with snakes is that they grow, and they grow fast," Auriel says. "I worked hard, hunted the ways that I could, and became bigger than my siblings. I traveled, I grew strong, and I came home and found as many of them as I could. They will never torment a young snake, ever again. While I was hunting my siblings, I met an eclipse-born porcupine that had the power to speak to the ants."

"No, Auriel—that's *your* power," Mez says.

"It is now," Auriel whispers.

Mez backs up toward the tree where her friends are.

"Your ability will prove very useful," Auriel whispers into Mez's ear. "The invisible can go anyplace, can overhear anything, can escape any fight. You have a power that is very, very precious."

"And you'll help me figure out how to use it?" Mez asks.

"Don't worry. We'll make sure your power is maximized," Auriel says.

Mez feels something brush against her back and startles, whirling with claws outstretched. "Someone else is here," she hisses.

"No. There is no one here but the two of us," he says.

"I know what I felt," Mez says. "Someone brushed . . . oh." As she whirls she steps on something thick and scaled. "It's you," she says, hackles rising straight up.

"That's right," Auriel says, voice even nearer, the

forks of his tongue tickling the sensitive hairs of her ear. "It's just you and me."

The colored scales surrounding his head glow, and Mez can see that there are five, all in different colors. She's not mistaking it. He's gaining colors. And looking stronger and healthier each time he does it.

"Auriel, your—your scales . . ." Mez stammers, mind racing. Considering how close he is to her, she can sense no warmth from Auriel's breath. It is as chill as the air from the Ant Queen's cavern. Mez's stomach, already plummeting, drops to the pads of her paws. She backs up but hits the wall of the ziggurat, much closer than she thought it was. Then she realizes it's not a wall: she's up against the coils of the constrictor, one on top of the other, as solid as stone.

She's been so naive. Growing up in her panther family, she was taught to respect Aunt Usha's authority above all else. Now, her unquestioning obedience has surely killed her.

"Auriel," Mez whispers. "You've gotten a new scale with each power you've stolen. You were down below with the Ant Queen. You killed Niko and the caiman and the kinkajou. The traitor is you."

21

"CLEVER GIRL," AURIEL says, his voice no longer the soft purr he'd put on moments before. His real voice is a sound no mammal could produce. He rasps, each vertebra along the constrictor's long body layering eerie echoes over the sound. "My original power is not speaking to ants—it is to suck out the powers of other eclipse-born. Like you, Mez. The other victims trusted me to the end, never figuring me out, even as they were taking their final breaths." He chuckles. "Of course, there is a while between that final breath and death, so maybe they figured it out then. But of course, they couldn't tell me. They couldn't say anything at all."

Even within her terror Mez hears a sound like the

rustling of leaves, a sound that brings to mind both death and dryness, and senses the rings of coils swirling in opposite directions around her, narrowing as they go. Hemming her in. As if patting down grasses to find a place to sleep, she turns a tight circle, looking for an opening.

"You said that you didn't want to interfere by appearing to Aunt Usha, but really you just were worried that she'd see through you. I was easier to trick on my own," Mez says.

"Don't let your final moment be one of struggle," Auriel says, "when it can be one of peace. How your death happens is all you have left in your control. You can't change your fate, but you can change how the end feels." He pauses, and when he speaks again his face is right beside hers. "I saw something like bliss on the kinkajou's face as it died. Being constricted can be pleasurable."

Mez leaps.

She doesn't leap forward—that would bring her right up against Auriel's coils—but upward, perfectly vertically, like she used to do when playing whisker-taunt with Chumba. By springing all her ankles at once, she pops into the night air. Then, once she's at her highest, she reaches her front claws out, scratching for purchase.

But her claws find only open air, and as she begins

to fall back down Mez starts thrashing desperately, the moves bringing her head over heels, the crown of her head the first thing to hit a tangle of thorny brambles. *Be invisible, be invisible,* she wills herself as she scrambles through the vines, finally getting to her paws. Her darkvision shows Auriel arrowing through the darkness, enough scant starlight to outline the rainbow of scales surrounding his face.

Mez goes still. Auriel is only roughly heading in her direction. Maybe she *is* invisible. She looks down at her paws. She can't see a thing, but that could be a result of black paws in black night. Even her darkvision could miss a midnight panther.

"You know that I hunt by vibrations, silly panther," Auriel says, emerald scales glinting in the starlight. "Your invisibility will do you no good against me."

Is that true? If it were, why would he tell her instead of simply hunting her down where she is?

What Mez wants most is to call for help. But Auriel would find her before her friends could get there, and he would have them all. Still, she readies herself to call out a warning the moment she feels the touch of Auriel's coils. If it's the last thing she does, she'll prevent the other eclipse-born from suffering her same fate. They can run away and save their own lives, even if it means leaving Auriel and the Ant Queen to hatch their plan without opposition.

For now, though, her only option is to hold still.

She won't be able to hide for long. Auriel's expanding to fill her entire field of vision: he's fanned out his long body, moving back and forth as he goes, waiting for some part of him to bump into Mez. The grasses make crackling sounds as clouds of startled grasshoppers flee the constrictor. Mez scrunches her eyes shut as they batter her face. All the while, Auriel moves ever closer.

As she waits for an opening, Mez's mind races. If Auriel wanted them all dead, why do it this way? He could have killed her the moment he separated her from Aunt Usha. Why wait so long, why bring her to the ziggurat only to secrete her away like this?

Mez sees Auriel heading off into the darkness. Maybe his random movements will bring him the wrong way. Her hackles lower slightly. She might have a few more minutes to live, to figure a way out of her plight.

That's when the touch comes. From behind her.

Auriel's tail. Mez holds perfectly still, hoping that Auriel won't realize he's found her. Maybe he thinks his tail hit a mushroom, or soft moss, or a spiny rat bumbling through the nighttime undergrowth.

Auriel hisses.

Mez crouches.

The constrictor suddenly streaks toward her,

impossibly long, somehow covering all paths of escape. Mez picks a direction and leaps, claws outstretched and jaw open, as if she'd have a chance of doing any damage to Auriel if she managed to bite him.

Mez lands right in the middle of a mass of coils, and they're immediately thrashing around her, closing in tight. Auriel is silent as he goes about his deadly work, wrapping himself around her. One paw is caught out at an angle, and Mez feels tendons and ligaments inside it tear as it wrenches painfully against her side.

Then the real squeezing begins. Invisibility is no help against this.

For a moment it does almost feel nice, like she's being loved, like back when she was a young cub and Aunt Usha would wrap her body around Mez's, telling her, with that simple motion, *I will take care. Don't worry.* Then it constricts, and Mez feels her fur pulling, her skin shredding, the bones of her spine and ribs grinding. Each breath is shallower than the last, and each time she tries to take in another her lungs only shrink, until she's no longer able to breathe at all. Until she's dying.

Mez feels a panic unlike any she's ever felt; it's a powerless panic, an otherworldly panic. She's acutely aware of the insects fleeing Auriel, of the wet scales of a millipede glinting in the pattering rain, of a tarantula disturbed by the commotion and making tentative steps from its den, of some stars produced by the struggling blood vessels of her eyes, of others that are real points of light in the night sky.

The ants that cover Auriel's body cover Mez now, crawling over her eyes and ears. As they do, she hears snippets of their song again:

> *Constrictor!*
> *Our queen hears*
> *all*
> *you may consume but five*
> *Niko you took right in front of*
> *our queen*
> *and he was four*
> *five does this panther make*
> *choose greed*
> *and greed will undo you*
> *for our queen will know*
> *all*
> *our queen hears you*
> *constrictor!*

So. Auriel and the Ant Queen are allies. Not that Mez will be able to do anything with the information. She can't even speak anymore. In the distance, she hears a macaw calling. Maybe it's Sky. Mez puts her mind fully into the sound of the macaw, listens to the harshness and the music of it. She can keep that sound for herself, even as she dies.

Poor Chumba, she thinks. After her sister, Mez's mind goes to her new friends, who might shortly face her same fate. She thought she'd be keeping them safe by being silent, but she knows now that she has doomed them. They'll discover the husk of her body, too, see that she's gone the way of the kinkajou and caiman and not know why or how she got that way. They'll flock to Auriel, hoping he'll save them.

I will never obey blindly again.

But the realization is too late.

Auriel's voice is right beside her face. "There you are, give it to me."

Sky revealed Mez's power, and now Auriel has led her off into the night to empty her out, just like he did Niko. Is Auriel's underling a knowing part of this plot to steal everyone's powers?

Numbness grows with the bands tightening around her, and Mez feels a curious lack of pain, a curious lack of any feeling at all. Her vision goes from black to white, and it takes longer and longer to open her eyelids whenever she blinks.

There are other sounds under the macaw's shrieks.

A monkey. Croaks of a frog. A bat's high-pitched voice crying: "Let her go . . . !"

Even with the sound of Lima nearby, the coils binding Mez tell her to give in. She again feels her fur tearing and her ribs grinding, only this time it's because the coils are loosening, sliding in opposite directions as Auriel releases his grip.

Mez gasps, her vision gaining color again, her mind filling with the painful bliss of taking in air, her ribs cracking as they fill. She hacks and sobs, her body falling limply to the jungle floor when Auriel finally releases her fully.

Inhale, exhale. Even though it's painful, there is no other work in the world but this.

As she gradually catches her breath, Mez's darkvision provides her with the sight of Gogi, scrawny little Gogi, standing in the dark, his arms outstretched and teeth bared, fury and terror mixed on his face. Licks of flames rise from his palms, but Mez can tell he doesn't know where to send them. He's a daywalker, and can't see anything beyond the dazzle of his own flames. He has no chance against a night predator like Auriel.

Mez gets unsteadily to her paws, legs splayed and uncoordinated. Lima and Rumi can see, of course, and Mez is dimly aware of them guiding Gogi, telling him when to turn or duck or jump. She doesn't know if they're avoiding Auriel or looking for her, but she can't bring her voice to work; when she tries to speak she can only shudder.

Mez startles when a wet leaf strikes her on the face, then realizes a wind has come up. Rumi must be using his powers.

Auriel's long coils are still all around, the smallest creatures of the night chirping as they flee him and Rumi's wind. Mez is only gradually able to make all the motion coalesce into shapes.

Auriel isn't hunting for her anymore.

He's racing up the ziggurat.

Despite pain lancing up and down her body, Mez struggles to make her jagged vocal cords come together into sounds. *He's going after the rest of you,* she wants to warn. But she can't.

Mez blunders through the night, tripping over vines and upturned earth. She manages to hurl herself into Gogi, nearly pitching him over in the process. He shrieks in fear, throwing fiery punches in the dark. "Oh, no you don't, I'll get you, I'll get you!"

Mez manages to get scraps of sound to come out of her throat. "It's . . . me!"

Suddenly the flames are out and Gogi's fingers are on her, grooming through her fur. It makes her chafed skin light up as if it's burning, but all the same she's grateful for the grooming, can feel tears filling her eyes at the touch of her friend. "The . . ." she gasps. "Aur . . . the zig . . ."

She hears a shrieking commotion from up above, the panicked hooting of Sorella and the sloth and the growling of the ocelot, Sky's caws above it all. Lima screaming, her voice changing pitch as she streaks through the night: "Flee! Everyone flee!"

"Come on," Gogi says, his arms under Mez's collarbone. "Let's go. I'll help you."

"No," Mez moans, her joints popping and grinding. "I can't move. Let me be."

"Sorry," Gogi says, releasing her.

"Leave me here. You go help," Mez says.

"Well, I can't really see anything, that's the problem," Gogi says. But, in true Gogi form, he bolts off into the night anyway, in the process heading directly *away* from the ziggurat and tripping over a vine, sprawling on his face.

"No, come back, this way," Mez tries to say as she staggers toward the ziggurat.

Her limbs are uncoordinated, lancing up and down with pain. She's got none of her usual speed as she limps toward the ziggurat even as Auriel rears up at the top, looming over the eclipse-born.

From this distance, even through the shroud of the

dark and rainy night, one thing is clear: Auriel has been hiding the true extent of his power. The creature at the top of the ziggurat is nothing like the gentle leaf-eating animal Mez first met. He opens his mouth wide, jaws open to the night, and the voice that comes through is powerful and raw. He might have no fangs, but Mez knows, from the agony still burning in her chest, that Auriel doesn't need them. His true dominance is through the muscles of his body. And those are in full play now, the bands of raw power beneath his scales turning and rippling as he maneuvers, flicks of his massive tail blocking any of the eclipse-born from escaping. The colored scales encircling his head glow with a fiery intensity.

Caught unawares, the desperate eclipse-born screech and scurry. Sky's strident caws are the loudest, but the rest of the animals express their shock in other ways, from roars to shrieks to claws scuffling on stone. Auriel is a whirl of energy, looming over the top. His topaz scale glows painfully bright, and then the very stone of the ziggurat wavers under him, like Niko would have once done, and Mez realizes she is probably witnessing Niko's very power, that Auriel constricted it out of him like he almost did to her, that it's the reason for that newest colored scale.

There is a giant grinding sound, and Mez realizes

the doors at the top of the ziggurat are opening. She sights Sorella, arms flung over the edge of the ziggurat, trying to grip the stone. But, though nothing is touching her, something is pulling at her. It's like gravity is yanking the uakari into the open top of the structure with many times its normal power.

Even the uakari monkey's fur is pressed flat, pulling back and down as surely as if a giant hand were yanking it. The roaring sound is loud enough to drown out the screams of the stricken animals.

It's like she's being dragged into a whirlpool. Like in the cavern.

It was Auriel who trapped Niko. Auriel isn't killing the eclipse-born now—he's entombing them inside the ancient structure! Mez hears more stones grinding as the ziggurat's doors begin to close. As they do the suction sound gets even stronger, and Sorella loses her grip, plummeting head over heels through the night. A flash of yellow-gold, and the trogon is gone, followed by Sky, the force pulling at him strong enough to send up a cloud of red feathers.

Despite the pain in her body, despite the scissoring of her own bones and joints, Mez staggers toward the ziggurat. She doesn't know what she will do if she's able to make it to the top, but knows she has to do *something* to help the rest of the eclipse-born. Rear legs dragging behind her, Mez tries to call out the names of her friends, but agony scrambles the sounds, and she hears herself only gasping and shrieking. Finally, despite the force of her will, her body fails her. When she tries to climb the first level of the ziggurat, the extra weight causes her front leg to wobble and give, sending her tumbling down to the muddy ground, sparks of pain in her eyes.

Then, as suddenly as all the commotion began, the thunderous sounds from the top of the ziggurat are finished. Gritting her teeth against the pain, Mez manages to raise her head and look up. She sees no one. The eclipse-born are gone. Auriel is gone.

No more screechings and scramblings.

Silence is back.

Cicadas, crickets, rainfall.

Mez drags herself into the shelter of a bush, burrowing amid ferns and flytraps and vines. As soon as she's hidden away she closes her eyes, letting darkness take over, falling deeply into her pain.

She doesn't know how much time has passed when she hears a rustling sound. Staggering awake, she whirls, teeth bared. Outlined in her darkvision, she finds Gogi still wandering about, groping his way right toward a looming tree, arms outstretched. "Guys? Guys?" he calls out, his voice hoarse. "Where are you?"

"Gogi!" Mez manages to say, the words coming out in an anguished gasp.

"Mez!" he calls, blundering through the night, batting aside fronds until he's near her, though facing the wrong way. "What happened up there?"

"Auriel," she says through gritted teeth. "He betrayed us!"

"Keep talking," Gogi says, stepping right into a big patch of nettles. "I can't find you without your voice. Ow! Why couldn't I have darkvision like you guys? Ow, ow, holy monkey butts, those *hurt!*"

"I'm over here," Mez says. She manages to get to her paws, though pain lights up her body.

Suddenly Gogi's grooming her, picking through her fur. She's glad for the closeness, but this time the pain is too much to take. "Stop, stop," she says.

"We need to find Lima to help you, right away," he says.

"Lima . . ." Mez says. Her mind goes to the little bat, and to Rumi. *Are they trapped down below too?*

"Lima!" Gogi calls into the night. "Are you there?"

"Not a good idea to go shouting off into the darkness, Gogi," Mez says through gritted teeth. "Not when we don't know who else is listening."

Gogi goes motionless for a moment. When he speaks again it's with uncharacteristic conviction. "I don't care. Let them come. You need help. Lima! Lima, are you out there?"

Mez won't try again to stop him. She needs the help too much.

They listen to the night. Mez's breath comes in ragged gasps—no matter how much she tries to calm it, she can't seem to get it under control. Gogi continues to shout Lima's name, and with every "Li—" and "—ma" Mez's imagination supplies more and more ferocious animals and monsters hearing Gogi's call and stalking through the night to eat them. Like an Ant Queen.

And, sure enough, something does come.

At first there's only a change in the air, a shifting in the sounds of the night. "Gogi," Mez whispers, "hold quiet for a second."

She feels the monkey tense beside her, then hears the sound of wings whisking over the night breezes. She tries to follow the movement, but it's too fast, too light— too small. "Lima?" Mez whispers. "Is that you?"

She feels a slight pressure on her temple, and she's soon suffused by warmth, her pain dissipating, like chill in the sun.

"Lima," Gogi whispers. "You're alive."

"Of course I am," Lima says between licks. "Mez, we saw you were missing, and we all came right down. I was near you while Auriel was attacking you, but there was nothing I could do. I'm so small, and my powers are to heal, not to harm, and I think you turned invisible, did you realize that? I'm sorry."

"I'm going to be okay," Mez says. "Thanks to those healing powers. So no apologizing."

"I'm so glad you're all right," Gogi says.

"I might be, but the others . . . I flew back up when Auriel went on the attack, but there was nothing I could do there, either. Everyone was fleeing, but no one was fast enough. Not even the trogon. I couldn't . . . I wanted but I couldn't . . ." Lima's voice pinches off.

"You did everything you could," Gogi says.

"He's gone," Lima says.

"That's right, Auriel isn't around anymore. We're safe," Gogi says.

"No. Not Auriel." Lima takes a deep breath. "It's Rumi. Rumi's gone."

Mez sits back on her aching haunches, stunned.

"We messed up, Gogi," Lima continues, tears in her voice. "You scampered down to help Mez, and I flew right down with you, but Rumi, he's just a little frog. I'm sure he was racing to keep up with us, but he was still up there when Auriel began to suck them all down and he—he got pulled right in."

Lima's voice becomes barely audible over the sounds of the night. "They're all gone. We're the only ones left."

"Then it's up to us to save them," Mez says.

22

SOMBER AND PENSIVE, the three catch their breath at the ziggurat's edge. Lima busily licks at Mez's most wounded parts.

"What do you think Auriel is doing to them down there?" Gogi asks.

"I saw it firstpaw," Mez says, wincing. "He's sucking away their powers. He tried to drain me, and if you two hadn't stopped him he would have succeeded. Now that he's got them all trapped in one place, he's . . . I'm sure he's draining them one by one."

"Isn't he scared of the Ant Queen, though?"

"He's been crawling with ants since we first saw him. And he was right down there with the queen before, because he was the one to constrict Niko. I think he might be working *with* her."

They all let that sink in.

"If his goal this whole time has been to steal our powers, I don't understand why he'd go through all this," Gogi says. "Wouldn't it be easier for Auriel to, you know, kill us off as he found us instead of bringing us here?"

"I've been thinking about that," Mez says. "It seems clear so far that the eclipse magic is very important to the ants, the original shadowwalkers. If Auriel is working with the Ant Queen, maybe he's promised us—and the eclipse magic inside us—to her. He brought us here under false pretenses. We were supposedly defending Caldera against her, but we're actually meant to be *sacrificed* to her. But he's been stealing our power on the side, siphoning as many away as he can before the Ant Queen emerges from her prison."

"Won't our families back home figure it out when we never come back?" Lima says. "And they'll rally against him? Well, your families. I bet none of the bats even noticed I was missing."

"Not if no one thinks Auriel is the one that killed us. Not if they think it's the Ant Queen. Not if the way it's always been in the rainforest is that animals keep to themselves."

"But—" Gogi says, before going silent. "Oh my. They'll all think we died defending Caldera!"

"And that valiant Auriel tried to bring us together, but was the only one to make it out of the battle alive—"

"—with all of our abilities, an Ant Queen, and the might of billions of ants at his side," Lima finishes.

"We have to stop him!"

"Yes, but how?" Gogi says, tapping his toes on the ziggurat's roof. "There's no getting in there. Assuming that's where Auriel is, of course. None of us actually *saw* him go in."

The night's chill thickens. Without speaking a word more, the friends draw tight.

"I mean, I'm sure he's probably sealed away, never to return. Sorry for even bringing it up," Gogi says, his arms wrapping around Mez. Her body is still sore all over, and she winces at the pain of his touch. But she does nothing to get him off her. Lima is between them, tucked under Mez's chin. They stare out across the top of the ziggurat, looking for Auriel, for the first sign that death is on its way.

"Well, I guess there's no point sitting around getting ourselves scared," Mez finally says. "We need some sort of plan. And we need to get off the ziggurat."

"We don't know who Auriel will start with, so from here on out we'll have to assume that he has access to any of the powers of the other eclipse-born," Gogi says. "Actually, we'll be able to figure out who he's . . . constricted by which powers he has access to."

"It's too terrible," Lima says. "What if Auriel uses wind? Then we'll know that he's . . . that he's . . ."

"No more of that talk," Mez says, shaking her head. "Here's what I'm thinking: We continue with our plan. We get ready to begin the ceremony to renew the Ant Queen's bonds at dawn. Now, if you guys would let me move, we could get searching to see where the removable sigils went during the fight."

"Sorry," Gogi says, Lima taking to the air as he disengages from Mez's front. "Sometimes I clutch a little tight when I get scared. Monkey habit."

"They've got to be here somewhere," Mez says, pacing the ziggurat's roof.

"Unless they got sucked into the ziggurat," Lima says from where she's riding on Mez's shoulder. Gogi must be searching silently behind them, as stealthily as she is.

Wait. Gogi, *stealthy?*

"Gogi," Mez whispers, "you're getting very good at sneaking!"

No answer.

Mez turns around, but Gogi is not there. She looks

farther back and finds him right where she left him, peering around in astonishment.

Eyes alert to any sign of Auriel, she slinks over to him. The jungle is quiet all around them as Mez pads near. "Are you really playing a *game* right now?" she asks.

Gogi shrieks in surprise and leaps high into the air. He lands on all fours, looking vaguely in Mez's direction. "Sweet monkey breath!"

"What is it?" she asks, spinning around with her ears back, looking for enemies.

"Mez. You're *invisible*."

She gazes down at her own paws. Not there. Oh. So she is! She's invisible! "Wow. That's got to be useful, right?" she asks.

"Useful? It's *awesome*," Lima says. Mez cranes her neck back and sees the bat gripping empty air, wings at her side.

Gogi nods in agreement, empathetic smoke rising from his hands.

"Okay, enough conversation," Lima says. "I'm still getting the creeps around here. It feels like the trees themselves are watching us. Let's get searching."

Mez and Gogi fan out, feeling along the ground with claw and hand and tail. "No boa constrictors, no boa constrictors," Gogi whispers as he hunts.

"If there's any sign of Auriel, we'll hide," Mez reassures him.

"Maybe *you* will, Little Miss Invisible," he says. "A capuchin daywalker is like a sitting sloth out here."

"You'll follow my lead," Mez says.

"No arguments here," Gogi says, a hand on Mez's invisible tail. "No boa constrictors, no boa constrictors," he continues to whisper. He must look faintly ridiculous, tiptoeing along, led by nothing at all.

"Any sign of the sigils yet?" Lima whispers from her perch behind Mez's ear.

"Not yet," Mez whispers.

"No boa constrictors, no boa constrictors," Gogi whispers.

"But *why?*" comes a voice from a tree overhanging the ziggurat. "We're so much fun!"

They freeze.

"You guys heard that too, right?" Lima whispers. "I didn't make it up?"

"Yes. I definitely heard that," Mez whispers back.

At first she thinks the shock of the sudden voice has her light-headed, that fear is what's making the night around her warp and waver. From Gogi's and Lima's gasps, though, she knows she's not the only one feeling it. It's not that just the air is shifting; the stones of the ziggurat ripple underneath her paws. Liquid rock bunches behind her back legs and nudges her forward, like a rippling wave, pulling ever toward the overhanging tree.

Gogi springs across the ziggurat's roof, sprinting hands over feet while Lima darts into the air. Mez leaps for a nearby palm tree, but the shifting stones prevent her from getting a good launch. She winds up striking the trunk with her shoulder and falling back to the ziggurat's surface, pitching over on the rolling stone. She struggles to get off her back as the waves in the rock continue to drive her toward the tree.

She'd thought it was draped by a large vine, but Mez sees now that she was wrong, that the vine is actually a snake, a snake she knows well, a snake that is slowly uncoiling and opening its broad triangular head, ready to receive her.

Something has changed about Auriel. His movements before were always a little stuttery, as if his body was struggling to remember how to move. Now he's almost molten, pouring like honey off the tree and onto the ziggurat's surface, his tail going in one direction and his head in the other, so that when Mez looks at one she loses track of the other.

She's mesmerized by his strange movements, her limbs going senseless. She knows this might be part of his strategy, some new ability he's siphoned out of one of the eclipse-born, but she's powerless to counteract it. Not that she could move to save herself anyway, not with Niko's stolen earth power sending the stones themselves rippling toward Auriel. The gravity power, wherever he got that, is also sucking at Mez, bringing her ever nearer the constrictor's coils. How can a small panther resist?

Mez hears Lima shriek, and looks up to see the bat, so much littler than she, courageously darting through the air toward Auriel. The constrictor snaps at Lima once she's near, but she is too small and the snake too big; his jaws close on open air, and Lima is soon hurtling past him. She doesn't get far before the gravity drags her back; despite Lima's frantic flapping she's motionless in midair, then zooming toward Auriel. He's ready for her this time, mouth open wide. Even without fangs, he could easily swallow her whole. Lima shrieks, wings flailing.

Mez wants to help, but she's got problems of her own. She's been pulled close enough to Auriel now that one of his rapidly unfurling coils strikes her on the head. Mez staggers under the blow, but she's soon back on her paws. With Auriel's attention turned to Lima, Mez takes the opportunity to sink her teeth into his side. The bite sticks for a moment, but then Auriel wrestles free,

Mez's sharp canines skittering. She spits out a mouthful of scales.

When Auriel whirls to defend himself against Mez, his gravity power momentarily lapses, giving Lima a chance to dart into the canopy. Even as Mez is pushed off her paws by one of Auriel's coils, she sees the tiny bat's feet hanging on to a branch for dear life, the gravity field causing the top of her head to point in a straight line toward the snake. Auriel's muscular, writhing coils bash into Mez again, sending her skidding along the ziggurat's roof in a spray of soil and leaves and insects.

"Heads up, snake-breath!" comes Gogi's voice. It's followed by a popping sound, then the scene fills with light.

A ribbon of flame streaks from the monkey's position at the far side of the ziggurat, as thin as a reed but hot enough to smoke the air. He's aimed it straight for Auriel's eyes.

The constrictor ducks so his eyes are clear of the line of fire, but the flame hits him squarely on the top of his head, and he seems dazzled, tendrils of smoke rising from his scales. As Auriel shakes his head to clear it, the stones cease their rippling, gravity magic no longer pulling Mez toward him.

"Gogi!" Mez shouts. "That was amazing!"

"Compliment me later!" he shouts back. "This is our chance—scatter!"

Lima zooms away, and Gogi scrambles farther along the ziggurat. Mez finds the tallest nearby tree and, going invisible, claws her way up it.

It's tough climbing, since by rotten luck Mez chose a tree whose trunk is clogged by the thorns and prickers of parasitic vines. Once she's at the top she finally allows herself to whirl and look for Auriel. When she spots him, she cries out.

Auriel is facing off against her friends, his long and powerful body dragging across the stones as he whips back and forth. Squinting her eyes, Mez realizes that Gogi and Lima are immobilized, pressed against the stone of the ziggurat, no—pressed *into* the stone of the ziggurat, as if embedded in clay, Lima's wings and Gogi's arms and legs spread out wide.

"Mez, wherever you are, save yourself!" Gogi yells into the night sky. Auriel whirls, looking out for invisible Mez, then snaps his attention back to Gogi when the monkey unleashes another bolt of fire. With his hands restrained, Gogi can't aim it, and the flame goes up into the sky, fizzling out in a flurry of sparks. Auriel rears back, enraged, as if to clamp the monkey in his fangless mouth. Mez hears Gogi cry out, unable to contain his fright, sending another bolt flaring into the sky.

But Auriel doesn't attack. Instead an ominous sound begins, a familiar grinding and roaring.

The ziggurat doors are opening.

For a moment Mez is too surprised to act. Then she's bounding down the tree, hurtling her way through branches and thorny vines, leaping and scrambling, hurling herself onto the ragged mossy stone blocks with claws that are soon bloody and aching.

The moment she lands, her invisible paws touching stone, Auriel's tail disappears inside and the doors give their final shudder. She was moments too late.

The roof of the ziggurat is empty.

Auriel has taken the last of her friends.

NIGHT FALLS AND yet Mez hasn't moved. She knows she should be hidden in the trees, but can't will herself to do anything but splay out on the stone, chin against rock. Her eyes flick open in worry whenever she thinks of what might be happening to her friends, sealed away with Auriel a few feet below, then drift closed as fatigue washes over her.

If only Auriel were here to fight. No matter how lopsided the battle, she'd give herself up to the combat, struggle until she couldn't, go out with claws and teeth bared. Anything but this dread that the end of those she cares about is happening right now, that she is powerless to do anything to prevent it.

She scratches at the seam where the stone doors meet, leaps into the air and down on all fours, the way Aunt Usha once taught her to puncture an underground rat den. Of course, the mammoth doors are motionless and unresponsive. No panther can claw her way into a ziggurat.

They'd all followed Auriel's will so blindly—he might have simply asked the eclipse-born to walk inside the ziggurat and they would have, if Mez hadn't turned invisible during his attack, escaped him long enough to blow his cover. The nights of following orders without question, whether they came from Aunt Usha or Auriel, are over. She will trust her instincts from here on.

Still, her realization has come too late. Auriel will suck her friends down, one by one, until he has all the powers of the eclipse-born. Unless the Ant Queen has her own ends for them.

If only the removable stone sigils were still there on top. But of course they're nowhere to be found. They must have dropped inside with the other eclipse-born during the attack.

Mez's tail thrashes angrily.

Whatever Auriel's goals, he now has all he needs to achieve them. He's already gotten power over gravity from some hapless animal, and now he has Niko's power over the earth, as well. If Sky's not useful anymore

Auriel can add his divination, which should augment Auriel's access to the knowledge of the ants. He'll soon have Rumi's wind power, and Gogi's fire . . . Mez shudders, imagining vortexes of flaming wind.

The only eclipse power Auriel doesn't yet have, Mez realizes, is *hers*. Is there some use in that?

As the day breezes waft over the roof of the ziggurat, over this empty stone space where her friends first gathered, loneliness threatens to make Mez collapse again. At least there's the possibility of a solution. She doesn't know how to use it, but she has a scrap of power. Auriel wants her. She could be bait.

The very place she shouldn't be, Mez knows, is right where she is. Here, Auriel will have no problem finding her. She gets up to four paws, slinks to the edge of the ziggurat, then drops down to the next level and then the next. Eyes alert for danger—*or prey*, she adds, her stomach growling as she descends the last level into the forest—Mez noses her way into the cover of the trees.

Hunting while literally invisible. Wow. That might make her feel a little better.

For the following night and day, she tries her best to worry about what she *does* have power over: hunting, finding the safest hiding places, even napping. Adult panthers spend most of their time alone, worrying only about food and rest. She's able to slip into that mode, beyond thought as she lets reflexes take over. It's the only way forward.

Her pathways often take her near the ziggurat, and each time she tries something new: she examines and reexamines the panels that are exposed, tugs at any images of the sun or moon to see if they might come free, leaps and claws at the seam on top. But the ziggurat is unrelenting. It rises silently from the rainforest, giving up no answers to what is happening inside. No sign of Auriel, no opportunity to confront him, no chance to enact her last desperate and useless revenge.

That evening, Mez steals near the structure at dusk, hoping that this time something will have changed. And this time, something has. Unfortunately. Only one sigil remains lit.

She returns to the jungle pathways that have become habitual to her, the scent trails that any panther hunting in the area would be drawn to, where the fattest forest birds nest and where tasty stout piranhas, rippled with fat and muscle, come near the surface. Her mind loops, again and again, to her friends. No matter how much she thinks on it, though, she can come up with no way to save them.

It's strange; it's like she must stop being herself, that she's only able to move and hunt when she forgets who she is and who she's lost. When she does remember the plight of the rest of the shadowwalkers, it's too much to bear, and stills her in mid-stride.

Twilight is the easiest. The night of hunting spreads wide before her, and feels like it might last forever. At dusk she's paused beside a still puddle to get a sip of water when she sees movement in the reflection behind her. Mez goes motionless, then slowly lowers her head, as if to take another drink. This time her senses are on high alert, watching for any sign of life, ready to turn invisible and spring away if Auriel attacks.

A branch cracks. Mez crouches, ready to leap, letting out a low growl.

The voice, when it comes, sets something thrumming deep inside her. It's from someone more familiar than anyone else Mez has ever known.

"Oh, Mez, it really is you!"

Her ears go flat and her eyes widen. How can this be? It's Chumba.

"CHUMBA*?!*" MEZ SAYS.

Immediately she's bowled over by a ball of calico fur, licked up and down her face. "Mez, Mez, it's you,   why-would-you-leave-like-that-it-can't-happen-ever-again-okay?"

The ziggurat is many nights' travel from their den. Auriel was the one who told Lima how to get here — Chumba shouldn't even know how. Even if she knew the way, how could Chumba have survived the journey alone? It's like Mez is seeing a ghost. Wary of Auriel's traps and schemes, she edges away from her sister.

"Mez, what's wrong?" Chumba asks, ears perking in worry.

Mez's mind races. Many of the eclipse-born didn't know their powers before they were sealed into the ziggurat. Maybe Auriel can steal powers away before the young animals ever know them. Maybe his henchman Sky is speeding through his divinations, unlocking powers as fast as Auriel can squeeze them out. Maybe one of those powers is the ability to create illusions. Maybe they've gone into Mez's mind and pulled out the thing she cares about most in the world and made it appear here in the jungle, to trap her.

"How—how do I know you're real?" Mez manages to stammer.

"What do you mean, how do you know I'm real?" Chumba asks, her pink-and-black nose trembling. "Mez, it's me!"

Mez hangs her head. "So much has happened, Chum. And I can't figure out how you can be here. I'm so confused." This looks and smells like Chumba. All Mez wants to do is go hug her sister, feel her closeness after all this time. But trust has proven dangerous.

"I'll explain how I'm here," Chumba says, eyes brightening. "But first, how about this, Mez? Remember the triplets? Remember whisker-taunt? Remember how we saw that big gooey slug stuck to Mist's tail, and we didn't tell him?"

A smile creeps over Mez's face. "Yes," she says, "I

remember all that." For a moment she's still hesitant, then she breaks out into laughter, relieved laughter, great peals of it resounding through the nearby jungle.

Mez approaches her sister and nuzzles close. The love that quickens both their hearts is no illusion. "How did you find me, Chum?"

"It was maybe ten nights ago," Chumba says. "We were on the hunt, and Mist was going really fast and I . . . I was falling behind. It's okay, don't worry about me, I've been fine," she says, seeing Mez's worried expression. "I was racing to catch up, and suddenly I had this . . . this *vision*. The whole vision felt like you, if that makes sense, like you were on the edges of everything I was looking at. You were on the side of this big stone pyramid thing, and you were crouched, and there was this bird, this red bird—"

"That's Sky!" Mez exclaims. "He was helping me discover my power."

"He had you in some sort of spell. I was yelling your name, but you couldn't hear me—"

"I *did* hear you, I did!" Mez says.

"And as I was yelling I saw you break out of the trance and you were wounded, and everything was all chaotic, but you were limping to the top of the pyramid, and there was a giant snake attacking all these animals and that's when the vision broke up. I tried to get it back, but it was like I wasn't making it, I was receiving it. It was like trying to force a dream to return."

"Sky suspected his power was more than divination, and he was right. It looks like he's able to *communicate* through his visions, too. Oh, Chumba. You don't know the worst of it. That giant snake was *Auriel*," Mez says. "He was bringing together all the eclipse-born—he said to defeat the Ant Queen. But he attacked us to steal our powers. I was tricked, Chumba."

"When the vision was ending," Chumba says, "it didn't blink out. It traveled back to me. It took me across a canyon and over a waterfall and then into the rainforest that I recognized, all the way to me, right into my eyeballs, and then it ended. So I knew sort of how to get to you. And once we were here it was a matter of finding that crazy pyramid thing, then looking for you."

"So Aunt Usha didn't exile you, too?" Mez asks.

Chumba shakes her head.

"I wonder if you also have powers," Mez says, "if Sky's vision was able to reach you like that. We were born around the same time, after all."

"I don't think so, Mez. There's nothing magical about me."

"You haven't daywalked, but I could *almost* wake you up during the day. And you're always the first up after the Veil lowers. All those long twilights when it was only the two of us awake, remember?"

"Those were my favorite," Chumba says, her voice husky.

"Mine too," Mez says.

"I don't know what this Sky character can do, but I don't think it's because of some magical power that I knew you were in trouble. I think it's just that, well, you're my Mez. I knew there would be a sign of you, eventually. It had to happen. We wouldn't be kept apart. Maybe that red bird knew that."

Something about Sky getting called "that red bird" makes Mez smile. Chumba's right, it's probably part of Sky's power to allow some communication in the reverse direction. Who knows what power he'll bring to his evil alliance with Auriel—if the treacherous constrictor lets him live.

Mez's whiskers droop. "I hate that night I got exiled, Chum. I should have fought back harder against Aunt Usha, I know now. But I was worried what Usha might do to me, and to you. I wish I had been braver. I told myself I was doing the right thing for Caldera, but now it turns out Auriel has sucked out the powers from four of us and the rest are probably getting sacrificed to the Ant Queen. Rumi is down there, and Gogi and Lima."

"Rumi? Gogi? Lima? Who are these panthers?"

"They're not panthers," Mez says, allowing herself to rest her haunches on the jungle floor. "They're a frog and a monkey and a fruit bat. Friends of mine."

Chumba rolls her eyes. "Wait until Aunt Usha hears about that!"

"Yeah. Has she cooled down? Do you think we can go home? We'll have time on our way back to figure out how I can tell her I'm friends with some non-panthers. I have to say, it's been nice being friends with other animals instead of just eating them. Oh, Chum, there's so much to catch you up on!"

Chumba's face goes serious. "Mez—I didn't come alone. Aunt Usha is *here*!"

"Wait, what?"

"Do you think I'd make it here on my own?" Chumba asks with a wry smile. "Haven't you been listening to anything Mist has been saying about me all these years?"

"Yes, Mez, you made me lose one of my sister's cubs; I wouldn't want to lose both of them," comes a deep and glittering voice. Aunt Usha. The beautiful panther emerges from the foliage and slinks along the far edge of the puddle, green eyes hard as gemstones.

Despite everything she's been through, Mez takes a submissive cub posture, head low and ears down, their tips pointing toward the nape of her neck. She never thought she'd be allowed to see Aunt Usha again.

"Shh," Aunt Usha growls. "I've heard enough of your conversation to know we should say nothing more out here in the open. Come to the den."

With that, as suddenly as she appeared, Aunt Usha heads into the leafy undergrowth of the rainforest. "Come on," Chumba says, gently nosing Mez. "I bet Aunt Usha has a plan. And she's right— panthers shouldn't be out in the open."

Mez plucks up her courage. "We should go straight to the ziggurat," she calls after Usha. "My friends are in danger!"

Usha's voice travels back, cool and clipped. "No other animal could be more important than your own kin, little one. You should be overjoyed that I have come all this way for the sake of an exiled cub. Stop that nonsense and come. Now."

With Chumba's gentle presence at her side, Mez reluctantly follows. Usha has made a day den that looks like a rattier version of the one they used to live in. It's still cozy, though, a snug warren under interlocking brambles and thistle. Whiskers sensitive to any ants or thorns, Mez pokes her way in.

Immediately she's plowed into by three puffballs, the triplets licking her face up and down. Overjoyed to see them again, Mez gives the nurslings playful little nips, knocking them onto their backs one by one, to fits of giggles.

"That's enough," Aunt Usha intones, the sound of her voice sending the triplets retreating to a corner of the den. The matriarch has already arranged herself in the tight space, mere inches away, her regal face composed and dignified. "Let's get right into it. There's no need to rush a rescue. We have been here one night already, watching the ziggurat while we looked for you. I saw the boa constrictor attack that monkey and bat. I saw him open the ziggurat. You have been tricked, and might have died. It is good that I finally allowed Chumba to convince me to come find you."

Chumba's mouth drops open at the almost-praise.

"I will only say this once, Mez, but I am sorry. I was angry and scared before, and I planned to pick you back up after our hunt once you had learned your lesson. But you'd already left. I did not know that constrictor was there to lead you away."

"Thank you, Aunt Usha. But please, we don't have much time to lose," Mez says. "Auriel is consuming the eclipse-born's magic one by one. He's getting more and more powerful with every moment—soon he'll release the Ant Queen, and together they'll rule all of Caldera."

"Tell me," Usha says, "what would 'ruling all of Caldera' look like? One does not 'rule' a jungle. We animals of the rainforest live secret and quiet existences, each keeping to its own kind. Such animals cannot be ruled, no matter how powerful any one of them may become."

"I . . . spoke to the Ant Queen, while I was on a mission belowground. Ages ago, the ants were in charge of Caldera, and the rest of the animals were enslaved to farm the land for them. She claims it was more peaceful then than now. But I don't believe her."

"My whole life has been lived beneath the Ant Queen's constellation of stars," Aunt Usha says. "But you're telling me that she is real?"

Mez nods, while she does so taking in more of the makeshift den. There's Usha, Chumba, the trembling triplets, and . . . Mez sees the pure white fur of an animal huddled at the far side of the den. Eyes narrowed, Mist makes no move to get up or join the conversation.

Something isn't right. If this really is Mist, why hasn't he made a snide remark yet?

Chumba nuzzles up against Mez. Although she doesn't look at Mist, Chumba's ear, the telltale right ear that Mez knows reveals her secret thoughts so well, flicks in his direction. Chumba is warning her.

"Don't you want to nuzzle me, too?" Mist says, his voice flinty and low. A sardonic, self-mocking smile spreads over half his face.

Half his face.

Mist gets to his paws slowly, almost lazily. Mez can see him better now. She gasps despite her efforts to keep quiet, then bites down on her lip to prevent any more sound from coming out.

His beautiful and blemishless face is still intact—on one side. On the other, though, where once was smooth white fur now are the knobs and twists of scars. A thick knot of khaki-colored hard tissue marbles his nose, and the side of his mouth is gone, clean gone, revealing the top and bottom row of teeth, turned an ocher color from the constant exposure to the air and elements.

Mez does her best to keep her face calm, but the sight of him makes her hackles rise, and there's no hiding that.

"Aren't you willing to even look at me, cousin?" Mist asks, a self-mocking laugh in his voice.

"Of course I am," Mez says quietly, forcing herself to meet his eyes without flinching. She senses her voice is about to tremor, and makes sure it is regular and even before she continues. "What happened to you?"

Mist looks directly at Mez for the first time. She

takes an involuntary step back: his expression is one of raw fury. "Funny you should ask," he says. "Because it's *you* that happened to me."

"I don't know what you mean," Mez says.

"Why don't we save this for—" Chumba starts to say.

"Enough from you, runt," Mist says sharply to Chumba before returning his attention to Mez. The sound of his anger is enough to set the triplets mewling and covering their eyes.

Aunt Usha watches on impassively, letting this power play work out on its own. Mist continues. "Some 'friends' you made along your way came looking for you, Mez. A family of boars heard about you from some howler monkeys and owls who live near a great water-fall. Apparently the monkeys and owls tried to stop a daywalking panther from passing through, only it managed to escape them. The boars formed a posse to hunt this—this shadowwalking *monster*. I see you're flinching. Of course, it's not you they found, you made sure of that. No, they found another panther entirely. I'm so easy to spot, after all—you've always enjoyed pointing that out."

"You?" Mez asks. "Mist, I'm so sorry they came for you. And all because—"

"Because I'm known as the panther who killed the great eagle," Mist says.

Mez looks at her cousin, baffled. He's kept up this false version of events, even after his lie nearly killed him?

"They waited until he was on his own during the hunt," Usha says primly. "And that's when they attacked. Turns out that boars are surprisingly intelligent, despite appearances."

"I've met lots of animals who aren't panthers here," Mez says quietly. "They're all smart." Her mind goes to the sweet but vacant-eyed sloth. "Well, *almost* all."

"At least this time of fraternizing with lesser animals will soon be over," Usha says. She turns to her son. "Come, Mist, if you've finished wallowing in your tragic tale of woe, we have an operation to plan. Though I do not fear a constrictor's misguided notion that he can somehow rule a rainforest, the Ant Queen is another matter entirely. Some ants, like leaf-cutters, are peaceful. But I've met army ants before. They'll consume everything in their path to grow their colony. The Ant Queen's scheme could ruin Caldera, and it must end now."

"But how?" Mez protests. "The removable sigils are the only way to open the ziggurat, and they're trapped inside."

"You seem to have forgotten that you are a panther," Usha chides. "You have been going about this all wrong. Panthers do not go racing into trouble. Panthers wait in the stillness for trouble to come. And we will be ready for it."

UNDER COVER OF night, fully in their element, the panthers steal toward the ziggurat. Aunt Usha is in the front—the nights when it seemed like Mist might soon lead the family are long gone. This new sullen version of Mist doesn't fight this arrangement, silently skulking at the rear of the group. Mez and Chumba stick close to each other in the middle. The triplets are nestled back in the den, too young for this outing.

The ziggurat looms, monumental and unnatural, before the stars that make up the constellation of the Ant Queen. Mez feels as she does each time she sees the structure—her instincts tell her it's not meant to be here, not meant to be anywhere in Caldera, that it represents a deep and profound wrongness. Once they're close enough, Mez presses her ear against one of the stones. But it is too thick; she can't hear any clue to what's happening inside. There's no way of knowing if the eclipse-born are fighting, or if they're long past the point of resistance.

Aunt Usha sniffs around the ziggurat's base, her head bobbing as she picks up whatever clues she can from its scents. Mez is the first to begin the climb, looking back at her family and nodding encouragingly. Chumba stares up at her in amazement, her outline stark in Mez's darkvision. Mez nods toward the top. *We go all the way up.*

Aunt Usha takes over the lead as they ascend, level by level. Mez assists Chumba up an especially high step, gently biting into the nape of her sister's neck to help her the last few inches. When he catches sight of it, Mist scoffs and hisses.

"I'm so glad to have you near again," Chumba whispers. "If Mist thought Aunt Usha would approve, I think by now he'd have—he'd have . . ."

"Shh, I'm here now," Mez says, knowing very well what Mist would do to Chumba if he could.

"You don't know the half of it," Chumba whispers. "Usha never talked about coming to find you until after Mist was attacked. So he thinks that—that—"

"—Usha needs me as part of the family now that Mist is maimed," Mez says. "I can only imagine what that's done to Mist's nasty side. I'm sorry you had to deal with him on your own. I should have been around to protect you."

"No. I don't need protecting, okay? I just want you to stay near. Love me, don't shelter me. Get the difference?"

"Yes," Mez says quietly. They'll have to continue this conversation later. They've reached the summit.

Chumba makes a low, astonished purr as she sees the treetops at eye level all around them, the endless greenery of Caldera spreading in all directions, night mists rising from broad swaying leaves, the edges of everything made silvery by darkvision. "To actually be *standing* on this thing," Chumba whispers. "It's eerie."

Mist is the last to arrive, springing above the level of the stones and landing silently on four paws. He's immediately scanning about for danger, whiskers twitching. Aunt Usha pads to the center of the ziggurat, nosing along the seam. "Take up positions on the corners," she orders. "Chumba, I need you to perch on the edge so that you can see the final glowing sigil. We'll need to know when it goes out. That's the only warning we're likely to get."

"So we wait, and then launch all together once the

Ant Queen or Auriel emerges?" Mez asks.

"Yes," Usha says coolly.

Mist speaks up. "Mother, you should be last to attack, to have the honor of the final blow. Let us harry the enemy first."

"No, Mist. Mez is correct," Usha says swiftly. "If we stagger our attacks, we lose our greatest advantage."

"I'm not wrong!" Mist suddenly screams. His teeth are bared and eyes wide, finally finding voice to the tortured feelings passing behind his eyes. "*Listen* to me, Mother!"

Usha tosses her head in irritation. "It is the truth, Mist. Stop mewling and prepare for combat."

Mez wrests her gaze from Mist and approaches Chumba. "You can stand watch over the sigil from over here, near me," she says out of the side of her mouth. She won't let her sister anywhere near Mist, not with that murderous expression on his face.

Once the other panthers are in place, Usha takes up her position in the shadows and closes her eyes, her face resuming its regal air. When her lids close, she disappears—though not as much as Mez would, of course, with her invisibility. Time enough to tell them about that later. She'll use her power during the fight, if need be, but otherwise she doesn't want to attract any more jealousy from Mist than she already has.

Mez's darkvision wavers, and she's worried that she's being magicked, that the attack has begun and Auriel is casting a spell on her. But then she realizes that the surfaces of the ziggurat are shimmering because they're covered in tiny moving creatures. She gasps in alarm as the shimmering begins to cover Usha, rising from her paws to her chest and head.

Chumba gasps too. Mez looks over and sees the shimmering is climbing up her sister, and then looks at her own paws and sees she's being covered too—by ants.

Mist yowls and snaps his teeth, trying to bite the ants off. Mez just watches them climb up. So far the Ant Queen has not used the ants to attack, and Mez can only assume that hasn't changed. They start to vibrate and hum, like they did belowground.

"Chumba," Mez says, "look at the last sigil. Has it gone out?"

"Yes!" Chumba reports. "Just now!"

"That's no coincidence. I think the Ant Queen is emerging, Aunt Usha," Mez says. "We must be ready."

"Yes, Mother, I—" Mist starts to say.

"It begins!" Usha exclaims. "Everyone get back!"

The doors below them are opening.

From her hiding place in the shadows, Usha's tail begins to thrash. Mist stares down, equal amounts of fear and unhinged rage in his expression. At the sight of the abyss opening beneath them, Mez's courage flags. How can any panther—even one as powerful as Usha, whose jaws can puncture a capybara's skull—hope to damage a foe as powerful as the Ant Queen? But then Mez remembers that her friends might still be alive down there. She can find the courage to continue for their sake, if not her own.

With a grinding sound and a shudder, the doors stop opening, hanging down into the ziggurat's interior. The ants that have been covering them melt away, pouring into the cracks between the ziggurat's stones. The roof of the ziggurat is left more quiet than ever. Even the surrounding frogs and owls go silent.

Without leaving their ambush crouches, the panthers stare into the void. It's fully dark, moonlight soon getting lost in its depths, rendering even their darkvision incapable of seeing anything beyond the first few feet.

"Remember what we agreed earlier," Mez whispers to Chumba. "Whatever's about to happen, you'll do what it takes to stay safe."

"Mez, didn't I tell you not to shelter me anymore?" Chumba says. Mez begins to protest, but Chumba silences her with an impish smile. "We'll finish this fight later."

The ants are returning, waves of them swarming

along the ziggurat's lips, thousands of legs chattering against rock. Like blood from a wound, more and more of them leak out across the stones, a pool of gnashing mandibles and waving antennae.

Usha holds still, and her family follows her lead.

Sky emerges from the ziggurat's interior and arrows into the night sky, coming to rest on the upper branches of one of the surrounding ironwood trees. His piercing eye fixes on the ziggurat's roof, and he launches into a shrill scream. "Auriel, beware! There is a white panther up here!"

Of course. Mist is the first one Sky would have spotted, his fur lighting up in the darkness.

The time for ambush is over. Usha lets out a furious scream, and Mez jerks her attention toward her in time to see her aunt flying through the air to clamp her jaws around something Mez can't see. Mez and Chumba slink around to find out what her aunt has pounced on.

It's Auriel.

Alerted by Sky, the snake has sneaked up through the darkness. Only it's not a snake. It's the *shape* of Auriel, but there's no skin. It's not flesh that Mez's seeing, either, but something more like pure energy, a raw and bright and crackling substance. It's like he's been filled by some magic, and it's made him something more elemental than animal.

Even if he's made of pure energy, at least Auriel can still be grappled, like any other snake. He whips around, but Usha's jaws have locked behind his head. Auriel's long body sizzles as he thrashes.

His eyes dart as he struggles to figure out who his mystery assailant is. Now that the moment of surprise has passed, Mez and Chumba and Mist instinctively circle the struggling constrictor, dancing around him, looking for an opening. Whenever the panthers lunge, though, their jaws close on open air, their adversary whipping too quickly for the young cats to get a bead on him. While they wait for an opening, all they can do is watch Usha wrestle him, and take care not to fall into the yawning gap in the ziggurat's roof.

Mez doesn't know which way the struggle will go. When a panther is as strong as Usha, no creature alive can loosen the jaws locked around its throat. But in this strange glowing state, Auriel is clearly like no other creature alive.

And where is the Ant Queen?

Hordes of ants continue to emerge from the ziggurat's opening, stretching their shimmering blanket far across the stones and into the night. They roll over Mist, who tries to claw them away, yelping in pain when they retaliate. "Chumba, avoid the ants," Mez warns, but Chumba is already a step ahead. She scrutinizes the ground as she backs away from the oncoming horde.

Despite Mez's attempts to avoid them, some of the ant soldiers have been able to climb into her fur. Pricks of pain light up her belly and back.

Auriel switches tactics, rolling and twisting along the roof, his crushing coils encircling Usha even as she tries to suffocate him. She's agile and unpredictable, her body leaping and snapping even as her jaws never leave his neck, the snake's looping body passing through open air and twisting around itself, nearly knotting tight as it winds itself up.

Chumba sees an opening and dashes forward, trying to pounce on Auriel's tail, claws of her one forepaw extended and ready to dig in. "No, Chumba!" Mez cries. "That won't help!"

Auriel seems to notice Chumba for the first time, and his thrashing tail whips toward her instead. She flees back to Mez, but her movements slow and then, with a thud, she's suckered to the floor. Auriel's gravity powers must be intact.

The constrictor seems to realize a new strategy in that moment, and Usha's fur begins to point directly to the ground, as if blown flat by wind. Still growling ferociously, she drops, belly pressing into the earth.

Auriel uses his stolen power to press Usha harder and harder into the stone, his trapped head dropping along with her. His topaz scale—the one that must represent his gravity power—glitters and glows, giving his head a brown-gold aura. Mez watches her aunt's eyes open wide, lips and ears pressing into the stones. Through it all, Usha never lets up her grip. There's a sizzling sound, and the sweet stench of burning fur. Mez has no idea how painful it must be to bite Auriel in his raw-energy form.

Through it all, Auriel continues to thrash, his tail thudding into the ziggurat's roof, sending up rains of ants and moss and mold and shards of stone. Mez dashes to Chumba's side, draping herself over her sister's prone body to shield her from any falling debris. She's turned herself invisible in hopes that it will decrease the chance that Auriel notices her, but it will be only a matter of time before Auriel's tail happens to touch her and he suctions her body to the ground, too.

Usha starts gasping in agony from her position flattened on the floor, eyes wide as her jaw muscles clench tight, their straining visible even through her thick fur. While Usha lies there, immobile, Auriel lifts his massive tail and brings it high into the sky, ready to crash down onto Chumba—and Mez.

Desperate, Mez sinks her nails deep into Chumba's hindquarters and pulls. It's difficult, but she's able to drag Chumba along the ground despite the magic pressing her down. Auriel's heavy tail thuds right where Chumba was a moment before, the impact strong enough to make the ground shudder, setting Mez's paws to tingling.

The tail rises right over Chumba and Mez. Desperately, Mez drags again, wincing as she does, ready for the strike from above that will end it all.

Only the strike doesn't come.

A flash of white, then a glimpse of a creature streaking across the ziggurat's roof. It's Mist!

He uses the opening to launch himself right at Auriel's softer underbelly, sinking his teeth in deep. The white panther drapes over Auriel, puncturing with his sharp canines while his back claws skitter across invulnerable scales. Before Auriel can bring his tail down and crush Chumba and Mez, he's writhing in agony, whipping through the air. Mist has clamped onto Auriel's underbelly as securely as a tick, and isn't going anywhere, even as Auriel brings him smashing onto the ground.

Mist. Mist has saved them.

Even as he thrashes, trying to bludgeon Mist against the stones, Auriel keeps his merciless eyes on Chumba.

Chumba's body begins sliding. Startled, Mez tenses her muscles and digs her teeth into Chumba's nape. But she's powerless against the movement. Chumba's lips draw back from her teeth as she fills with panic. "Mez, what's happening?"

"I don't know!" Mez says. But then she sees Auriel still staring at Chumba, and she realizes that he's using his gravity magic to send the little panther down into the abyss. Down to the Ant Queen.

The thought of her sister tumbling away into the darkness scrambles Mez's senses. From somewhere above comes Sky's strident caw: "Auriel! Mez is here. She just became visible!"

All Mez's attention is on Chumba. There's only a short distance between her sister and the gaping void, and Auriel's power is dragging her into it tail-first. Chumba desperately tries to grip into the stone, but neither her clawed limb nor the pawless one can get any purchase, and she's sliding helplessly, faster and faster.

Mez scrambles and pounces toward her, but it's too late. Mez is still in the air when Chumba's eyes widen more than ever, her mouth opens into a scream, and then she whips down into the darkness.

Chumba is gone.

FOR AN INSTANT, Mez is motionless. There's Sky above, cawing out his warnings to Auriel. There's Usha, powerful jaws locked behind the constrictor's head. There's Mist, clamped onto his belly, digging in as best he can.

Then there's Chumba, somewhere in that darkness, tumbling into the pit of ants and their queen and whatever is left of the trapped animals.

Chumba, Rumi, Gogi, Lima, the remaining eclipseborn—that's where Mez's heart lies. She'll have to leave Auriel to Mist and Usha.

"I'm coming, Chumba!" Mez cries as she springs toward the opening and leaps in. As soon as she's falling, she flings her legs out in four directions so she'll kite in the air.

She looks back as she falls to see Sky still screeching away his warnings, Mist hanging on tight to Auriel, teeth bared as he tries to find a spot to bite down.

Then Mez hits the bottom, yelping and shaking the pins of pain from her ankles. She is in a cold and cavernous space, full of scents of metal and old air with dank undercurrents Mez has never encountered before. Since she can't see in this pitch black, she has to rely on scent to find Chumba. She picks up a trace of her sister not too far off and approaches, hesitantly slinking forward, not daring to speak.

The floor crunches underpaw, almost like it's covered in old leaves. But it does not smell like leaves. Each step brings up the sharp, two-toned scent of . . . not bone, quite, but something like it, plus acid and guts. *Ants*, Mez realizes. *I'm crushing ants!* Even as she pauses and scents the air, she can feel them in her fur, climbing around her ears. *Maybe I'm wrong*, she tells herself, unnerved. *Maybe this is my imagination.*

The last sigil has gone out, which means the Ant Queen is probably free, could be anywhere around them. Shivering in the frigid air of the ancient ziggurat, Mez creeps toward Chumba's fear scent.

Why can't I hear any of the other eclipse-born? she

wonders. *Are they dead?* She wants to call out their names, but knows the Ant Queen could be listening.

She feels something brush her nose, and seizes in panic until she picks up the scent underneath and realizes that it's Chumba's tail. Chumba doesn't say anything out loud, but continues to run her tail under Mez's chin, silently acknowledging her sister's presence. As she huddles near, Mez's sensitive whiskers tell her Chumba is looking up, and she follows her gaze skyward. Stars wink within the rectangle of open sky. They can hear the fighting growls of Mist and Usha, but there's no getting back up to join them. Unless there are pawholds carved into the walls, the sisters are trapped below.

As they slink blindly through the pitch black, Mez tries to adjust to her new and strange-smelling surroundings. With every pawfall the ground crunches, each step bringing with it the smell of sap and insects. She's squishing a horde of ants as she goes. At least they don't seem to be biting back or singing any creepy Ant Queen–inspired songs. For now.

Suddenly Chumba halts, her whiskers beside Mez's own. Her voice is the slightest whisper: "Mez, over here. I felt a monkey foot."

Heart sinking, Mez follows her sister through the

dark. Sure enough, there's a monkey's foot. Only the foot. Stranger still, it seems to be floating in midair. Her whiskers sense the five toes, the warm pad in the center, but as she moves around it the monkey . . . ends. Not into thin air, though—there's rock surrounding it. The monkey has been embedded in rock!

At least its flesh is warm. At least it isn't dead. Soft toes dart under Mez's whiskers, like the monkey is responding to a tickle, and she hears the faintest hint of a cry. Gogi.

A glow begins within the stone. At first Mez thinks she's seeing a glint of starlight within the rock. Impossible. Then she realizes that Gogi's making his fire within his prison, sending glitters across the surface of the nearby rocks.

Mez swivels, knowing that the scant light Gogi's glow has cast will be enough for her darkvision to take in more of her surroundings. When she sees what's around her, she cringes back in shock.

The ziggurat is hollow all the way down from the open stone doors, and the walls around her are covered in vines and dirt, all of it swarming with ants. The floor, too, is teeming with them. Ants crawl over Mez and Chumba, they crawl over the vines, and they crawl over the walls themselves, up and along the runes carved into the massive stone doors suspended from the ceiling.

In the walls, embedded in the stone, are animals. Many animals.

Beneath the growls and smashes from the fighting on the roof above, Mez takes a closer look. The animals aren't chained up in any way—it's more like they've been pressed into the stone while it was soft, and then it set around them. There are no faces visible, just a wing here, a claw there, the entire back of Sorella. The submerged animals continue around the entire cavern, evenly spaced, except at the end, where there is a gaping hole, shards of rock all around, ants swarming even those. It's like that imprisoned animal has been forcefully yanked out.

There's no way to be sure, but Mez thinks she knows what she's seeing—Auriel trapped all the eclipse-born here in the ziggurat, and he's taken one out already and constricted it. Or fed it to the Ant Queen. He's probably planning on working his way through all the remaining animals in time.

Auriel is still above. But where is the Ant Queen?

Mez gets Gogi's foot between her teeth and tugs as gently as she can, but he yelps, stuck tight in the rock. "Come on," Chumba whispers beside Mez. "Now that there's light, the Ant Queen can probably see us. We should hide."

"I'm sure she doesn't need light to sense us," Mez whispers back, shivering. "But hiding definitely sounds like a good idea. Where?"

"Wherever it's darkest, obviously," Chumba says, for a moment sounding just like Usha. She leads them toward an edge of the chamber, where wall meets floor. They slink along and keep their hackles low, so they're half hidden in the shadows at the chamber's edges.

Mez takes advantage of the pause to take another look around. There are the feathers of the trogon, peeking out over the surface of the stone. There's Sorella's lustrous tail, knobby after, she'd once confided, it had been broken in a squabble with another uakari. Where each animal is embedded in the rock, there is also a blank bubble within, glowing in shades of brown from Gogi's fire. Mez figures those air pockets must be to keep each prisoner alive until Auriel or the Ant Queen consumes it. Every embedded animal has a bubble prison, except one. The ocelot.

The cat's tail dangles limply beside Gogi's foot. Mez can't see a bubble, though—it's like the stone has been filled in. Alert to any movement of Auriel from above, or any movement of the Ant Queen from here below, Mez stalks nearer to get a better view.

The filled interior of the air pocket throbs rhythmically. It's hard for Mez to make out exactly what she's seeing, but it looks like a giant knobby heart, breathing in and out. Slowly she's able to make out more details—it's like a frozen combat in there, like the ocelot was battling some other animal before they both got trapped in sap.

Then Mez sees the shape of two mandibles locked around the ocelot's neck. Realization comes in a rush: This is the Ant Queen. Feeding. She's twice the size of the cat. Even if he weren't trapped inside the stone, the ocelot would have had no chance of defending himself against her.

"Oh, Mez," Chumba says. At the sound of the panther's voice, Gogi strengthens his fire, and the ruddy glow casts ribbons of light into the thin stone, illuminating it like a mud pool in a sunbeam. Mez can see the ocelot's body now, limp within the embrace of the giant insect, head lolling to one side.

"What's she *doing*?" Chumba asks out of the side of her mouth.

"I think she's . . . eating him," Mez says, shuddering.

The Ant Queen begins to move within the stone, one leg and then another lifting and lowering. The stone surface begins to shiver.

"And it looks like she might be on the move again," Mez says. "We have to come up with a way to get the trapped animals out, now!"

Instinct brings the two sisters low to the ground, legs tensed and tails thrashing. "Maybe if we surprise her . . ." Mez says, but her voice trails off. Two inexperienced panthers against a giant armored insect—they don't stand a chance.

The glow intensifies, and then the stone crackles, sounding like a bush after a lightning strike. Rock shards rain on the panthers, clattering on the stone around them. As one, Mez and Chumba go still.

After the hail of stone bits, the next thing to tumble out is the ocelot. He pitches headfirst, and Mez expects to see him hit the ground on all fours, like any cat would. But he slumps right where he strikes the stone, his legs making unnatural angles. The ocelot is dead.

Mez has no time to think about him. The Ant Queen will be the next to emerge.

There is no hesitancy to her movements—this is a creature who has never had need of fear. The Ant Queen lifts her heart-shaped head, antennae dabbing the air while her mandibles open and close. The stiff yellow hairs that sprout along her head and abdomen only accentuate the unbroken invulnerability of her plate armor. She is as large as Usha, but has none of the softness of a mammal. The only way Mez has ever known to kill an insect has been to crush it. But how can she crush an insect that's bigger than she?

The broken body of the ocelot reminds her how impossible the task before her is.

Mez wills herself to be as stealthy and unnoticeable as she can, and sure enough, her paws disappear beneath her. She doesn't know if the scent of her pantherfear will be enough to warn the Ant Queen, but she can't do anything to control that.

"Chumba, stay hidden here for a moment," Mez says. "I'm going to use my invisibility to ambush her."

Mez expects Chumba to protest, but instead her sister's words are cool and confident. "I love you, Mez. I'll join the fight as soon as you start the attack."

The ants continue to surge toward their queen, collecting into streams and rivers, their teeming bodies rising to Mez's belly and entangling in her fur as she picks her way along. The Ant Queen remains motionless, head raised and mandibles outstretched, antennae waving while she senses the world around her.

Then she makes a shriek, an otherworldly grating sound, and her legs undulate. She skitters around the chamber, her ant minions swarming her and raising up their strange harmonic song as she goes. Chittering all the while, she sprints toward a soft furry body trapped in a stone pocket, lit by the ruddy light of his fire. Gogi.

Oh, no you don't.

Fury gives Mez speed, and she can't help but release a low growl as she nears the Ant Queen, now only a few panther-lengths away. Double-checking her invisibility, Mez edges closer. Closer.

The Ant Queen whirls toward Mez, mandibles flaring, but they snap over open air. She doesn't seem able to detect Mez, at least not yet. The Ant Queen scurries the last few paces toward Gogi.

Where will Mez try to bite? She settles on one of the narrow joints where the three sections of the Ant Queen's body join. Those seem weakest. Mez's mouth, which usually waters when a successful kill is ahead, is fully dry, proof of how hopeless this is.

Closer. Closer.

The ants raise their ghostly song—if they're making words, they're lost in the echoes of the chamber. The Ant Queen lifts her forelegs to the stone and begins to clatter her sharp mandibles against it.

Mez maneuvers so she's approaching behind the Ant Queen's head, hoping that being out of view will give her more chance of staying undetected. She fixes on the joint where head meets abdomen.

Now's the hardest part: the tide of ants has risen around their queen, and Mez will have to ford through them. She gingerly places one invisible paw into the stream of ants, then another. Whether unaware of the panther because of her invisibility or too much in thrall to their queen, the ants don't bite Mez, even as they get crushed under her paws. Her covering of insects must make her more visible, but hopefully the same layer of ants will help mask Mez's scent.

She's near enough to the Ant Queen now for her sensitive nostrils to pick up the sharp scent of the acid wetting the queen's mouth. Her massive rear section pulses, and for an irrational moment Mez thinks it's the spirit of the ocelot, still moving inside her. But then she realizes that she's probably seeing eggs form, already in motion within their mother, ready to be laid by the millions.

Why haven't the ants informed the queen that Mez is stealing toward her? Maybe her invisibility has them confused—whatever the reason for this stroke of luck, Mez knows she must take advantage.

She gets into position, standing on her back legs in the middle of the swarm, jaws open as wide as possible. To reach the Ant Queen's height, Mez has to balance precariously while proceeding. She's near enough now to hear the creaking of the queen's armor, could reach out and swat the Ant Queen's antennae with a paw if she wanted to.

Mez looks back toward Chumba, who is still in her

hiding place, staring in her sister's direction. *I love you,* Mez beams. Then she cranes forward and clamps her jaws around the Ant Queen's neck.

Instead of feeling the acid tang of exoskeleton crackling under her paws, the moment Mez contacts the queen the chamber is gone, Chumba is gone, the ziggurat is gone. It's all replaced by a void, the Ant Queen floating in the space, facing Mez, her legs curling and uncurling in waves, up one side and down the other.

Mez tries to growl, but no sound escapes her. Her limbs swim through open space.

While the Ant Queen's shining black eyes in their crimson armor stare right at Mez, words appear inside the panther's mind: *I wish to talk to you, Mez.*

Mez looks down at her own body. She's suspended in the void too, paws outstretched. Air does not exist anymore. But neither is she suffocating. She thinks her response. *Don't hurt my sister.*

I might let her live. If you obey me.

Why are you killing us?

Auriel killed the ocelot. He constricted him to seize his power. I had just awoken from my long sleep and made the climb up from the watery lower reaches after the two-legs' foul prison finally released me. I was famished, my eggs were withering with my starvation, and the ocelot was dead. I did what I had to. Auriel is the murderer here: if it didn't take him time to recover after each constriction, all the eclipse-born would already be slain. Forgive me for eating a dead cat. I am sure it disturbed you. But you are a hunter too. Those teeth and claws of yours have killed many an animal. My unborn children would have died if I hadn't consumed the ocelot. If you really consider it, I do not think you will find that much that needs forgiving.

What do you plan to do? Mez asks. Her mind is spinning. Does the Ant Queen consider her an ally?

It is simple, the Ant Queen says. *We ants have always surrounded you. But we have been living in separate colonies, fighting one another as often as we fight others. What the ants have needed is a strong leader, and now I am free. I herald the return of the era of ants. You cannot change that.*

We will stop you, Mez thinks.

But why should you want to? the Ant Queen asks. *If you help me extend the rule of the ants, you will have all their power at your back.*

Mez shakes her head. *I saw the panels. The two-legs were in agony as the ant horde ripped them apart. I'm sure all of us would get the same fate, sooner or later.*

Ah, the two-legs, the Ant Queen says. *If only I could have allowed them to live. Do you know what makes the ants and the two-legs similar? Communication. The ability to coordinate the movements of hundreds and thousands, for* one individual to control a horde. *As their world got less habitable, the two-legs would not cede it to its rightful inheritor: the ants. And so they had to perish.*

Auriel betrayed us, Mez thinks. *There is no way we would work alongside him.* She extends and retracts her claws as she takes in more of the Ant Queen's fearsome body, suspended in space. The pulsing eggs in her abdomen, the claws along her legs, the efficient blades of her mouth.

The emerald boa was useful to me. He diligently brought all of the eclipse-born here. But Mez—the same combination of night and day magic that made you all shadowwalkers is what animates the ants as well. It used to be all under the ants' control, but when your generation of shadowwalkers was born, some of that magic came to reside in you. When you join me, the eclipse magic that dissipated will be brought back together. Auriel double-crossed me by taking your powers for himself. He will not be allowed to survive such insolence.

He might already be dead. My aunt Usha has been fighting him on the surface. Instinctively, Mez looks up, but there is only this strange black void all around her.

Then he will die one way or another, by your aunt's doing or mine. Mez, we must act quickly. Your friends, those animals that Auriel trapped in the stone—convince them to join me. I will launch my army, and we will all rule Caldera together.

If you free them, I can try. But how do I know we can trust you?

You are not in a position to ask for trust, the Ant Queen says. *But think of this: You are crawling in ants. I let them bite your sniveling white cousin, but I have kept you safe. If I wished to kill you, I would merely need to release the right pheromone and they would all have bitten you at once. You would be instantly paralyzed, and no fragile little mammal can live with a heart that has stopped.*

Mez looks down at her body floating in the open space, at the mess of calico patches and ribbons that is her mother's legacy. *I don't have any ants on me.*

Yes, you do.

The cavern swoops back in, the chamber swoops back in, the ziggurat stones above Mez's head swoop back in.

Chumba's paws are batting her face. "Mez, Mez, Mez!"

Mez's sensitive whiskers set her snorting and sneezing, and she recovers to see Chumba's wide, tearstruck eyes staring back at her. "Mez, I thought you were gone. I thought I was all alone down here."

"No," the Ant Queen says coolly. "You both have me. And you have my army."

Chumba gasps.

Mez looks down. She's swarming in ants. Soldiers with fat heads and mandibles as long as her own claws. Workers streaming along, tapping their antennae against Mez's fur and skin. They're covering Chumba, too, on her whiskers and in her ears. Mez shivers in fear, and when she does, the ants on her stall, waving their forelegs in the air before continuing on their way.

"Mez. The time has come for you to decide," the Ant Queen says. "Will you serve? Or will you die?"

"What's she talking about?" Chumba asks.

Mez's mind races. If the Ant Queen can speak directly like this, why take her into that weird void? There's only one answer: to isolate her. Just like Auriel kept her isolated from her family when he asked her to leave with him, all those nights ago.

Mez takes a deep breath. "I'd rather be on the side that wins than the side that dies. I'll convince my friends. Release them and I'll speak to them. We will serve you and the ants."

"You've made the right choice," the Ant Queen says.

27

THE ANT HORDE drains off Chumba and Mez, flooding to the walls instead. The insects swarm up the ziggurat, covering the thin walls that imprison the surviving eclipse-born. The chamber fills with the crackling, tinkling sound of ant mandibles on stone. Most of their flailing efforts don't find any purchase on the rock, but a few are able to work their jaws under outcroppings. Dust of pulverized stone fills the air.

"Mez," Chumba whispers, "what have you agreed to?"

"It's the only way to survive," Mez yells. "The ants are the way of the future. They'll keep us safe."

"But Mez—"

Mez flicks her right ear, their secret sister sign, as she stares up at the progress of the ants. Chumba goes quiet.

Openings are broadening in each of the stone prisons, more and more of the trapped eclipse-born coming into view. Lima is the first to emerge, flitting out into midair. When she sees Mez, she zooms over and lands on her head. "Oh Mez, hooray. It was terrible in there, my echoes just rebounded right back to me so I couldn't even tell where I was but now we're free so that's good, let's get out of here—oh, hi, panther, you must be Chumba, Mez has such nice things to say about you— there are so many ants here, GAH! WAIT, WHAT IS THAT?"

Lima has seen the Ant Queen. She darts into the air. "Shoo, shoo, get away," she says, waving her wings in the Ant Queen's direction. Busy overseeing her minions' work, the Ant Queen doesn't notice the little bat.

The small animals must be the easiest for the ants to free. Rumi is next to emerge, then the trogon, tumbling onto the ziggurat floor and looking around groggily. Mez points at the ground in front of her, and they come to join her, taking the long way to avoid going too near the Ant Queen. Rumi looks up at the opening, and the stars above. "How do we get out?" he whispers to Mez, before his eyes return to the giant ant.

"Auriel and our aunt Usha were battling up there, but there's no sound from them anymore," Mez says softly, aware that anything she says can be overheard by the Ant Queen. She imagines Mist and Usha triumphant over the corpse of Auriel, or Auriel wrapping his coils around the lifeless bodies of her cousin and aunt.

Finally Gogi and Sorella are out. Mez's heart swells at the sight of them, but she forces her face to remain impassive. There's too much to pull off here—she can't go revealing herself early.

The Ant Queen turns toward Mez. "Tell them what you have agreed to."

Terrified, the eclipse-born stare at Mez, waiting for her to reveal what's going to happen next. They have so little fight in their eyes. The surprise attack by Auriel must have exhausted them. Even Sorella looks overwhelmed.

The Ant Queen is watching. Calculating.

Mez takes a deep breath.

Then she begins to yell. "Rumi, make your wind. Gogi, add your fire!"

The Ant Queen catches on to Mez's betrayal before the eclipse-born do: Mez's friends stare at her in confusion while the Ant Queen begins to hiss and whirl, the ant hordes descending the walls to come to her aid. Sorella is the first one to realize what Mez is proposing. "You heard her! Everyone next to the frog, unless you want to be crisped up."

The eclipse-born throng around Rumi, who groggily peers around, startled. Then the plan clicks. "Oh, Mez," he says. "Finally having our powers combine. This is a most admirable strategy!"

"Just start!" Mez says, watching as, like a flash tide, gnashing ants surge toward them.

"Gogi, are you ready?" Rumi asks.

"Am I?!"

"Yes, are you?"

"It's a figure of speech! Rumi, you go first!"

With a loud croak, Rumi emits a sudden wind. He's got more control over it now than ever before, and is able to curl it into a column of air around the eclipse-born. Mez gasps in amazement, the sound soon lost in the rising roar. Ants are caught up in the wind currents, darkening the air. Some tumble through to the inside of the tornado, and the trogon goes about pecking at them, eating as many as he can. The rest of the eclipse-born crush themselves against one another, trying to smash the stinging insects between their bodies.

Except Sorella. She's grooming *Gogi*, shockingly enough, because Gogi has the more important work of making fire. He holds out both hands, palms open and wrists linked. A jet of fire starts in the center of each hand. The two streams join, forming a flame stronger than any Gogi has produced until now. It enters the cylinder of air and lights it up, fire dispersing up the tornado, suffusing it with a hot orange glow.

It's gorgeous—and deadly. There's a sizzling and popping sound as the ants in the stream light and crisp, then the sound becomes a roar of steam as more and more of the insects incinerate.

Mez can't see the Ant Queen through the wall of fire, can only imagine the ancient monster's fury as her minions go up in ash and smoke while Rumi expands the tornado farther and farther out. The little tree frog begins to lift off the ground with the effort, and Mez places a paw over him to keep him from flying away with the blast, hoping he hasn't released his skin poison by accident.

The tornado's radius has extended enough now that it edges up against the stones of the ziggurat. "Oh no, oh no," Chumba says, seeing what's happening the same moment that Mez does.

The ziggurat is coming apart.

It's *lifting*. The heavy stones that make up the structure are sighing into the air, the flaming ants are whirling up, the vines are loosening and whipping free into the night. It's like gravity is reversing, like everything now wants to tumble up into the sky instead of away from it.

But soon those giant stone blocks will start to fall.

"Rumi, it's too much, stop!" Mez cries, lifting up her paw and yelling in the frog's ear. But the wind prevents him from hearing any of her voice. He seems lost in his power, unaware of what's happening around him. Mez watches an extra sheen emerge on his skin. She removed her paw just in time to prevent getting poisoned.

Gogi has seen what's happening, and stops adding his streams of flame to the tornado. The red firelight of the chamber returns to the grays of moonlight. Until Mez's eyes adjust, she'll be nearly blind. A great stone beneath her—one of the stones that made up the floor of the ziggurat—soars upward in a blast of wind, sending out a spray of soil and mud and charred ant bits.

Mez's eyes are still dazzled when she spies a big shape plummeting toward her. She can't get her body to move in time, but there's a calico blur from the side and then Chumba has barreled into her, rolling with her to one side while the stone thuds into the ground. "See?!" Chumba says. "Sometimes *you're* the one who needs rescu—"

They've rolled just far enough to enter Rumi's wind tunnel, and the panthers are whisked into the air, separated by the currents and hurled up into the dark.

Mez can only hope Chumba and the other eclipse-born are safe as she swims through the air, barely clearing another giant flagstone hurtling toward her.

Either Rumi has realized what he was doing, or he's been crushed by flying stone. Either way, the wind calms. Now Mez is gently floating back toward the ziggurat floor, gaining speed until she lands on freshly upturned soil. She looks in time to see a sharp stone falling right toward her, and barrel rolls to the side, barely clearing the spot where the stone crashes in a spray of dirt and ants.

More stones are plummeting all around, and for a few long moments Mez is pure instinct, leaping and dashing and leaping again. Light flashes in the corner of her eye, and she sees that Gogi is clinging to a flagstone a short ways to her side, nervous fire sparking from his palms as he peers into the chaos around him.

"Gogi!" Mez cries. "I'm right here! Have you seen Chumba?"

Gogi races toward her, his expression turning from fear to joy. "Mez!" He turns to one side. "Rumi, Rumi, Mez survived!"

More rocks shatter and tumble, and Mez weaves to dodge them, shards of stone cutting her face and cheek. She leaps to avoid a dagger of rock, and falls into a hole, the soil churning beneath her. A black-and-red body appears on the edge of the widening pit, and she realizes it's Sorella. The uakari monkey grips the stone with one hand and reaches toward Mez with the other. "Up we go, panther!" she cries.

Then Mez's paw is firmly in Sorella's hand, and then she's vaulting through the air.

In that hurtling moment, Mez gets a better sense of her surroundings. The floor of the ziggurat is in chaos. The sloth lopes in front of Mez, searching for a way out, the nightblind animal miraculously avoiding piece after piece of falling shrapnel. Mez can still see the rectangle of starry sky above, but its edges have become ragged. The great doors have already tumbled down.

"Holler if you see the Ant Queen anywhere with your darkvision," Sorella says, then peels away, grunting in anger. "What I wouldn't give to have those two brittle antennae under my hands right now."

But there is no sign of the Ant Queen. The floor warps under Mez's paws, the stones raking and pointing upward like fins. The trogon flits up and away into the night sky, and Mez can only hope Lima has already escaped. The landbound animals are left cowering, scrambling about in fear as the ziggurat continues to crumble.

As soon as she's yanked Mez to safety, Sorella releases the panther and hops away, narrowly escaping a stabbing spike of stone. Mez staggers up to four paws and casts her eyes about, hoping to find Chumba. There's no sign of her sister. What Mez does find is Rumi.

The little yellow frog is trying to pick his way out of a pile of fang-sharp shards, shuddering in exhaustion as he falls back yet again. "Rumi!" Mez calls out.

It takes him a few moments to realize he's seeing Mez, then his mouth widens into a big grin. When he speaks, his voice is almost gone. "Mez!"

Rumi's expression changes when a giant rumble comes from the shifting stone around them. It's in all directions this time, like all its stones are about to fall at once. "Don't touch me!" he warns. "I accidentally envenomated while I was using my power. By the way, this whole place is going to implode, have you noticed?"

"Yes, I definitely have noticed," Mez says. She gently grips a flat piece of stone between her teeth and uses it to spade Rumi out of the pile of shards.

"Perhaps we should escape now," Rumi says, hopping away.

"Very good idea. If you have any thoughts on how we can do that, let me know!" Mez shouts.

Rumi starts to rise into the air, wind gusting out of his mouth. He immediately goes off at a tilt, careening into a wall. "Okay, okay," he mumbles as he gets back to his feet, "I think I'm too tired to try that trick again."

Even though Rumi's powers might have been what got them into this situation, they won't be much help getting them out of it. Invisibility won't do much good, either.

Mez's eyes go up to the world outside the ziggurat, where Mist, Usha, and Auriel still are, if they're alive. *Usha, help me and Chumba and my friends out of this.* But Aunt Usha isn't here. It's up to Mez.

The roof stones have tumbled together, forming a rough arch. They quiver, and any moment the formation could fall, but for now the roar of falling rock has quieted.

Mez can now hear the panicked calls of the trogon, the grunts of Sorella . . . and a skittering sound. She trains her ears, trying to figure out where it is that she's hearing giant ant legs tapping against rock.

Lima's voice comes through the dark, right nearby. "Mez. The Ant Queen—she's straight ahead!"

"Lima, you should have flown to safety by now!" Mez says.

"Not without you guys," Lima says. "Who would have just echolocated the Ant Queen if you didn't have me around, huh?"

"Have you seen Chumba?"

"No, I'm sorry," Lima says. "This way to the Ant Queen."

Mez pads in the direction Lima indicated, tail straight and ears perked. The ceiling above starts to grind again, and Mez knows they'll soon be buried. But in front of her she sees the pulsing, throbbing abdomen of the Ant Queen, she and her thousands of eggs disappearing from view as she forces two stones aside and slips through the space between.

Through that space is starry sky—not above, but straight ahead. Of course; as the ultimate underground creature, an ant would be the one to find a way out.

"This way, everyone!" Mez cries before taking off at a sprint, her claws skittering against the shifting stones. "Chumba, if you can hear me, come!"

As she dashes, there are more grinding sounds from all around, almost like a giant animal's roar, then the stones above give way. Mez hears moans and shrieks following each crash, but tries to keep her focus on the shifting passageway before her.

"Right behind you!" Rumi calls, and though Mez can hear movements of other animals following, she has no idea which ones.

Debris rains from the sky, clods of dirt and twisting bodies of ants filling the air. Even with her darkvision, Mez stumbles as she goes, and can only imagine how the daywalkers are doing—assuming any of them have survived this far.

Chumba, please tell me you've already found a way out.

Mez's sensitive nose detects sweeter air, not clogged with dust and ants, and her heart lifts. "Rumi, are you still back there?" she calls as she races.

"Yes!" he croaks from his spot on her back. "And guess who came up behind me?"

"Hey, Mez," cries another voice, ragged and nearly out of breath. "Don't think you were going to get away from a seventeen that easily!"

"Gogi!" Mez says. "There's no seventeen I'm happier to hear from. Come on!"

Before them is the night sky itself, no stone in view, as if they've been traveling across the heavens all this time and not through a tunnel of fractured stone. Only a short way to go and they'll be back out in the rainforest, into night air and majestic trees.

The tunnel curves, and as it does the Ant Queen comes into view.

There, on the far side of her, right at the tunnel exit, is Auriel.

He's been desperately wounded. The emerald tree boa lies amid the shivering rock, dirt spraying on him from the unstable ceiling. He's got a huge puncture wound behind his head, blood welling where Usha clamped down tight. Because of the deep wound, he's only partially able to lift his head, and the eyes that regard the Ant Queen's approach are hazy and unfocused.

Light returns to his face when the Ant Queen skitters near. Mez is just close enough to hear what he says: "You are finally free! We can begin your new era. Help me, Narelia."

Narelia. The Ant Queen has a name.

She comes nearer and nearer, mandibles wide. The Ant Queen is plenty strong enough to carry Auriel—it won't slow her at all to bring him to safety.

As she and her friends continue to steal toward the tunnel exit, Mez watches Auriel's expression turn from expectant to confused to despairing as the Ant Queen speeds past into the night, not taking even a moment to acknowledge him.

"Narelia, save me!" he calls after her. "I brought the eclipse-born here. It is because of me that you can now harvest them!"

The Ant Queen doesn't slow, and spares only a few short words for Auriel. "The ants owe you nothing. You are a fool."

Then she skitters toward the tunnel exit, leaps into the stars, and disappears.

The tunnel continues to disintegrate, so there is no time to spare. Mez continues forward, toward the stars and the mists of the rainforests that open out below. And toward Auriel.

The constrictor tries to shuffle forward, but his wounds are too grievous. Meanwhile, the tunnel continues to break apart, half of the starry sky ahead disappearing from view as a boulder drops and blocks it.

As Mez barrels forward, alongside and then past the stricken Auriel, she sees that they're emerging out on a bluff, the nighttime rainforest rising from the mists below. As she escapes out into the cool air, Mez's exhausted muscles finally give out, and she planes through the ferns and grasses chin-first.

As soon as she can get her paws under her Mez stands again, only to see Rumi soaring through the air, his sticky fingers wrapping around her neck to stop himself from hurtling farther. He hugs himself tight to her. Gogi is next, unable to stop in time and crashing into the two friends, rolling them down the ravine. Mez staggers back to four paws, whipping her attention to the ragged tunnel exit as soon as she can.

It's gone. The falling rock has sealed it tight.

No one else is coming.

She realizes with a start that they are high enough that the ziggurat should be in plain view. But it's not there. In its place is a pile of rubble, giant stones and shards of stones crushing or entombing anything trapped within—Auriel included.

Mez returns her attention to the sealed exit. Chumba isn't here, so she must be buried too.

Rumi is on the grass, staring at rock-clogged space where just a moment before Auriel had been struggling to escape after the Ant Queen refused to help him. "I guess evil turns on itself," he says.

Gogi puts his warm, furry arm around Mez. She hides her face in his elbow, stunned, tears in her eyes. "They're all gone, Gogi. I thought that flaming tornado was the right plan, but I—I . . ."

"Mez, shh, Don't be so hard on—"

"We *failed*, Gogi! The Ant Queen got away. And they're dead. The rest of the eclipse-born. And Chumba!"

"Would you stop your blubbering for one moment and listen to me? Look!"

Mez and Rumi turn to see where Gogi is pointing.

There, huddled under the broad shelter of an iron-wood tree, are a bedraggled and shivering trogon, bat, uakari monkey, and sloth. Farther along, sitting apart from the rest, is a group of panthers.

"Some of us made it out," Mez says, dumbstruck.

"Yes," Gogi says softly. "Some of us made it out."

28

IN THE BLUE-GRAY light of dawn, an improbable group of seven animals sits in a circle. Three nightwalkers, four daywalkers. Five walkers, two flyers. A trogon, a uakari, a sloth, a bat, a frog, a capuchin monkey, and a panther.

They do not know that they are being watched.

The frog speaks. He is slight, and young yet, but his words carry wisdom and quiet gravity. "We cannot linger. The falling of the ziggurat must have been heard far across Caldera. Even now the animals that would like to see us destroyed are surely approaching. The ants have a queen again. Whatever she's been planning over the last eon will begin soon. And the eclipse magic we contain seems to be important to her plans. I don't think we'll be able to rest while she's still alive."

"What do you suggest we do, Rumi?" asks the sloth. Mez looks at him in surprise. He's barely ever spoken before. His eyes shine sweetly, though she still suspects that might be because there isn't very much between them and the back of his skull.

"We cannot stay together, I'm afraid," Rumi says. "With the Ant Queen on the loose, there will be even more ill will toward the eclipse-born, and the moment someone spots a bat traveling with a uakari, we'll be found out. Though I think we should separate, I would like to stay here. The inside of the ziggurat was covered in engravings, and they're now exposed. There is much knowledge locked into them. Careful study might allow me to solve the mystery of why the ziggurat was here in the first place, of what our powers mean. The removable sigils must be somewhere in this rubble too, and might still be of some use." He smiles ruefully. "A single tree frog shouldn't attract too much attention from our enemies."

"Some of us could risk staying together, right?" Mez says. It's not a very panther thought, but she can't stand the idea of being separated from Lima and Rumi and Gogi. Granted, it would look strange for a capuchin to be living in a panther den, but Lima could find a way to nestle out of view somewhere.

Mez casts an eye to the next hillside over. There, Usha and Chumba and the triplets sit in silence, waiting for Mez to come join them. Mez knows Usha is in great pain from the wounds she received during her battle with Auriel, but she manages not to show it, maintaining her regal expression.

Chumba is scratched all over, tufts of her fur missing where she got singed by the flaming tornado. She hadn't needed Mez's help at all—the resourceful panther discovered the exit before anyone else, had escaped even before the Ant Queen. Mez can't wait to hear the whole story, but there will be plenty of time on the way home for Chumba to tell it again and again.

Usha reported that Mist slinked away during the fight on the roof, and he still hasn't shown up. Assuming he survived the ziggurat's collapse, maybe he's run away for good.

Alone with Aunt Usha, Chumba keeps glancing over at Mez: *It's awkward over here. Hurry back!* The triplets are watchful and anxious, motionless except when they nip at itches under their fur—apparently a stream of ants passed through the den on its way to the queen.

Gogi clears his throat. The others turn their attention to him, startled. "Can I say something? I think we might be forgetting something more important at stake.

Auriel was one enemy. A powerful one, sure, but just one snake. The reason he was able to get so close to killing us all was because he approached each of us on our own. We didn't know better than to trust him, because we didn't know about each other. We couldn't share our information. We couldn't warn each other."

To her surprise, Mez sees Sorella *nodding*. At Gogi the Seventeenth!

He continues. "Of course, Auriel's now buried under tons of stone, so that takes care of that. But we'll have the Ant Queen to contend with—and there might be other eclipse-born out there, who could become shadowwalkers with their own goals, for good or for bad. I say we all return to our homes. I'm ready now to convince my troop that I'm not unnatural, that I'm like any other animal. Except for the shadowwalking part. And the fire, I guess that's unique, too. Okay, maybe we are unnatural—shoot, got to figure out my wording."

"Gogi," Lima says, "stay on track, buddy."

"Right. Anyway. Most important is that we keep an eye out for the Ant Queen. Between all of us, we can cast a net broad enough to cover all of Caldera. Let's change being scattered from our greatest liability to our greatest strength."

Mez looks at Gogi in astonishment while the other animals murmur in agreement. Even the trogon, usually distractible and anxious, nods solemnly. "Gogi's right," Mez says. "While I spoke to her, the Ant Queen revealed that she thought our lack of communication was our greatest weakness. She's counting on our not staying united. Even though we separate now, let's meet here in a year's time to pool our information."

From the jungle tree line, they hear the calls of the howler monkeys. The group goes silent and tense. The Veil has lifted, which means their daywalker pursuers will soon be out in full force.

"It's a plan," Sorella says. "For now, we must scatter!"

Lima wraps her wings around Mez's neck. "I'm going to miss you so much," she says.

"You should travel with my family at least as far as your cave," Mez says. "It's on the way, after all."

"Gladly," Lima says, relieved. Then she looks apprehensively over at Usha. "As long as your aunt doesn't try to make me into a snack."

Gogi joins the hug. "Did you see the way the other animals looked at you just now?" Mez asks, her voice muffled by monkey fur. "Our true leader was here in front of us the whole time. We just didn't notice it."

"I don't know about that," Gogi says bashfully, suddenly fascinated by his toenails.

"Sure as pond scum, Big Rumi will be waiting in my home swamp for me to show up," Rumi says. "I'm glad to stay here. If I can decode even one of the sigils on the stones in the rubble, maybe we can figure out some of the mystery of our rainforest!"

Mez shoots the frog a penetrating look. *Maybe sometime you'll tell me why you kept your power a secret for so long.*

"Mez," Chumba calls from the hillside, "the triplets are getting antsy. Usha says we have to go!"

"Coming, coming!" Mez calls back. "I'll be dying to hear what you find out," she says to Rumi as she gets up to four paws. "But I'm afraid my aunt might leave without me if I don't get over there right away."

Aunt Usha glowers over the scene, impatient. "Looks like we're in for a *really* fun journey back," Lima says out of the side of her mouth.

"I know," Mez says. "Forget about the howler monkeys. I'm worried I might not survive my *aunt*."

With murmured good-byes and calls of "back here in one year," the friends part. Lima on her shoulder, Mez rushes to her waiting family. Before she's even arrived, Usha haughtily strides off. Mez nuzzles Chumba and then, stepping in unison, the sisters follow their aunt toward home.

"Has Usha mentioned Mist?" Mez asks out of the side of her mouth.

"Not once," Chumba whispers back. "It's really

uncomfortable. The only time she said his name was to tell me about how he fled during the battle against Auriel, and that no son of hers would run from danger. Since then, it's like he never existed."

"And now I'm needed back in the fold," Mez says, shaking her head. "There's no predicting fate, is there?"

Under the calls of the approaching howler monkeys, the eclipse-born disperse.

Unnoticed by any of them, a bedraggled and wet panther stands amid the wreckage of the ziggurat, hidden in the deep shadows between the shattered stones, flexing and unflexing his claws. He scowls in the direction of his departing family. The panther's fur is the purest white.

Mist is not alone. Right above him, also hidden within the deep shadows of the rubble, is a red bird. His eyes glitter with intelligence. Sky has been watching. Sky has been listening.

A Q&A

WITH ELIOT SCHREFER

Q. You traveled into the Amazon to research this book. What can you tell us about your experience there?

A. I flew from New York City (where I live) down to Lima, Peru, then onward to Puerto Maldonado, the last airport before the jungle takes over from civilization. From there it was an hour's drive along dirt roads, then a few hours by boat, an overnight stay at a jungle lodge, and six more hours along the Tambopata River to the research center where I stayed for a week.

Each time my guide took me into the jungle we went deeper, eventually leaving entirely the trails established by the local people. Instead, he took his machete to branches and led us through nameless bogs and dense spiderweb-clogged stretches of forest. The second time we trekked, we started particularly late in the day. Twilight was near, and at the equator, when sundown comes, it comes fast. Soon we were in half-light, tromping through bogs and marshes, tree frogs chirping all around (hi, Rumi!), caimans staring at us, their eyes unsettling red orbs reflecting back in the light from our headlamps. These reptiles were only three feet long or so, but still! It was plenty unsettling to wander through the dark with them on all sides.

Oscar Mishaja Salazar, my guide, showed me a different world by night. There was no sign of any of the daytime animals we had seen just hours earlier—it was like they'd vanished from the rainforest entirely. Frogs, tarantulas, cats, and bats replaced the tamarind monkeys and the bees. Click beetles buzzed heavily through the night, their glowing abdomens as large as marbles. When one landed on me, I could feel the heaviness of it.

I'd read about how completely the jungle was divided between nocturnal and diurnal animals, but never experienced it for myself until then. The magical Veil that separates day and night in *The Lost Rainforest* felt actual. Two kinds of animals really do inhabit the same rainforest without knowing much at all about each other.

Q. Clearly ants had an important role in this book— and will continue to have one, we sense, in the next book of the series! How did that come about?

A. I'd thought my biggest discomfort staying in the deep Amazon would be the mosquitoes. But I didn't get a single mosquito bite during my whole time in the rainforest!

No, the real problem was the ants.

Really, they're the only constant of jungle animal life. Ants are active all day and all night. It got me to thinking about how, in the Peruvian jungle, humans and ants are the only creatures up at all hours. Both are the rare examples of hypersocialized creatures, in which groups of thousands and even millions of individuals can cooperate and coexist—and therefore dominate their world. The shared human-ant tendency to overrun our environments led Abbott Lowell to once observe that ants, "like human beings, can create civilizations without the use of reason."[1]

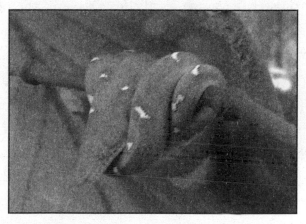

*A juvenile emerald tree boa I met in the Amazon.
Everyone's cute in baby photos!*

---

1.   Quoted in Bert Hölldobler and Edward O. Wilson, *The Superorganism* (New York: W. W. Norton & Company, 2008), xviii.

From there, I started to think about how the other animals of the rainforest are comparatively self-contained and self-sufficient. A fantasy story that takes place in the jungle, I realized, wouldn't run like a fantasy story in the temperate climates. There would be no kingdoms or organizations. In fact, a villain could easily take advantage of the rainforest animals' lack of organization to work his or her plans in secrecy. (Hi, plot twist!)

It's hard to think of humans as being in charge of the planet once you take a good look at ants. There are between one and ten *million billion* of them, weighing approximately as much as all the people of the planet put together.[2] They've been on this planet long enough to have been biting the ankles of dinosaurs.

Winter keeps ants in check in North America, but in the Amazonian jungle they are truly awesome to behold. Army ants might be fearsome, but bullet ants are the biggest danger at the Tambopata Research Center. About two inches long, they are solitary hunters. Their bite isn't fatal to humans, but they get their name from how painful it is. They'll wander over any surface, and it's very easy not to look where you're putting your hand, go to pick up a coffee mug, and

2. Hölldobler and Wilson, *The Superorganism*, 5.

wind up spending the following day writhing in bed in agony.

Thus the Ant Queen was born. Although there are no humans alive in the world of *The Lost Rainforest*, the queen and her minions represent the social conquerors of the rainforest, able to spread far beyond the constraints of the more solitary animals. I've given her additional magic in these books, but even everyday ants are pretty magical, when you think about it. Consider this: ants use their antennae to smell the hydrocarbons in the exoskeleton of other ants, and in so doing know who's from which nest, what their social status is, and how old they are. Neat trick!

As far as the Ant Queen is concerned, she's not finished with our eclipse-born animals—Mez, Lima, Gogi, Sorella, Rumi, and the rest will have to race to organize themselves to fight against her as their story continues.

Q. The rainforest starts to feel like its own character in the book, with its own mysteries and revelations for Mez and her friends. What other tidbits came up for you in your research?

A. Nineteenth-century explorers talked of the rainforest as a "counterfeit paradise." It looks lush and full of richness, but life within it is an eternal struggle to find enough to eat, and to avoid being eaten. What defines a rainforest is—you guessed it—the rainfall. They get over eighty inches a year. It's easy to focus on its cool animals, but with high amounts of water and heat, the tropical rainforest can support some aggressive, giant plant life. Vines are everywhere. These colossal plants are engaged in their own combats against one another. Those fights are just as violent and lethal as those among animals, but occur over a longer period of time.

This fight, between a vine and a tree I met,
has been going on for many years.

As a result of this ferocious competition for sunlight, life in the rainforest has moved from the floor to the canopy. We as humans have learned to look *around* us for food or danger, but something I noticed about the rainforest was how often I wound up looking *up* to see wildlife. There's a whole extra axis for rainforest animals to worry about.

The rainforests cover only a small fraction of the earth, but are thought to be home to over half of the planet's plant and animal species. They remove a tremendous amount of carbon from the atmosphere and therefore mitigate global climate change, provide resources to indigenous people, and are an essential part of the global water cycle . . . yet they're being cut down rapidly. I hope that some of *The Lost Rainforest*'s readers will join me in helping them.

Q. Could you share some of the resources on the rainforest and its inhabitants that you found most useful?

A. Yes! Here are my favorites:

I'm a big fan of www.mongabay.com, which has many informative articles about the rainforest, with sections geared for kids and for older readers. As a place to start, they have a great handout available at http://kids.mongabay.com/lesson_plans/handout.html, including a quiz for classroom use!

For a more in-depth account, John Kricher's book *A Neotropical Companion* is rigorous and accessible and taught me many of the details of jungle life.

On the film side, the very best I can recommend are the riveting "Jungle" episodes of the *Planet Earth* and *Planet Earth II* documentary series that the BBC released in 2006 and 2016.

For those who become ant-obsessed like me, I recommend the documentary *E. O. Wilson: Of Ants and Men*, which is a portrait both of the study of ants and of one of our most important scientists. The BBC series *Life in the Undergrowth* is also an excellent source of information, and of filmed accounts of invertebrate life. For books, Bert Hölldobler and Edward O. Wilson's *The Ants* and *The Superorganism* are the bibles of the field. I found Deborah Gordon's *Ants at Work* very useful, too.

Q. Were there more rainforest animals that you wish you could have included in *Mez's Magic*?

A. Yes, so many! I hope maybe some young writers out there will choose a new rainforest animal, figure out whether it's a nightwalker or a daywalker, and come up with a personality and a magical ability for the new eclipse-born. Maybe you could even write an adventure for the animal to go on! Did Auriel come looking for this eclipse-born, too? What happened next?

There are so many rainforest animals out there, but here are some that almost made it into *Mez's Magic*, but I just didn't have enough space in the pages:

hoatzin	tapir
capybara	Brazilian porcupine
peccary	Arrau turtle
glass frog	fer-de-lance (pit viper)
opossum	

Author trying to look like a tough jungle guide.
Maybe should have taken the glasses off.

ACKNOWLEDGMENTS

This book wouldn't have happened without Melissa Miller. I was over the moon the day that she wrote to ask if I'd work on a series about rainforest animals for her. THANK YOU, Melissa. Caldera is yours! (In a non-creepy-Ant-Queen way, of course.)

I couldn't be more pleased with the team at Katherine Tegen Books. You've been great caretakers, and Ben Rosenthal, this book found a terrific editorial home with you. I feel very lucky.

For making my Peruvian Amazon trip so amazing: thank you, David Veinot, Sarah Ducharme, Isabel Galleymore, EmmaLeen Tomalin, Oscar Mishaja Salazar, and the rest of the staff at the Tambopata Research Center.

As always, many thanks to my agent, Richard Pine, and this book's essential early readers: Daphne Grab, Donna Freitas, Marianna Baer, Jill Santopolo, Anne Heltzel, Marie Rutkoski, Eric Zahler, Kathi Rudawsky, Gloria Lepik Corrigan, and Barbara Schrefer. (Take note, world: moms make great line editors!)